The Wind Comes Sweeping

MARCIA PRESTON

The Wind Comes Sweeping

MIRA®

MIRA

Recycling programs
for this product may
not exist in your area.

ISBN-13: 978-0-7783-2630-4
ISBN-10:   0-7783-2630-6

THE WIND COMES SWEEPING

www.MIRABooks.com

Printed in U.S.A.

First Printing: April 2009
10 9 8 7 6 5 4 3 2 1

Oklahoma—where the wind comes sweeping down the plain.*

Prologue

THE LEGEND OF SILK MOUNTAIN

Oklahoma Territory, 1895.

This is the way the story came down to me. The way it might have been.

Even before daylight, Leasie awoke to the yawling wind. It rang across the flat plains and scoured the shale rocks on Silk Mountain. It whistled through cracks in the cabin walls so fiercely that she could feel it on her cold cheeks where she lay in bed, cocooned in three quilts. Nothing was safe from the long, prying fingers of the wind. Day and night, it never ceased.

Jacob was already up, dressing on the other side of the curtain that served as their bedroom wall. She heard one boot clunk on the wood floor after he'd laced it, then the other, and the rustle of his coat as he pulled it on. The cabin door opened and sucked the curtain outward, the cry of the wind suddenly close and loud until he shut the door again.

She ought to get up. Jacob would need a hot breakfast when his chores were finished. She lay for a moment longer inside the warm quilts. The cracks of sky in the log walls were getting lighter; the sun would be up soon, but inside the cabin it was still hazy dark. She pictured Jacob forking prairie hay into the pen for their horse, Brownie, and for the mule and the milk cow. Grain was scarce, but he rationed one cup a day for the mash of milk and table scraps he fed the hog. The scrawny pig would become bacon and ham and chops and fatback, meat to last through the next arduous winter.

The last thing Jacob would do before coming in for breakfast was to break ice on the half barrel where the animals drank, and bring a bucket of the water inside. She would have to boil it to make it safe for cooking or drinking or washing dishes. Every two days he hauled water from the river. Come spring, he would try again to dig a well. When they had a well with a windmill, Jacob said, the days would be easier for them both. She pictured the paddles of the windmill spinning in the endless wind.

Leasie rolled to the edge of the bed and stuck her stockinged feet out from under the covers. Jacob had lit the fire in the cookstove before he went out, but its heat never reached the floorboards or the corners. She pulled yesterday's clothes from the chair next to the bed and dressed herself under the quilts. Three petticoats, for warmth. Her camisole, then the coarse muslin dress, and her apron on top of that. She couldn't face going out in the cold to the outhouse before breakfast, so she used the chamber pot in the corner and covered it with a square board. Then she laced up her brown boots and ran a brush through her hair, twisting it up behind her head in a vertical roll. It had grown so long that the ends sprouted like a turkey's tail at the crown of her head. She secured it with the four hairpins she'd laid on an upturned bucket beside the chair.

She ducked past the curtain, leaving the bed to air out before she made it, and set about making breakfast. All the while, the frenzied wind licked around the cabin walls, through the cracks at the window. It curled up from the floorboards and snaked beneath her skirts. Her feet were already cold inside her boots. She made bacon and biscuits. With yesterday's boiled water she made coffee. Lots of strong coffee.

Before the biscuits were ready, Jacob came in, riding a gust of wind into the house. Whatever heat had accumulated inside the cabin was sucked out the door. He didn't even say good-morning, just stood beside the stove and warmed his backside.

Jacob was thirteen years older than Leasie, and sometimes he acted more like a father than a husband. A strict father, at that. She was nearly nineteen; she didn't need a father. She needed a husband who was soft sometimes, especially in the bed they shared. A husband who would talk to her about something besides the plowing and the crops. Most days he disappeared into the fields after breakfast and she didn't see him again until supper. She was by herself all day in the tiny cabin, no bigger than one room of the house in

Kansas City where she'd grown up. When he came home and she asked him about his day, he would talk about the work that still needed doing, and complain about the lack of rain. Once he'd seen Indians in the distance, on horseback. She questioned him about that, but he didn't know what tribe they were, or where they were going. Then he'd fall silent, concentrating on his food. He never asked what she'd done all day. Maybe he knew how lonely she was and didn't want to hear about it.

In warm weather she could spend her time outdoors. She tended a garden, spindly though it was, and washed their clothes in a big iron pot. Sometimes she walked out across the prairie until the cabin was no more than a dot in the distance, then turned around and walked back. If she went too far and lost sight of the cabin, she might lose her bearings and never find it again.

Once, though, she had kept going. She walked all the way to Silk Mountain. Jacob said people called it Silk Mountain because after a rainstorm, if the sunlight broke through the clouds just right, the mountain's flat top turned silver and shiny. She'd watched for that the first spring, and the second, but she never saw it happen.

There was no way to judge the distance out here, and the mountain looked closer than it really was. It took a long time to get there, and when she stood at the foot of the rocky outcropping that rose so unexpectedly from the grassy prairie, she was disappointed. Up close, Silk Mountain didn't look like a mountain at all, just a big upheaval of boulders. Still, she would have liked to climb up and look off from its top. But she was already going to be late getting home to start supper.

Jacob never said a word while he waited on his meal that evening, and she didn't tell him she had walked miles across the prairie and thought of never coming back.

She crossed off days on the Montgomery Ward & Co. calendar Jacob brought home from the mercantile store. The nearest settlement lay a full day's ride to the east, and when he went for supplies, he was gone two nights and three days. She couldn't go along because somebody had to stay and tend the animals.

On the first week of spring weather in 1895, Jacob put on his cleanest clothes and hitched the horse to the wagon. "I'll be back as soon as I can," he said, meeting her eyes briefly before he climbed onto the wagon seat. His eyes were lake blue and always seemed to be looking at something she couldn't see. He had loaded the rifle and hung it beside the door within her reach. "Don't shoot nothing you don't have to," he said.

That year the weather went from winter to summer with only a week of spring in between. The day Jacob left turned hot and windy. At first she enjoyed being on her own, not having to cook big meals. She worked in her garden, fed the livestock and milked the cow. But that night, lying alone in the drafty cabin with the wind huffing at the door, she heard coyotes nearby, their howling lonesome and eerie. Finally she drifted into frightening dreams and was awakened by the echo of a scream on the wind. She sat up straight in the bed, her heart pounding.

People said the cry of a panther sounded like a woman screaming. She didn't want to know which one she had heard. She was afraid she was that woman.

What if she became pregnant and had to bear her baby out here alone, no friend or midwife to help her? What if the creatures from her dream were attracted by the sharp aroma of blood and came to devour the child? Leasie didn't sleep the rest of the night.

The next morning she arose exhausted but with a sense of purpose. She put up her hair and made the bed and cleaned the kitchen. She threw the quilts across the clothes-line to air out. The day was even warmer than yesterday, and windier. For miles around her the prairie grass rippled, undisturbed by animal or human. A lone hawk circled high above Silk Mountain.

She thought of writing a letter to her family back in Kansas City, but after the first few words she stopped. That world didn't exist anymore; there was only this place, and the wind.

Leasie filled the big iron pot in the yard with soapy water and carried a bucket of it to the cabin. She took off her dress and left it outside the door. In her petticoats and camisole, she got down on her hands and knees and scrubbed the wood floor of the cabin. Her knuckles were raw and red. When she'd finished, she left the door open so the floor would dry.

She put both her dresses in the wash water, swishing them up and down, then rinsed them in a separate bucket. Dust whipped across the trampled yard and stung her bare arms. Her wet clothes would get dirty again just hanging on the line, but that couldn't be helped. She turned the two dresses wrong side out to lessen fading by the sun and hung them on the clothesline next to the bedding.

She dumped the soapy water, poured the rinse water onto her garden and set out walking across the prairie.

It was late morning and the sun warmed her shoulders. She imagined her camisole and full petticoats as a white sundress, like a Kansas City girl might wear to a party. She picked a yellow flower from the knee-high grass and wove its stem into her hair. A jackrabbit startled from the grass and bounded away, and three shiny crows crossed the sky. She saw no people, no houses.

The sun was straight overhead when she reached Silk Mountain and began her climb. Her brown boots wedged in rock crevices and her palms reddened with shale dust where she grabbed on to boost herself up. She had forever, so she took her time.

She was sweating by the time she reached the flat rock at the top. From the ground it looked square as the bottom of a buckboard, but once she'd climbed onto it, she found the south edge was cropped off like a bite mark and it slanted slightly to the west. She stepped over two gaping cracks and stood at the flaking edge of a shale boulder that faced east. The slab jutted over the rocky slope below like the prow of a ship.

Her hair had come undone and it whipped around her face. She held it back with both hands and looked across the land in all directions. Somewhere there were towns and people, but here the land was empty and endless and offered no respite from the wind. The only feature besides rolling grassland and a line of trees along the distant river was a rocky ridge, not as high as Silk Mountain, several miles to the north.

Leasie spread out her arms. Closed her eyes. Tipped her head back, and fell forward over the edge.

Only God knows what she thought of in those few seconds, the warm wind ripping past her white skin until she went to ground.

It was days before Jacob found her body. The vultures had found it first.

He didn't bury her remains on his little homestead, nor on Silk Mountain. For reasons known only to him, he buried Leasie on the slope of that rocky ridge she'd seen in the distance. Later he married a Kiowa woman who'd received ownership of the ridge as part of her tribal allotment. Jacob Youngblood was one-eighth Indian himself, though no one remembers which tribe.

Gradually Jacob and his second wife bought or traded for her relatives' allotments and the adjoining unassigned lands. They amassed two thousand acres, more or less, that became the original Killdeer Ridge Ranch. His Kiowa wife didn't live long either, but she bore him three sons. One of those sons was my grandfather.

Jacob Youngblood was my great-grandfather; the Kiowa woman called Tia-Ma my great-grandmother. I never knew much about Tia-Ma, but the legend of Leasie was kept alive through the generations. Sometimes I think Leasie was my true ancestor, more than Jacob or the Kiowa woman whose death from influenza was much less dramatic.

Oklahoma gained statehood in 1907 and Jacob married again, a woman named Naomi who helped him build the ranch into a prosperous cattle operation. The ranch passed down to my grandfather, Stone Youngblood, who bought out his brothers, then to my father, J.B. And now to me. My name is Marik Youngblood.

Hard times took a toll over the years, and the ranch isn't the sprawling two-thousand acres it was a century ago. I left it once, intending to be an artist and a teacher instead of a ranchwoman. But as the saying goes, if you want to make God laugh, tell him your plans. At my father's graveside on Killdeer Ridge—in the family plot that grew up around Leasie's bones—I promised J.B. two things, hoping to make up for all the ways I'd failed him. One of those things was to preserve what was left of Killdeer Ridge Ranch and keep it in the family. The other was to find his only heir and grandchild, the daughter I'd given away.

Chapter One

Killdeer Ridge Ranch

Before sunrise, Marik drove her father's old truck along the white gravel service road that wound up the ridge to the giant windmills. Dust funneled up behind the pickup's tires, and a chilly wind gusted through the passenger window, stuck permanently halfway open. The pickup's heater poured warm air on her boots. A preseason thunderstorm had blown through the night before, with plenty of bluster but only a spattering of rain. Spring was weeks away.

She took it slow over a patch of graded ruts, coffee sloshing against the lid of its thermal mug in the console, the arthritic joints of the pickup creaking. Her dad had named the truck Red Ryder, after an old-time hero of cowboy comics. Every time she climbed into the cab to make her morning rounds on the ranch, she caught her father's scent, though he'd been gone nearly two years.

She was nearing the apex of the ridge where she stopped every morning to watch the sun rise over the ranch and the river valley. Against a blue-gray sky, forty-five giant wind turbines towered above the horizon, catching the first rays of sun in their long white arms. Below them the earth waited in shadow.

The first time she'd seen windmills like these at the White Deer facility in West Texas, their stark beauty and clean design had stopped her breath. Their slow, rhythmic turning sounded like a heartbeat, the mystical pulse of the earth itself. Regardless of storms or heat, the white giants stood inscrutable, heads turned to the wind. These forty-five turbines produced enough electricity to power nearly a million homes, and this was only phase one of the wind farm.

Marik parked Red Ryder at her usual spot on the highest point of the ridge. That's when she saw it—a dark mass on the rocky ground, something that didn't belong. It lay at the foot of Windmill 17, where the service road wound back on itself before disappearing behind the low hill.

She leaned forward against the steering wheel and squinted into the predawn light. The blackish mound was about the size of a newborn calf, nearly hidden by last season's sagebrush and dried yucca. But it couldn't be a calf; the cattle were in the lower fields now, on winter-wheat pasture. Maybe a runaway trash bag that blew up here in the night? But it looked too solid for a trash bag, and heavy.

It wasn't moving with the wind. She had the sinking impression that whatever it was, it had once been a living thing.

She searched the dusty floorboard for the binocular case. The binocs, too, had been her dad's. She could see his calloused hands on the metal when she removed the beat-up glasses and got out of the truck. Wind whipped her ponytail and the loose ends stung her eyes. Should have brought a stocking cap. It was always cooler up here than in the ranch yard, where the ground was flat and trees sheltered the buildings. She zipped her jacket and stood on the running board with the door open, steadying her elbows on top of the cab.

The sun had breached the horizon now, and the slim rotors of the windmills cast moving shadows across the land. Next month wild verbena and prairie daisies would thrust up from the rocky soil. But in February the ridge was a tonal study in pale gold and shades of russet brown. She liked to paint it that way, but those paintings were hard to sell. Buyers wanted more color.

She held the binoculars to her eyes and searched the landscape for the alien object. Low brush and shadows obstructed her view, and the lenses of the old binocs were fogged with scratches. She tossed the field glasses on the truck seat and walked down the service road toward number 17.

Gravel crunched beneath her boots. The only other sound was the unhurried soughing of the windmills.

An immense canopy of sky arched cloudless from

horizon to horizon. Severe clear, her pilot father would have said. It was the kind of day her grandmother had written about in diaries, a diamond of hope after a long, cold winter. Soon when she walked here she'd have to watch for killdeer eggs at the edge of the road, the speckled eggs perfectly camouflaged among the rocks.

When she drew closer to the dark object lying in the scrub growth, she saw the wind ruffle its edges—like feathers. Her chest closed up. *Please, not an eagle.* But no other bird would be that large. She left the roadbed and crossed open ground, stepping over clumps of dried timothy and prickly-pear cactus. Another few feet and she stood over the fallen bird. *Damn.*

Her artist's eye cataloged the mottled colors—burnt umber, sienna, Payne's grey. Highlights of gold oak. A golden eagle, she thought, though she'd never seen one this close. She crouched beside it.

The head was bent beneath its body. One wing lay unfurled and obviously broken. Even inert, the hooked talons looked macabre. Those claws could seize a slippery fish right out of the water, or rip apart a small animal to feed the eagle's young. She touched the bird with the toe of her boot, hoping for movement and a chance for rescue. There was none. The body felt stiff.

From a distant pasture a bull claimed his territory with a wheezy bellow. Above her head, the windmill blades kept up their leisurely *whough, whough, whough, whough.* She looked up at the turning rotors. The carcass lay right below them, no more than twenty-five feet from the tower base, as if the eagle had simply dropped from the sky. The fiber-glass rotors appeared to turn slowly, but that was an optical illusion. Each hollow blade was more than a hundred feet long. The tips of the blades could reach 156 miles per hour and still look slow to the human eye.

Was it possible the eagle had flown into one? She couldn't imagine that. Eagles' eyesight was legendary; they spotted prey on the ground or in the water from hundreds of feet above. Nevertheless, if her neighbors found out about the dead eagle, that's exactly what they'd claim—that the bird had been killed by the blades. Burt and Lena Gurdman had objected to the wind farm from the begin-ning and had delayed construction of the first phase with their complaints. Folks around here were stoutly protective of the migratory birds that wintered along the river, and Marik had no doubt Burt Gurdman would use the eagle's death as ammunition for another battle.

The dark feathers glistened in angled sunlight. The bird's wingspan must be seven feet, at least. Even dead it looked beautiful and strong and utterly wild. Carefully, she rolled it over. Thank God it didn't have a white head. She was fairly sure bald eagles were still on the endangered-species list, though the U.S. Fish and Wildlife Service had recom-mended delisting several years ago.

She ran her fingers over the satiny breast feathers. "What happened to you, big brother? I wish you could tell me."

The coming furor rose in her imagination like a bad movie. It was illegal to be in possession of an eagle feather, let alone an entire animal. If he could, Gurdman would use this new argument to stop construction of the last twenty-five wind towers.

Don't borrow the jack before the tire's flat. It was her father's voice, clear as ever in her head. His easygoing ways had endeared him to everyone but had also led the ranch into deep debt. She'd had no idea how deep until his sudden death.

Marik laid an arm across her forehead, shading her eyes from a brilliant sunrise. Her gaze traveled down the slope and across the wide fields near the river.

She saw three choices. She could turn the bird over to a county official or wildlife ranger and meet the consequences head-on. Or she could haul the eagle to the river, let it be found in its usual habitat—but on the opposite bank that was part of the state wildlife preserve. Not on her ranch.

Or she could bury the creature where it lay and keep quiet.

All three options stunk. But when she thought of the impending brouhaha over the eagle's death, it was damn tempting to go home and get her shovel.

Her battle of conscience dissolved with the growl of tires on gravel. Somebody was coming. The sound drifted to her across the ridge before she spotted the vehicle winding through the switchbacks and up the rise.

Double damn.

Marik straightened her spine and stood beneath the giant turbines, facing into the wind. Waiting for trouble.

A white pickup tacked toward her at a leisurely pace. She had not closed the gate at the main road and, despite the

No Trespassing signs, the driver apparently took the open gate as an invitation. The men who tended the windmills drove white pickups, but she could already see this one was a stretch cab and the power company's gold logo wasn't painted on the door. None of the neighboring ranchers drove a truck like that, either.

She lost sight of the vehicle behind a rise and then it emerged again on the high ridge. The truck stopped beside Red Ryder and a tall, lean man got out. He wore jeans and low-heeled boots with a quilted vest over his long-sleeved shirt. She didn't know him. He clamped a wide-brimmed hat on his head and started down the slope toward her with a rolling stride.

His face looked friendly enough until he saw the mound of feathers at her feet. When his eyes fixed on the eagle, all hints of a smile faded away. He didn't speak as he approached but knelt immediately and put his hands on the bird, turning it over, spreading out the feathers on the underside of the tail.

"Bad news," he said. "It's a bald eagle."

He looked up at her with gold-ochre eyes. She frowned. "There's no white head."

"It's a young one. They don't get the distinctive white feathers on the head and tip of the tail until they're at least four years old."

"How do you know it's not a golden?" she said, still hoping.

"The feet, for one thing. Golden eagles have feathers all the way to the claws. This one doesn't. And see that grayish color of the feathers on the underside of the tail? That's distinctive to a young bald eagle. A golden would have white on the tail, up next to the body."

"It's sure big to be immature."

"Probably a female. They get larger than males. I'd guess it's two or three years old."

Perfect. Not just an eagle; it's the freaking national symbol.

The stranger looked younger than she was, early twenties maybe, except for those case-hardened eyes. "You talk like a biologist," she said.

"Not exactly. But I majored in it, along with land management. I'm Jace Rainwater, your nine o'clock appointment."

He brushed his hands off on his jeans and stood. Six-four, she guessed, even without the big hat. He paused as if waiting for her to introduce herself or offer a handshake. She did neither. She was supposed to interview him about the foreman's job—two hours from now. Nowadays people called it *ranch manager,* but she figured if *foreman* was a good enough title for Monte, her dad's old friend, it was good enough for whomever she hired.

"Sorry to be so early," he said. "I drove from Amarillo and made better time than I expected."

"You must have left in the dead of night to get here by sunrise."

He offered no explanation. Maybe he awoke hours before daylight the way she did, worming over the things she could change and the ones she couldn't.

"There was nobody around down there," he said, gesturing toward the cluster of ranch buildings at the foot of the ridge, "so when I saw the truck up here I figured it must be you."

She glanced at the eagle again. "Early would be a good trait for a ranch hand, any morning but this one."

"At least the eagle's a young one, probably not half of a breeding pair," he offered.

She blew out a breath, looking across the fields to the west where the Gurdmans' farm abutted her land. "My neighbors won't care how old the bird is when they try to block construction on the other windmills."

"Your neighbors object to the wind farm?"

"*Those* do."

He followed her gaze toward a distant clump of trees where the glint of a white farmhouse reflected the early sun. "What for? It's pollution-free energy and it's quiet. Cattle can graze right under the turbines."

"Exactly. But the windmills might emit *harmful rays* that cause cancer and birth defects."

"Good grief."

"Not to mention that the Gurdmans missed out on the lease money from Great Plains Power & Light. The company wanted only this high ground that's not sheltered from the wind."

"Ah," he said. "So it's about money."

"That's what I think, but they won't admit it. All the farms and ranches out here are struggling financially. The wind farm bailed me out, and the Gurdmans resent me for it. And now, of course, they can say the windmills kill eagles."

"Maybe. Maybe not." His attention was on the eagle again. "You need to take the carcass to the state wildlife office in Pacheeta. I'll load it in the truck for you."

"Thanks," she said without enthusiasm. Pacheeta was the county seat and fifty miles away. "But I thought I'd just call the local law to come pick it up."

He shook his head. "I wouldn't. No telling what might happen to it before a wildlife ranger got to see it."

For a man who'd just arrived on the scene, he had plenty of opinions. She wondered if Rainwater was an Indian name. He didn't look any more Indian than she did, with her light brown hair and blue eyes. But half the folks in Oklahoma had some Indian heritage if you traced their lineage back far enough.

He pulled a pair of gloves from his pocket and lifted the eagle by its feet, staying clear of the talons. And then he leaned in to smell the bird.

"What are you, the animal CSI? Don't tell me you can tell how long it's been dead by sniffing."

"No. But I think this bird's come in contact with Diazinon. That might have something to do with why it died."

"Diazinon—the stuff you spray to kill ticks and fleas?"

"Right. It was outlawed a few years ago, like DDT before it, but lots of people still have some sitting in their storage sheds."

"How would an eagle get hold of that?"

"Good question. Maybe by accident, but it would take an awful lot of it to be lethal for a bird that size. Even DDT usage didn't kill the adult birds, just weakened their egg-shells so the babies didn't hatch."

A crawly feeling rose up her back. "You think somebody poisoned it on purpose?"

"Look, the smell might be something else," he said. "I'm just guessing. You need to have a wildlife official examine it."

She followed him up the rise to where they'd parked, and he laid the eagle carefully on the stained bed of her truck. "You don't happen to have a garbage bag, I guess."

"The whole truck's pretty much a garbage bag."

He didn't dispute it. "Wait a minute. I might have some-thing." He rummaged in a storage box mounted behind the cab of his truck and came out with a lightweight tarp. He opened it in her truck bed, laid the bird in the center and wrapped it up.

"Good idea," she said. "I don't need everybody in town to see my illegal cargo."

"Not just that. We want to keep it in the same shape you found it, without damage in transit."

"We?"

"I'll ride with you if you want," he said. "I know some guys in the U.S. Fish and Wildlife Service. Maybe I can help smooth any ruffled feathers."

She made a face but he didn't seem to notice the pun.

"It couldn't hurt," she said. "We can talk about the foreman's job on the drive. Follow me down to the house and you can park your truck there."

He touched two fingers to the brim of his hat, like John

Wayne in an old cowboy movie, and walked back to his vehicle.

For the space of time it took to open Red Ryder's mulish door, she watched him go. She'd read the résumé he'd e-mailed. He had good credentials and a background in conservation that was a plus in her view. But a résumé didn't tell much about a man's temperament or his character. Could she trust this guy to live within a stone's throw of her house, with no one else around for miles?

Then she thought of the eagle again. If Rainwater was right about the Diazinon and the bird was intentionally poisoned and dumped beneath the windmills, there was no doubt in her mind who'd done it.

Chapter Two

Red Ryder burped smoke and lurched into gear. With Rainwater following, Marik zigzagged down the ridge toward the two-lane blacktop road that people around here called a highway. This time she closed the gate behind them.

The ranch buildings—her house, the foreman's cottage and two barns—sat at the base of Killdeer Ridge half a mile from the windmills as the crow flew, a mile and a half by road. From the paved road she turned beneath a cedar-log archway with Killdeer Ridge Ranch branded into the wood. The gravel on the quarter-mile driveway was nearly worn away, the one-lane road in need of grading.

They passed the foreman's quarters first, where Jace Rainwater would live if she hired him. The two-bedroom cottage sat vacant, its windows dark and lonesome. For months she'd resisted hiring anybody to replace Monte. After J.B.'s accident, Monte had deflated like a wrinkled balloon, his seventy years coming upon him all at once. He'd decided to retire but agreed to stay on a few months to help her get a handle on running the ranch. The few months turned into a year. Monte was her surrogate grandfather when she was growing up, a fixture at the ranch since before she was born. Without him the place didn't feel right. Marik still held a mean little resentment toward his daughter, who'd finally come down from Oklahoma City with a U-Haul and taken Monte and his things back with her.

She parked Red Ryder in the graveled space in front of the cobblestone ranch house originally built by Stone Youngblood, a grandfather she never knew. The original structure was two-storeys and square as a shoe box. Marik's mother had supervised several additions, including a southern-style front porch, a carport and a master-bedroom suite on the ground floor at the back. If it wasn't architecturally harmonious, the big house was comfortable inside and definitely unique. It might have grown even larger if Julianna Youngblood hadn't taken her plans with her to the grave when Marik was six years old.

Marik wondered if Jace Rainwater could sense the history that lived among these cobblestone buildings, or if he saw only the shabby remains of a once-prosperous enterprise.

His truck pulled in beside her and rolled to a stop. She shouldered her door open and started up the rock sidewalk to the house. "Want some coffee for the drive?" she called. On a ranch, coffee was one of the basic food groups. She'd been addicted since high school.

"No, thanks. I drank about a gallon on the drive out here," he said.

"Then you'd better come in and use the facility before we go."

She directed him to the bathroom, then clumped up the split-log staircase to her bedroom and pulled on cleaner boots for the trip to Pacheeta. If Rainwater had waited until nine o'clock to show up for their appointment, she might have fixed her face a bit before then. Or she might not. At any rate, she didn't see much point in it now.

When she came back down he had gone outdoors. She refilled her thermal mug and turned off the coffeepot but didn't bother locking the house. Her dad believed that locks kept out only honest men; a thief would break down the door or smash a window. She found Jace checking the cargo still wrapped securely in the bed of her truck.

Red Ryder's springs squawked as he settled onto the seat, his shoulders filling up his side of the cab. Marik coaxed the truck into reverse and they wheezed down the driveway toward the highway, leaving his nice airtight truck parked by her house. She hoped the old red pickup was up to the trip.

They rattled over the blacktop, watching shadows recede across the landscape as the sun ascended. She saw him try the window handle once, but when it didn't respond he said nothing and zipped up his vest. He didn't talk much, which was okay with her. Her social skills had regressed since she'd moved back to the ranch; after Monte left, she often went several days without talking to anyone.

A coyote trotted along a fence, heading toward a grove of leafless trees. Far to their right, above the line of trees that concealed the Silk Mountain River, a dark swosh etched the blue of the sky. The wingspan was too large for a hawk. It was another eagle, probably scanning a pool where the water was deep enough to hunt for fish. The sight of it sent a new pang of dread through her middle.

Rainwater saw it, too. "The river is the south boundary of your ranch?"

"Correct."

"Does it border your neighbors' land, too? The ones opposing the wind farm?"

She nodded. "The wildlife preserve butts up to me on the south, across the river," she said. "The Searcy ranch is to the east, and the Gurdmans' farm on the west. The land to the north is owned by somebody who lives in Oklahoma City and never comes out here. The elk from the refuge have sort of taken over the pastureland there."

"Cool."

"Yeah, they're beautiful. In the fall you can hear them bugling." Her mouth twisted. "Burt Gurdman runs 'em off his land with a shotgun."

Rainwater said nothing, just shook his head.

Marik pulled a folded paper from above the visor and handed it to Rainwater. It had come in yesterday's mail from the office of Earl Searcy, mayor of Silk. The notice invited local residents to attend a community meeting for the purpose of discussing the rural water system, a proposal to hire a full-time police chief and a possible moratorium on construction of twenty-five additional wind turbines on Killdeer Ridge. GPP&L had already paid half the lease money for phase two of the wind turbines. Marik had used the money to retire some of her debt and to buy a lustful young bull and a new bunch of heifers. If construction was blocked, the company might want that money returned.

The mere sight of the flyer made her angry all over again. The least Earl Searcy could have done was phone her about it in person. Silk didn't have a mayor when she was a kid, and she liked it better that way.

Except for the Gurdmans, the Searcys were her closest neighbors and good people. Earl had been a friend to her dad. His sons, Jackson and Cade, often helped out on the Youngblood ranch. None of them had ever said anything about opposing the wind farm.

"I don't know where they get off discussing construction on private property," she said. "My ranch isn't inside city limits. There's no question of zoning or public access or any other damn thing that should concern city government, such as it is. The construction is phase two of a project that was thoroughly discussed, state permits obtained, all the legalese dotted and crossed months ago."

He handed the flyer back to her and she stuffed it behind the visor again. "But if this eagle was killed by the windmills and some federal agency gets involved," she said, "that's a whole new ball game."

"You need a necropsy on the bird before that meeting."

She glanced at him. "What's that? An autopsy for animals?"

"Exactly. That's why you want to turn it over to the wildlife department instead of a county sheriff."

Maybe it was a good thing Jace Rainwater showed up early after all.

"During the first phase of construction, somebody put sugar in the gas tanks of the big dirt-moving machines," she told him. "Shut them down for several weeks. The site boss said they had trouble like that sometimes, but not usually in such an isolated spot. He thought it was probably teenagers, but I had my doubts even then."

Rainwater nodded but made no comment. She dropped the subject, regretting that she'd aired her grievances to a stranger.

After a minute he pointed through the windshield toward a rocky mound in the distance. "Is that Silk Mountain?"

"Yup. That's it. The town was named for the mountain, but people dropped the *mountain* part years ago and just call the town Silk." A neat irony, she thought, for a village of maybe two thousand that was anything but silky.

The mountain wasn't much of a mountain, either, just a geographical anomaly that had thrust a tall, red mesa far above the surrounding level terrain. Flat shale boulders stacked up like a deli sandwich that narrowed to a square, treeless summit. Between the mountain and the road they were driving lay a wide, flat plain veined by creeks that drained into the river. In the heat of summer, the creek beds dried up and stranded the resident crawdads.

"I read how Silk Mountain got its name," Rainwater said.

She nodded. "Did the guidebook tell you about the ghost that lives up there?"

He glanced sideways, his face skeptical. "No. I guess it left out the good parts."

"They say a young pioneer wife who lived out here before there was a town or a road, or anything, went crazy from loneliness and the unrelenting wind. One day while her husband was gone, she scrubbed the floor of her cabin, fed the milk cow and hung her only two dresses wrong side out on the clothesline. She was wearing a camisole and petticoats and farmer's boots when she climbed to the top of Silk Mountain and jumped to her death." Marik didn't mention her near relation to the young wife. "Sometimes on a moonlit night, people see her ghost standing on the edge of Silk Rock."

"Great story." He looked toward the shale outcropping and smiled. "So have you ever seen her?"

Marik paused. "I don't know you well enough to answer that." It might have been just a trick of the light.

The blacktop road led them directly down the unnamed main street of Silk. It was still early, and only a few dusty pickups and the postmistress's PT Cruiser were parked in the slanted spaces beside the street. Half of the storefronts sat vacant, sad reminders of somebody's retail dreams gone up in dust. Around windows dimmed by gray grime, the painted facades peeled like a bad sunburn.

"There's the P.O.," Marik said as they rolled past, "and the grocery store—slash—drugstore, and the DHS office."

"Every little town needs a welfare office," he said drily.

"It isn't just welfare. Daisy's an area supervisor for Child Protective Services." Daisy Gardner was the sole full-time employee at the local Department of Human Services office, and Marik's closest friend. Actually her only friend, now that Monte had gone.

There was one traffic light in Silk, perpetually blinking yellow, never red. "The bank's a branch of Pacheeta Farmers and Merchants," she said. "Up ahead is the farmers' co-op where I buy feed, and here's our Sonic, the only fast food in town."

"How's the food?"

"Anything I don't cook tastes great to me. And their cherry limeade is outstanding."

Outside the little town the speed limit rose again. She urged Red Ryder up to sixty, its top speed, and the shimmy magically disappeared. The gas gauge jittered on a quarter of a tank; she would have to fill up in Pacheeta.

Her companion cleared his throat and segued into his job interview. "Did you have a chance to look at the résumé I sent?"

"I did, and it's impressive. But that doesn't tell me about your work ethic, or whether you'd have trouble being bossed by a woman."

"Depends," he said. "How bossy are you?"

"Huh. *I'm* supposed to ask the questions."

"I see," he said, and smiled.

"Frankly, with your background and work history, it makes me wonder why you'd want a job out here, which most people consider the middle of nowhere. You could make more money working for the USDA or even the state, in some environmental capacity."

"That's what I was doing in Amarillo, at the county level. Believe me, the pay wasn't that great." His gaze traveled across the land in front of them, from horizon to horizon. "I need more space, and I love this country. I came from Oklahoma originally."

"So you're not employed now?"

"I quit my job last week. For personal reasons," he added. "I didn't get fired."

"Are these personal reasons going to follow you to the next job?" She glanced sideways and saw a muscle in his jaw tighten.

"My marriage is on the rocks. My wife just took a job she likes in Amarillo and she doesn't want to move. We're going to try separating for a while."

He set his mouth in a way that let her know that's all the personal information he cared to discuss. Fair enough. But a shaky marriage could mean that he'd be here just long enough to become helpful and then hightail it back to his wife.

The trouble was, the only other person who'd shown any interest in the job was not somebody she wanted on the place. She wouldn't admit it aloud, but sometimes it was eerie living out there by herself after Monte left. And some of the work simply required more physical strength than she had. She was five-seven and strong, but even now she was nursing a strained shoulder from hefting sacks of feed into the back of the truck. She would reserve judgment about Jace Rainwater. If he could help her out of this eagle mess, that was a definite mark in his favor.

"Okay. Your turn to ask questions," she said.

"Tell me about the ranch."

"Twelve hundred and eighty acres, more or less. Small by ranching standards. Dad had to sell a piece of it a few years back. What's left is about two square miles, though it isn't square because of the river. I inherited it when my father died and my sister didn't want anything to do with it." She had a quick flash of Anna at the oak table in the kitchen, signing over her rights to Marik the day after their father's funeral. Neither of them knew then that the ranch was immersed in debt.

"My sister's five years older and escaped to California right after high school. I stayed here with Dad and helped him run the place along with Monte, the previous manager." In those years they'd all assumed she would take over the ranch someday. But that had changed after she went off to college and fell in lust.

"Anna's husband is a producer in L.A. and makes a ton of money. She said I deserved the ranch because I always loved the land." Her smile twisted. "She thought she was doing me a favor." Her sister's jewelry alone could pay off most of the ranch's debts, but Marik would never tell her that.

"I didn't know how much trouble Dad was in until I moved back and took over," she said. "The cattle market went to hell a few years back and he'd made some bad decisions. I had to sell off most of the herd to pay a note that was overdue. I was hanging on by a thread when Great Plains Power & Light came out here and proposed leasing the ridge for a wind farm. I studied the concept and really liked what they were doing. It seemed like a good use of the land, not to mention keeping me out of bankruptcy, so I signed a fifty-year lease. Monte and I thought Dad would approve."

"The wind farm was what attracted me to the job," Rainwater said. "I've always thought we ought to find a way to harness all this wind energy. It wasn't the railroad that settled this part of the West—it was the windmill. If windmills can provide water for cattle and homes, why not electricity?"

"Why not, indeed."

"But you still run cattle?"

"Oh, yeah. It's a working ranch, just not a profitable one. I'm slowly building up the herd again, but I can't manage more cattle until I have some help." She shrugged. "I paint pictures, too, and during the leanest times I started selling a few to help pay the bills. There's a big landscape I did of Silk Mountain hanging in the local bank."

"My mom encouraged me to paint when I was a kid," he said. "The kitchen, the living room, the barn…"

Marik laughed. "I do some of that, too."

They'd gone another mile before he spoke again. He cleared his throat first, and she heard the hesitation in his voice.

"I have a son," he said. "If you hired me, I would want

to make sure it was okay for Zane to spend some time with me here. Mostly weekends, maybe longer in the summer." He looked out across the fields beside the road, as if the thought of his son made him sad. "He's a quiet kid, not rowdy."

Maybe that had something to do with his wanting the job—a good place in the country for his son. Marik smiled. "I like kids. I was teaching school before Dad died and I came back here. As long as it didn't interfere with your work, I'd have no problem with your son coming to visit. How old is Zane?"

"He's eight."

The same age as my daughter. She squinted toward the road ahead and waited out a sensation like her insides turning over.

Somebody else's daughter.

Chapter Three

A July morning, eight years and seven months ago... From the right seat of the single-engine Cessna, Marik looked out across a bluestem pasture beyond the runway of a country airport. The bleached tips of the grass rippled like an ocean in the Oklahoma wind. The pasture looked solid enough to walk on, but looks were deceiving; the thigh-high grass could conceal a coyote or a newborn calf, or even a person. She imagined lying down in the grass, hiding from the ache that filled her spongy stomach.

A clear sky umbrellaed the landscape. Far to the southwest, toward the ranch, a few clouds hugged the horizon. She leaned back on the padded seat and watched her father on the tarmac, going through his preflight checks. He examined the gas sumps for water, lifted the cowling and checked the oil stick. She'd done it with him dozens of times, but today she had no desire to copilot, or to be in charge of anything. She was just a passenger, sore and tired, going home without a baby in her arms.

She closed her eyes and saw a tiny face, ruddy with frowning, the puffy eyes squinted shut. *My daughter,* she had thought, trying on the phrase like an unfamiliar wrap. But not for long.

The alarming red imprint of forceps just behind the temple. No harm, the nurse said, perfectly normal for a first delivery. The mark would go away.

The only thing beautiful about a newborn, she thought, is the fact of its being, the miracle of its life.

Then the nurse took her away.

The attorney sat in the hospital administrator's office, his hair streaked with gray. A crucifix on the wall of the office...the smell of furniture polish. On the desk, a photo of two small children, a boy and a girl. She glanced at them and turned away.

Manicured hands laid the papers before her.

The room felt cold. She pulled the collar of her robe around her neck. Beneath her robe she wore the pajamas her father had brought her, cream with pink roses. His hand lay warm and familiar on her shoulder.

"Are you sure, honey? Once you sign these papers, there's no going back." His voice low, his face creased and tight.

They had talked it over endlessly; nothing else to say.

"It's the right thing. Isn't it?" Her voice raspy, not like hers.

"I believe it is, yes."

Now she picked up the gold pen, scrawled her name, handed it back without looking up.

"I know it's hard," the attorney said. "But they're a wonderful couple."

Her father's arm supported her when she tried to stand.

In the antiseptic-scented hallway, a woman in a seersucker robe passed them and peered at Marik's puffy face. Marik turned away, laid her forehead on her father's shoulder.

"I couldn't get through this without you," she whispered.

"You don't have to," he said, petting her hair. "I'll always be here."

Her father ran his hands over the prop blades, checking for blemishes. A yellow sun flowered in the east, heating the cockpit through the high windshield. The Cessna rocked as J.B. tested the flaps and trim tabs, manually working the ailerons and rudder. Marik thought, not for the first time, how young her father looked. Too young to be a grandfather, she told herself, but didn't believe it.

A widower for fifteen years, J.B. was still lean and fit. When he came to visit her on campus her freshman year, her roommates had flirted with him. If he had moved to town instead of staying on the isolated ranch after her mother died, he probably would have remarried. But he loved the ranch, and he wanted to raise his daughters there.

Now lines of worry etched his sun-weathered face, and she was responsible for those lines. She would make it up to him, stay on the ranch and help him run it, like a son.

J.B. climbed inside the four-seater and buckled himself in, yelled the regulation warning out the window—"Clear the prop!"—though there was no one close enough to hear.

The Cessna's engine fired to life and the plane shuddered.

She watched the oil pressure come up while her father checked the fuel gauge and the alternator. He tested the magnetos one at a time, listening for roughness. Queenie was running like a dream. She always did.

J.B. looked at her. "How are you doing?"

Her episiotomy pulled like barbed wire and her swollen breasts throbbed with every vibration of the engine.

"Fine," she said.

"Let's fly."

He handed her a headset and she put it on. The engine revved and the Cessna strained forward, lusting for the sky. At the end of the runway her father brought the plane around, checked the mags again, switched the radio to tower. They were the only aircraft on the strip. Clearance for takeoff came immediately and Marik laid her head back, waiting for the plane's slight sideways skid after liftoff, like a feather caught in a breeze.

J.B. banked right. Wind buffeted the plane like a motorboat on choppy water until they gained altitude and leveled off. The hospital was several counties from home, where she could remain anonymous, but the flying time would be short. There was nothing to do but watch the horizon until they approached the grass landing strip on the ranch.

Her dad's hand reached over and covered hers. "Are you hungry?"

"Not really."

"Once we get you settled in, I'll drive to town for some groceries. And anything else you need me to pick up."

Like extra maxi-pads. Breast pads, a prescription. Would

the clerk at the Pacheeta Wal-Mart recognize him and wonder about his purchases?

She hadn't been off the ranch since she'd come home, sequestering herself in the house, her car in the barn. No one else had known she was home and pregnant except Monte, whose silence was ironclad, and Daisy Gardner. Daisy had put them in touch with a private adoption agency, and she, too, would never breathe a word.

All of them would protect the awful thing Marik had done.

Chapter Four

The clock atop the county courthouse showed ten minutes before nine when Marik drove into Pacheeta with a dead eagle in the back of her truck. Half the parking spaces along Main Street corralled pickups and SUVs, and the lighted windows of the Corner Café displayed a late-breakfast crowd. There were no boarded-up storefronts here; compared to Silk, the county seat swarmed with commerce.

The regional office of the Oklahoma Department of Wildlife Conservation sat next to the courthouse and across from the town square. In the square, a community pavilion flaked white paint onto the dormant grass, and a statue of Will Rogers stood sentinel above a concrete pool drained for winter. A lariat dangled from Will's hand, and his bronze hat sat askew above a face expertly modeled with his whimsical smile. Unlike the state's amiable native son, Marik had met plenty of men she didn't like. But she'd always loved that sculpture.

Beside her on the breezy seat of Red Ryder, Jace Rainwater observed the town without comment. Except for the sculpture, Pacheeta looked like a hundred other small towns, and Rainwater looked as if he'd seen them all before.

She circled the block, past the *Pacheeta Tribune* that supplied the county with local news and gossip. An alley ran behind the wildlife building and she turned into it, hoping to unload her cargo away from the eyes of curious pedestrians. Two vehicles occupied a potholed gravel area next to the alley. Marik parked close to a metal door with ODWC stenciled in white letters on its brown paint.

The door was locked, and nobody responded to her pounding. She went back to the truck, where Rainwater was securing the tarp around the eagle after its windy trip. "I guess we can leave it here for a few minutes while we go inside," she said.

He nodded. "Not much traffic back here."

They walked down the alley and turned on to a quiet, spider-veined sidewalk. A brittle sun warmed their shoulders until they rounded the next corner, where the shade swaddling the front entrance of the building still felt like winter. Rainwater opened a glass door and held it for her. Marik stepped onto the industrial-strength carpet of a small outer office.

A young woman with straight, jaw-length hair sat behind

a desk, staring into a computer screen. Her hair looked too black to be natural, but it was striking against paper-white skin. One or two strategic piercings and she could be a Goth girl. The phone on her desk rang and she held up a red-nailed finger. "Be right with you."

"Department of Wildlife," she said into the receiver. There was a long pause while the girl rolled her eyes. "Gee, you're the first guy who thought of that joke," she said. "Is there something *else* I can help you with?" Another pause. "Just a moment, I'll see if he's in."

She punched the hold button and hung up. Her eyes flickered over the lanky form of Jace Rainwater and she smiled brightly. "Now then. How can I help you folks?"

"We need to see a ranger, if we can, or some other conservation official," Marik said.

"You're in luck. Ranger Ward is actually in this morning." She turned her head toward a hallway behind her desk and hollered in a voice that could have brought cattle in for milking. "Roger? Somebody here to see you!"

In seconds a wiry, fortyish man with a fairy ring of brown hair appeared in the opening to the hallway. He wore jeans crimped at the knees, cowboy boots and a tan-colored shirt with a Wildlife Department logo on the pocket. "We do have an intercom, Kim," he said to the receptionist, but his voice was as mild as the rest of him.

Kim shrugged, grinning. "Sorry." The hold button on the phone continued to blink.

"Morning. I'm Roger Ward," the ranger said, offering his hand to Marik first.

Marik thought how she would sketch him: oval head, round bald pate, oval wire-rimmed glasses, oval body and thighs. He wasn't fat, though, just compact, and no taller than she was. She introduced herself and her companion.

The ranger shook hands with Rainwater. "Come on back to my office."

Ward's office was just what she expected. Battered wooden desk, cluttered bookcase, a faux-tile floor that felt slightly gritty underfoot. Dusty but impressive portraits of Oklahoma's larger wildlife hung on the walls— whitetail deer, bobcat, elk, even a woolly black bear. Marik recognized the artist's name. From atop the bookcase, mounted specimens of bobwhite quail, wood duck and wild turkey fixed them with glassy stares. There was almost room to sit down in the two straight chairs Ward offered.

"Actually," Marik said, "the reason we came is out back in the bed of my truck. Can we bring it inside?"

Ward's interest perked up. "An animal?"

She saw a sharp intelligence in the faded blue of his eyes. "A bald eagle, we think."

The eyes widened. "Alive?"

"Unfortunately, no. I found it on my place this morning."

"Killdeer Ridge, right? Where the wind farm is."

"Right." He had recognized her name, like everybody else since the windmills went up. Sometimes she missed being debt ridden and anonymous.

"Let's take a look." He grabbed his oval ranger hat from beneath the turkey's wattle.

Why did men around here never step outdoors without a hat on?

In the alley, Rainwater carefully uncovered their cargo and they all leaned over the truck bed, arms on the sidewalls. Ranger Ward whistled through his teeth. "Isn't that a beauty."

"I'm guessing an immature female," Rainwater said.

Ward checked the tail feathers. "Good eye. Most people can't tell an immature bald eagle from a golden." He looked up at Jace. "It isn't banded. Any idea what killed it?"

Marik and Rainwater glanced at each other. "No visible blood or bullet wound," Rainwater said.

"Huh. Exactly where was the eagle when you found it?"

"Up on the high ridge," she said.

"You found it beneath the windmills?"

She nodded, her face glum.

"Uh-oh," he said.

"You know the Gurdmans, my neighbors?"

"Not personally, but I'm familiar with their complaints about the wind farm."

Marik sighed. "I'd like to keep this quiet until we know for sure what killed the eagle."

"No need to make an announcement. Let's get the carcass inside and look at it closer."

In a back room, the ranger laid the eagle out on a table and checked it over. Within a minute, he leaned over and smelled it.

"Diazanon?" Rainwater said.

Ward gave him a sharp look. "That's what I was thinking. Why the heck would an eagle smell like tick poison?"

"Good question," Marik said. "My friend here suggested a necropsy."

"Absolutely. We can learn a lot from a carcass. Birds have practically no sense of smell. It might have eaten poisoned meat despite the odor. Eagles do eat carrion sometimes."

Ward bagged and tagged the bird, then laid it gently in a chest-type freezer. "I'll put in a call to our chief biologist in Oklahoma City. Either he'll get a local vet to do the necropsy, or we'll send it to a special U.S. Fish and Wildlife installation in Wisconsin."

"That could take a long time."

"Yup. That's why we're going to freeze her. If Wendell can't come get the carcass, I'll have to pack it in ice and haul it to the city."

"Maybe we should call Sam Sullivan," Rainwater said, "up at the Sutton Avian Research Center in Bartlesville. I know they keep records on Oklahoma eagles."

"Good idea," Ward said. "They've coordinated with the department on migratory-bird incidents before." He smiled. "You know Sam?"

"Went to school with him a year or so. And I did some volunteer work at the research center."

"Sam's a good guy. Knows his stuff." He washed and dried his hands. "We need to fill out a report. Where you found it, date and time, any other circumstances."

He led them back into his office and cleared off a space in the center of the desk. After two tries, he found a ballpoint that worked. Marik and Rainwater sat, their knees touching the front of the desk, while she supplied the information the ranger asked for. He finished the paperwork and sat back in his chair, the springs squeaking.

"There's a town meeting coming up in Silk in about a week," she told him. "I'd sure like to know what killed the eagle before that."

His frown looked doubtful. "It usually takes longer. But I'll do what I can to hurry things up."

"Do you believe an eagle would really fly into those windmill blades?"

Ward shrugged. "It's unlikely, but it's possible. Out in California, there was an incident like that, but those windmills were built directly in the eagles' migration path, and it isn't a migration month here. The trouble is, there's a shortage of science on how the windmills might affect the ecology. Since the power companies don't announce where the wind farms will be built much before they build them, nobody's had a chance to map the ecology of a location beforehand. There's no control data, we don't know the natural patterns of the wildlife or even the plants in the area before the windmills—only after.

"Some biologists think the eagles might view the windmills as perches when the blades are still, and try it again when they're moving."

"That seems hard to believe."

"Yeah, it does. But we don't know about the songbirds or game birds in the area, either. Some might not nest there anymore because they view the wind towers as raptor perches, or the flickering shadows as raptor wings."

Marik frowned. "Even if that's true, wouldn't they just move over to the next pasture or creek?"

He shrugged. "Probably."

"Well, there aren't any trees on Killdeer Ridge, but the killdeer still nest all over the ground up there."

Ward smiled. "That's good to know. Wildlife is pretty darned adaptable. If it weren't, we wouldn't have any left. If you want my personal opinion, we've got to do something to cut down fossil fuel consumption, and for producing electricity, at least, wind farms are the best idea yet. The long-term benefits to the ecology far outweigh any short-term potential for harm." He shrugged. "But the real scientists want more proof."

"I don't think my neighbors' objections have anything to do with science," Marik said. She took a paper from a cube on his desk and jotted down a number. "That's my cell. It's the best way to get me." She stood up. "I appreciate your time."

He gave her a direct look. "Thanks for bringing the bird in. You did the right thing."

"Yeah, well. We'll see if good deeds go unpunished."

She followed Rainwater out through the front entrance. Kim was multitasking, the phone receiver gripped under her chin while she typed an e-mail and waved goodbye.

Marik filled up with gas at a Love's Country Store at the edge of town. On the drive they talked about her ranch operation and the proposed second phase of wind turbines. Rainwater said all the right things, but she listened for subtext that might signal problems. She didn't fault him for the wall of privacy around his family; she wouldn't discuss her personal life with a stranger, either. The main things that concerned her were the estranged wife and his over-qualification. She didn't want to train a ranch manager for six months only to have him quit and move on to a better-paying job.

Wind whipped through the passenger window and the truck bounced along the two-lane road. "Okay, direct question," she said. "And remember that I can check on this. Have you ever been arrested or jailed for anything?" She glanced at him sideways.

"No." He smiled. "Check all you want to."

"Then why are you willing to work for the pay I'm offering?"

He took a breath before answering. "I don't like cities, even if that's where the money is. And I would expect that after six months or so, if you were happy with my work, you'd be willing to raise the salary."

She nodded but said nothing. Her finances were too iffy to make promises.

It was eleven o'clock when they approached Silk. "How about a Sonic burger and a cherry limeade?" she said. "I'm starving."

She pulled into a drive-in stall and killed the engine. The day had warmed, and with their jackets on, the cab was comfortable even with the half-open window. She let him look over the menu a minute before she punched the call button. A teenage voice with a West Texas accent emerged with a hail of static from the speaker box. Marik wondered why the girl wasn't in school.

"I'll have a bacon burger and onion rings," Marik said and looked at Rainwater.

"Broiled-chicken sandwich and a side salad with Italian." She gave him a shocked look, but repeated his order into the speaker and added two cherry limeades.

"High cholesterol runs in my family," he said.

"Ah. You had parents."

He smiled. "Grandparents, too, so I'm told."

Marik's cell phone vibrated in her jacket pocket. She glanced at its tiny window and smiled. Daisy Gardner had seen her truck in town.

"Excuse me," she said to Rainwater as she flipped the phone open. Then to Daisy, "You'll never get your paperwork done if you keep watching out the window."

"In my job it pays to be nosey," Daisy said. "Can you stop by the office?"

"I've just ordered lunch, actually. And I'm not by myself."

"I know, and it looked like a *man* in there."

"What, you're using binoculars now?"

"Why are you riding him around in that old wreck of a truck instead of your perfectly nice SUV?"

"Long story. How about lunch tomorrow? I want to come in and get horse feed anyway."

"Okay, but call me this afternoon when you're alone. We need to talk. Today." She sounded pissed off.

"What's up?"

"I'll tell you later. And you can tell me who that is in your truck."

"Right. See you."

Marik closed and pocketed the phone. "My friend Daisy," she said to Rainwater. "Just another reason there are no secrets in this town."

Which wasn't quite true. Daisy had kept at least one secret for eight years.

The carhop brought their food, and after the obligatory rustling of sacks and paper-clad straws, they settled down to eating. Static crackled sporadically from neighboring speaker boxes, and from the top of a power pole, a mockingbird sang a forecast of spring. Marik kept thinking about Daisy's warning: *We need to talk.*

Had Daisy somehow learned about the private investigator she'd hired?

"You're right about the cherry limeade," Jace Rainwater said, his mouth half-full. "Good sandwich, too."

That afternoon she drove Rainwater over the parts of the ranch he hadn't seen earlier—the north quarter, hilly and forested, where elk sometimes passed through; and next to it the upper pastures, still dormant in February. Killdeer Ridge bisected the ranch at a slight angle from east to west. South of the ridge, two herds of cattle were grazing on winter wheat in the flat fields close to the river. A large pasture also bordered the river, part of it fenced off around a sheet-metal hangar and a grass landing strip for lightplanes. Today the airstrip was unmowed and looked abandoned.

"The foreman will be the only full-time hand, at least for now," she told him. "I'll hire extra help for jobs like cutting and branding."

Rainwater's hands clenched and unclenched on the knees

of his jeans, as if they were anxious to get to work. He asked smart questions, and she saw the thirsty expression in his eyes when he looked at the landscape. "It sure would be good to work cattle again," he said.

She knew the feeling. Marik loved cattle and she loved the land, even though she had once abandoned it. Monte used to say, *You can't beat out of the hide what's bred in the bone.*

Jace Rainwater was her best prospect for the manager position, and she could use an ally who had an appropriate education to back up the things she knew instinctively about ranching. Marik had majored in art and education— not the sort of credentials that carried much weight with a bank or her ranching neighbors. But she couldn't afford to make a quick decision about someone she'd be working with daily, who would live a few steps from her house. She sent Rainwater back to Amarillo with a promise that she'd make a decision within two weeks. Meanwhile, she could phone a couple of his references and have the P.I. do a background check. Might as well get something for her money.

She stood on the gravel driveway and watched Rainwater's white truck drive away, wishing Monte were here to help assess his possible replacement. Monte was a better judge of character than anyone she knew.

Wind swept across the yard and solitude surged around her. She was the only living person for farther than her voice could carry. If she dropped dead like that poor eagle, no one would know and few would care.

Okay, that's pathological. Cut it out.

The place was too damn quiet. She ought to get a dog.

The last dog on the ranch was Monte's old basset hound, a low-slung submarine named Rush Hour. The dog was lovable and useless, and when he died Monte was so broken up neither he nor J.B. got around to replacing him. What Marik wanted now was a big, furry ranch dog that would set up a ruckus if a stranger came onto the place.

She carried a bucket of horse feed and dumped it into the feeder in the corral. A ranch without horses was just wrong, so she had kept Lady and Gent. The blaze-faced mare and chestnut gelding coexisted in the small pasture behind the barn. When she was a kid and the ranch was prosperous, they'd had a string of twenty.

Her melancholy persisted, and instead of calling Daisy back right then, she walked toward the small barn next to the corral. It used to be a hay barn, but now it held something altogether different.

Her boots crunched in the silence. The barn door's curved handle felt cold in her palm when she rolled it open. In the barn's shady interior, the remnants of her father's green and white Cessna airplane lay mangled on the dirt floor.

Chapter Five

Marik stepped into the triangle of light on the barn floor and paused to let her eyes adjust to the surrounding shadows. No matter how many times she confronted the wreckage, her breath caught hard in her chest. J.B. had worshipped that plane, a sweet little Cessna 210 that he treated like royalty. Marik had loved it, too, once. But something faulty with its engine or wiring had killed her father. It was hard to look at the ruined fuselage, but even harder to have it hauled away as junk. To her the aircraft was still an indivisible part of J. B. Youngblood.

The musty smells of mice and old hay closed around her, and beneath that the metallic scent of engine oil. Overhead, sparrows chirped from the lofted darkness. When she was very young, the hay barn had been a magical place. She remembered two little girls scrambling over a mountain of hay bales that reached to the rafters. In a crevice between the prickly bales, they'd found a nest of sightless kittens. Nowadays hay was packaged in giant round bales and lined up along fences like Jurassic caterpillars. Today's ranch kids didn't know the joy of playing in the hay.

She took a deep breath that stuttered in her chest as her gaze settled on the ruined airplane. The left side of the cockpit was torn raggedly open, as if bitten away by monster teeth. The monster was a grove of hackberry trees that had ripped J.B. from his seat as the plane cartwheeled. She tried not to imagine the horror that must have seized him as he vaulted through the sky, out of control. Did images of his life pinwheel before him? Did he think of the granddaughter he never knew?

In her nightmares she flew with him and felt it all.

They'd found his body hanging in the branches, fifty yards from where the Cessna finally scraped to a halt. He was only twenty miles from the ranch when he crashed, on his way to pick her up for a visit. She was living halfway across the state at the time, a traveling art teacher for a sprawling rural school district. If she had promised to drive home for spring break, maybe he would be here today.

Funerals should be held in the gray chill of November, or in August's punishing heat. Not in springtime with the pasture singing flowers. After he was buried, she'd made the hay barn available to FAA officials for their investigation. Aeronautics experts brought the aircraft here piece by careful piece and laid it out like a jigsaw cadaver, just as it remained now. Their verdict was inconclusive. The plane had undergone its required annual inspection and maintenance only a few weeks before, and J.B. never did trust those annuals. He said something was more likely to go wrong with the plane after it was tinkered with by unfamiliar hands. Maybe he was right.

The Cessna was the last thing her father had touched, and he felt more alive to her here than in the little family cemetery where she and Anna used to play. When they were six and eleven, they had set up their dolls on their mother's grave and talked to her when the lonesomeness got too strong. But they grew older and the memory of their mother dimmed. Anna stopped going to the cemetery, but Marik never did. Now both her parents lay in the tall grass beside two generations of grandparents, a bachelor uncle, several family dogs and Leasie, the ghost lady of Silk Mountain. All of them watched over by the towering windmills.

Marik walked around the tail section of the airplane and looked down at the grounded right wing, the only part left completely intact. She'd made her first solo flight in this plane when it was new and she was seventeen—her dad waiting with a magnum of champagne when she returned, even prouder than she was. Anna was gone by then, but Monte was there to help them celebrate. In the barn's artificial dusk, she saw J.B.'s jubilant face that day—and then the quick contrast of his wounded eyes four years later, the day she'd driven home from her apartment at the University of Oklahoma.

He couldn't avoid staring at the expanse of her stomach when she'd dragged her lumpy suitcase up the front-porch steps. She read his disappointment—his artistic, college-educated daughter caught in a clichéd mistake, her bright future in jeopardy.

She had called her father to tell him, to ask if she could come home. But she hadn't said she was already seven months along, having hidden from her college friends by moving off campus, dropping her classes when she began to show. She'd intended to go it alone, but she chickened out. He must have expected her to look the same as always, not showing yet, with options still available.

"My God, Marik," was all he said, and her heart was a boulder in her chest.

"I'm sorry, Dad." It was the first in a litany of apologies, but her father had already wrapped her in a hug.

Two months later she'd taken her last flight with her dad, coming home from the hospital. Marik knelt in the dust and put her hand on Queenie's metal skin. It felt strangely warm.

A whirlwind swept through the barn door and sifted dust into her eyes. She wiped them on her shirtsleeve. Stood up and straightened her back.

For months after the baby was born, she had continued her self-imposed exile on the ranch, cooking for her dad and Monte, painting landscapes with too many dark colors. Hiding out, waiting for a vacuum to refill. She had no appetite and she spent sleepless hours in the middle of the night. Her father tried to get her to talk; so did Daisy. But she had no words for the emptiness inside her, the strange weightedness of her limbs.

Finally her dad had insisted she shouldn't give up on her degree with only two semesters left. She was to be the first Youngblood to graduate from college. To make him proud, she'd agreed to go back. She moved to campus, two hours' drive from the ranch, and rented a room from an elderly lady whose house smelled of lavender and dust.

A week before graduation, she'd received a job offer from a school district three hundred miles from home. The prospect of earning her own way, in a place where no one knew her, felt like absolution. Instead of going back to the ranch, she'd moved away to start her life over.

She'd been teaching four years at the time of J.B.'s accident. Suddenly her father was gone, denied the only grandchild he might have known. Her grief was a cyclone, for her dad and for her unknown daughter—the last of the Youngblood line.

When Marik came out of the barn, Daisy Gardner's dust-colored Honda was parked on the circular driveway near the house. The sight of it gave Marik an uneasy moment; she had not heard a car drive up. She rolled the barn door shut, latched it and walked across the yard toward her friend. A distinct chill had diluted the February sunshine. In less than an hour the sun would drop behind Killdeer Ridge and cast the outbuildings into premature dusk.

Daisy was leaning against the fender with her arms crossed, one loafered foot angled over the other. She was still in her work clothes, an embellished cotton jacket and khaki slacks that smiled at the knees. Daisy knew what was inside the barn and had chosen not to interrupt, but she didn't look happy.

"You were supposed to call me," she said.

"Sorry. I had company until a little while ago. An applicant for the foreman job."

"The guy who was in your truck today."

"Right. Seems like a good prospect."

"Is he married?" Daisy asked.

Marik chose the short answer. "Yes."

Daisy sighed heavily. "The good ones always are."

"Come on in," Marik said, starting toward the house. "It's happy hour."

Daisy followed her up the cobblestone path with her tote bag hanging from one arm. She wouldn't cross the street without that bag. It was her portable office, stuffed with case files, feminine necessities and more snacks than a vending machine.

Beneath the carport, they climbed three concrete steps to a side door that opened into the large, lived-in kitchen. The room stayed a bit too warm, even in winter, but this evening the kitchen's warmth felt good to Marik. She took off her jacket and tossed it onto a chair.

Daisy parked her tote bag beside the battered oak table that had been the hub of Youngblood family life for fifty years. In the open top of Daisy's bag Marik saw the toaster tarts and fruit roll-ups Daisy used to calm frightened child clients, and minisacks of Dorito chips to which Daisy was addicted.

"Wine or something harder?" Marik said.

"How about a good stiff scotch. It's been one helluva day."

"Uh-oh." Marik took wine and scotch from a cabinet and two glasses from another, adding ice to one. The Chivas was left over from J.B.'s stash. Marik didn't drink the hard stuff and had given up beer because of the calories. Her friend had no such restrictions.

Daisy sank her plump backside into a chair at the table. "First I had to repossess a two-year-old from a foster home where he was in great hands and return him to his worthless mother on a court order. And then—and *then*—I find out you've hired a private detective to hunt for your daughter! In violation of your signed legal agreement."

Marik sighed. "What did he do, call you for information after I warned him not to?"

"Not quite that klutzy. He had somebody *else* call me." She made a noise like a snort. "I got more information out of her than she did from me."

"What a surprise."

Marik set Daisy's scotch on the table and sagged into a chair with her wine. "I haven't broken any laws yet. Only when—and if—I actually contact her or the family."

Daisy fixed her with a direct look, her hazel eyes large behind her frameless glasses. "If you do contact her, I will report you to the judge."

Marik looked at her and knew this was a promise. "Thanks for your support."

"You know how I feel about this. You signed a Consent

to Adoption. I have told you she's healthy and well cared for, and that's all you get to know. Not only is it illegal for you to meddle in her childhood, it's selfish and wrong."

Marik looked into the red depths of her wineglass and said nothing. But Daisy wasn't finished.

"The parents could get an injunction," she warned, "maybe even get you arrested. And you'd deserve it."

The force of her words silenced them both. Daisy sat back and drank a lusty draft of her scotch.

There was more gray in her brown hair than Marik had noticed before, and age spots speckled her efficient hands. Despite the difference in their ages, they had always been close. "I promised Dad I'd find her," she said quietly.

"Graveside promises aren't binding." Daisy's eyes softened. "I know you miss J.B. so much you can hardly stand it. And you regret that he never got to know his grandchild. Believe me, I get that. I miss him, too." She blinked several times and traced a damp circle on the table beneath her glass. "I guess I was more or less in love with your dad for twenty years."

Daisy had never admitted this before, but Marik had seen the way Daisy looked at her father. If he'd shown the slightest interest, Daisy might have been her stepmom. Instead, because her own early marriage had dissolved without children, Daisy looked after the interests of dozens of kids on her caseload. She delivered tough love and strict ethics, but there was nothing she wouldn't do to help a child in need—and that had always included Marik.

The kitchen clock ticked, and Marik heard the wind gust through the carport.

"I've regretted giving her up a million times," she said, her voice low. "I wasn't thinking of the best interests of the child, or even my dad. I was only thinking of me, that I wasn't ready to be a mother. Dad supported my decision so I could go on with my life like the self-involved college kid I was. He would have loved to raise a granddaughter here on the ranch. But I chose not to think about that."

Daisy shook her head. "You're too hard on yourself. You always were. But that doesn't give you the right to renege on your decision."

Marik met her eyes. "My daughter is all the family I have left."

"You have Anna."

"Not really. I haven't seen her since Dad's funeral, and before that it was years. Anna never even knew I had a child."

Ice cubes clinked in Daisy's empty glass. "You wouldn't be able to leave it at just finding your daughter. I know you. If you saw her you'd want to be involved in her life, and that isn't fair. Not when she's so small and innocent."

A realization popped quiet as a soap bubble in Marik's mind. "You know where she is, don't you?"

Daisy's eyes didn't flinch. "I have always known. I kept track so I could assure you—and J.B.—that she was loved and happy. And she is."

"You told Dad that?"

"Yes, I did. Several times."

Marik's nose burned. At least he knew that much. "Have you seen her?"

"Not for quite a while."

The light outside the window had turned dusky pink and Marik felt the coming sundown in her bones. "I wonder if she looks like Dad."

"Maybe she looks like her *own* dad," Daisy said pointedly.

For all her ethics, Daisy was excruciatingly curious. Marik had never told anyone who fathered her child—not J.B., not even the baby's father—and Daisy never missed an opportunity to prod for clues. Marik guarded that secret as faithfully as Daisy protected the privacy of adoption.

Daisy sighed and pushed herself to her feet, her knees cracking. "I've got to go. Mounds of paperwork yet tonight." She shouldered the tote bag. "I guess you know about the town meeting and what's on the agenda."

"I know, all right."

"The power company will no doubt send a representative. Maybe they'll make a good argument."

"Hmm."

At the door, Daisy turned. "I'm serious, Marik. Do not go looking for that child. She doesn't belong to you, and she hasn't since you signed those papers."

Marik watched the taillights disappear down the driveway, feeling Daisy's censure like an anvil in her chest. Finally she refilled her wine and put on her jacket.

She passed through the living room without turning on a light. The glassy eyes of a bull elk and two whitetail bucks glittered from the high walls below a vaulted ceiling. They were J.B.'s trophies from years ago, his hunting phase. Someday she'd get rid of them, but not yet. Her boots thumped quietly on the padded rug, noisily on the hardwood floor at the room's perimeter, and out the front door to the cedar-planked porch.

The porch was wide and deep, her favorite place to watch the evening come down. She eased into a wooden glider that centered a cluster of chairs in the shadow of the overhang. All those chairs—as if company might drop by at any moment. Nobody else had sat here since Monte cleared out months ago.

It was a credit to their shockproof friendship that she and Daisy could disagree and move on with no permanent damage. They'd done it before. But Marik wasn't sure that would hold true this time, not if she actually contacted her daughter.

Was Daisy right? Was her desire to find her child selfish and wrong?

Her decision to give up her baby had hinged to a large extent on the fact that she couldn't be a single mom without the father's knowing. And she had reason to believe he'd be a lousy father. She had told herself the baby deserved better parents, but part of her wanted to punish him for disappointing her. Maybe that was selfish, too. But none of it changed her desire to find her child.

She'd given up her legal rights, but how did you give up regret, or the knowledge of a shared biological link? She remembered the feel of that heartbeat inside her, the wrinkled reality of those tiny hands.

Marik drained her wine, inhaled against the vise of her rib cage. The glider squeaked back and forth. If she lost Daisy's stalwart friendship, she'd be even more alone than she was now.

Up on the ridge, the windmills turned steadily, reflecting the last rays of a winter sun that had slipped behind the horizon. She watched the fading light climb the towers. When shadow swallowed the highest rotors, darkness fell quickly. Uncountable stars dotted the sky. Here there were no streetlights, no neon signs of civilization. Only the tiny red beacons atop the wind towers, blinking like sleepy eyes.

An owl called low and haunting near the barn, and from the windbreak behind the house, his mate answered. Halfway up the ridge near the cemetery, a coyote sent up its lonesome yipping, sounding like a whole pack.

This was her life now. Was she tough enough to be alone?

She understood why her father spent his life here even after her mother died. He'd loved the solitude. Anna had hated it. Marik wondered how their mother had coped with such exquisite isolation, an East Coast girl who had found her way west. Did Julianna love it as much as her free-spirited husband? Or was she like the ghost of Silk Mountain, driven to the edge by the terrifying beauty of so many stars?

In Marik's oil paintings, the outline of a hidden figure, feminine, invariably appeared somewhere in the background as if it painted itself. Sometimes she thought of the figure as her mother, who'd died from an ectopic pregnancy too far from a hospital. Other times she thought of the hidden figure as herself, and sometimes as the daughter she had given away.

"I never did belong here the way you do," Anna had said on the afternoon she signed over her share of the ranch. "We both know that deep down you're a hard-assed Oklahoma rancher, just like Dad." And Marik heard the envy in her soft voice.

Maybe Dad wasn't hard enough. Maybe I'm not, either.

She pulled the cell phone from her pocket and pushed a button to light up its address book. She scrolled down to Casey Scott's number, the cowboy-booted P.I. who had inadvertently tipped off Daisy about her search. He answered his cell phone on the third ring.

"Casey, it's Marik Youngblood. Can you talk a minute?" In the background she heard voices and the clank of silverware. "Sounds like I caught you at dinner."

His baritone came back with predictable breakup. "No problem. I'm eating alone. What's up?"

"I have another job for you. Just a small one. I need a background check on a man who's applied for a job here on the ranch."

"Easy done. Give me his name and whatever else you can." She pictured him taking notes on a paper napkin, barbecue sauce on his chin.

"Jace Rainwater. Went to school at TCU, living in Amarillo now. He listed the USDA as a job reference there."

"Okeydokey," he said. "How soon do you need it?"

"By next week, if you can. I don't need the whole family tree, just enough to know whether I'd trust him to live here on the ranch."

"Got it. Should be able to call you back in a few days."

"Any progress on our other project?"

"Not much. The adoption records are sealed and the hospital was a dead end. Couldn't find anybody who worked there eight years ago. Whole staff has turned over since then." She could hear him chewing.

"And you didn't find out a thing from Daisy Gardner, either," she said pointedly.

"Had to try. She's the only link so far."

Marik blew out a deep breath, watching a sleepy red eye wink off and on, off and on. "Let's put that on hold for a while," she said.

"You sure?"

"Yes. Save anything you've got for future reference and send me a bill. But for now let's just check on this guy who wants to be my foreman."

Chapter Six

Ranch work went on, regardless of anyone's personal issues. The bucket calf woke up before daylight, bawling his curly head off to be fed. No need for an alarm clock when Bully was on the job. He was gradually learning to eat the calf pellets Marik put in his feeder, but he still needed his milk.

She went out in the semidarkness to feed him. In the big barn she mixed calf formula in an aluminum bucket that had a long nipple on one side and a hook on the opposite rim. She lugged the bucket to a pen in the back of the barn, behind the milking stall that hadn't been used for years. Tools and horse tack covered the barn walls. In its open center, two tractors, a hay baler and a brush hog gathered the dust of disuse. Her father had bought the big John

Deere tractor on credit just a year before he died. She still hadn't paid it off, nor found the heart to sell it.

The calf's plaintive cry echoed from the rafters. "Hey, Bully," she called. "How's it going today?"

Twice a day she hung a bucket of milk on the railing of the pen and held on with both hands. Bully attacked the nipple with an eagerness that made her laugh. His petroleum-colored eyes, fringed with long white lashes, looked depthless in the shadows of the barn. She loved his hot, milky smell and the way foamy white slobber dripped from the corners of his mouth when he drank.

She leaned over the railing and scratched his bony forehead. "You don't know enough to miss your mama, do you, Bully?"

A feral cat peered down at her from the loft. Barn cats came and went, and this one looked like a descendant of an old tom she remembered from childhood. When Bully was finished, she poured the last dribbles from his bucket into an old pie pan her father had used for the same purpose, and left it by the door.

It took three tries to crank Red Ryder to life for her pilgrimage to the windmills. The wind was back in the north this morning, chillier than yesterday. On the crest of the ridge, she parked the pickup and stood on the running board, her eyes scanning dried cactus and sage for a mound of indigo feathers. Finding nothing, she exhaled a deep breath. The impending town meeting hung over her like a heavy boot waiting to drop. She'd never been good at waiting.

Across the valley, ribbons of gold light snaked between violet clouds. A group of elk, dark umber smudges at this distance, grazed at the edge of a creek. An urgency arose in her to paint the feeling of that cool light above the river. She'd been away from the canvas too long. When she checked the cattle in the pastures by the river this morning, she would take along her portable easel and do some plein-air work.

At the house again, she loaded her art supplies into the truck. She'd intended to drive to town today, but that could wait. She still had a few days' horse feed and calf pellets in the barn. Soon Red Ryder was jouncing over a flat field where wheat grew ankle high and shamrock green.

When she'd counted all fifty Herefords, Marik turned a wide circle in the field and rumbled back over the cattle guard at the gate. She checked on a herd of heifers, then drove to a fenced field where the airplane hangar hunkered in shaggy grass. J.B. would not approve of the neglected airstrip, but nobody used it now.

She parked beside the hangar, unloaded her gear and backpacked the folding easel, paint box and camp stool across the runway toward a flat spot near the river. Here the slow copper current made a bell-shaped turn around a rock outcropping and then flowed off to her right, reflecting the color of the sky.

Painting on location sounded romantic to nonartists, but in practice it wasn't always productive: the light changed and the wind blew and bugs got stuck in the paint. Either that, or it was a serendipitous joy. Today held promise for the latter. The morning was warming up, with a diffuse light filtered by thin, high clouds.

Marik tramped through dried grass to a place where an opening in the trees framed the bend of the river in the foreground and a hazy profile of Silk Mountain in the distance. She had painted this scene many times from various angles but was never quite satisfied. Maybe this was the day. She set up her easel with a sense of exhilaration she hadn't felt in a long time.

She described her composition with a few lines, memorizing the way the light looked on the mountain's flat crown right this moment, and began to lay down her dark colors first. She painted fast, standing up, with the quiet flow of the river in her pulse and the tremolo of a meadowlark like light on the grass. Time slipped away without notice.

When at last she stepped back to appraise her work, her shadow lay bunched beneath her feet. The field study was nearly finished and she liked it. She walked away, stretching her shoulders and painting hand, wishing she'd packed a lunch.

The monotone of a lightplane engine purred across the valley. She stood on the open runway and squinted toward the western sky. The airplane was flying the river line, sunshine glinting from its wings. For a disconnected instant she thought maybe it was her dad, and she couldn't wait to see him when he landed. When the illusion dissolved, there was a lump in her throat.

The plane was a low-wing, probably a Piper. The pilot

decreased altitude near the grass landing strip. The strip was still marked on aviation charts, but with no maintenance it would be dangerous to land there.

The plane dropped lower, and her heart rate increased. She stood in the landing path and waved both arms: *Go away!* The small plane buzzed over, then zoomed southward into the sun. She should notify the FAA that the airstrip was inactive. But that wouldn't help if a pilot was using an old chart. She didn't want any accidents here; she'd better mow the grass.

If she had a foreman, she could send him to do the job.

As if by some weird telepathy, her cell phone shimmied in her jacket pocket and when she answered, it was Jace Rainwater.

"Wanted to thank you for lunch and the tour yesterday," he said. "I really enjoyed seeing the ranch." Following up on the interview. "I talked to Ranger Ward," he said. "They're sending the eagle carcass to the U.S. Fish and Wildlife Service for the necropsy."

Marik frowned. "Good grief. How long will that take?"

"I know the regional director for the USFWS. If you like, I could phone him and explain the situation, see if he can speed things up."

"I'd appreciate that. I hate to walk into that meeting without any information."

He signed off with a promise to call if he learned anything. Rainwater was making himself valuable.

Back at her easel, she assessed the painting and with a fine brush added a dark arch in the sky—an eagle patrolling the river. Then she packed up her things and drove back to the real world.

That evening the wind turned sharp and the temperature dropped. One last night of winter. A charcoal sky descended, and in the morning fog lay thick around the outbuildings. The sky had just begun to clear at midmorning when the rural mail carrier drove his truck up to the house to deliver a carton of new canvases she'd ordered from an art-supply catalog.

She carried the carton to her studio. Hazy sunshine lit the north windows. Yesterday's field study sat on the table beside her easel where she'd been laying out the same scene on a larger canvas. The message machine on the landline phone was blinking. She pushed the button and heard a pause and then the click of someone hanging up. Probably a wrong number, but it reminded her to phone Betty Jane Searcy, the mayor's wife.

Marik had known Betty Jane since grade school, though Betty was ten years older. She taught piano students at her home for pocket money and she laughed a lot. Best of all, she didn't take her husband's position as mayor too seriously. When Betty Jane answered, Marik inquired about her family and then came to the point.

"Do I need to sign up in order to speak on behalf of the wind farm at the community meeting?"

"We're really not that formal," Betty Jane said in her leisurely drawl. "Anybody who wants to can talk. We just hope they don't all talk at once." Her laugh was contagious. "I'll put your name down anyway, so you'll be sure to get your turn. Personally I don't understand why anybody would oppose the wind farm."

"I appreciate that," Marik said. "I hope Earl feels the same way."

"He does," Betty assured her. "Say, I've been meaning to call you. Jackson's fiancée saw your painting of Silk Mountain down at the bank and had a fit over it. I'm wondering if you'd consider doing one like it, maybe a little smaller, that I could give them as wedding present. I'll be glad to pay whatever you usually get for those."

"I'd be happy to. When's the wedding?"

Marik made some notes and hung up feeling encouraged.

Pilots have a definition for flying: hours and hours of boredom punctuated by moments of sheer terror. Marik thought the same description applied to life in general. For weeks nothing much had changed at the ranch, and then there was a dead eagle, Jace Rainwater and the threat of that town meeting. So she wasn't surprised that afternoon when the construction contractor who'd erected the windmills called her on the phone.

"We want to get started on development of phase two," he said. "Can I come out tomorrow morning and walk the site with you, get everything squared away?"

Two possibilities flared in her mind. Either word hadn't trickled down through GPP&L that the town was considering a moratorium, or else the bigwigs did know and figured the opposition would have a tougher time stopping a project that was already under way—a sort of corollary to *possession is nine-tenths of the law.*

Either possibility was fine with her. "Come ahead," she said. "Eight o'clock too early?"

From the white gravel road beneath the windmills, they walked down the south slope of the ridge toward the family cemetery. Lou Benson, the construction chief, had supplied Marik with a hard hat from the stash in his pickup. The protective hat was required attire for walking beneath the towers, and she put it on without mentioning that she came here every day without one.

She had first met Benson during the construction of phase one, the first forty-five windmills. Benson had a great face, weathered but clean-shaven, with distinctive bone structure. She seldom did portraits, but he would be an interesting subject, with his graying sideburns and a ponytail that trailed out beneath the hard hat and over his jacket collar. Benson allowed no profanity by his work crew and no littering. On a chain around his neck he wore the small silver outline of a fish.

He had brought along an engineer named Jim Blake who was armed with a map of the completed layout of the wind farm and a pocketful of stakes topped with blue streamers. "We'll mark the preliminary boundaries this morning," the engineer told her, "then survey it this afternoon."

The new windmills would sit lower on the ridge than

the others, catching the updraft of south wind on the slope. The dirt movers would arrive Monday morning, weather permitting, and start carving out the extension to the access road.

During phase-one construction last summer, Marik had done her daily chores with the grinding of the big machines in the background, modern dinosaurs chewing up the earth. She'd spent time on the ridge watching the spectacle, fascinated and unnerved by the gargantuan scale of it, the magnitude of the engineering.

This morning a soft wind swept up the hill, smelling of spring. Just like the day of her father's funeral, only cooler. "My main concern is the cemetery," she told Benson, pointing west where the rocky ground softened into buffalo grass. "I don't want the cemetery driven over or disturbed in any way."

"By all means," Benson said. "Let's go flag it right now."

Marik approached the plot with a feeling like famine in her stomach. Her father's grave was easily discernible, the soil above it still slightly rounded and not quite covered with grass. The others were hidden in matted pasture and marked by grayish, knee-high stones. No fancy granite monoliths here, not even for J.B. His stone, still smooth and new, was similar to the modest memorial he'd chosen for his wife. Leasie Youngblood's marker, the earliest occupant, was a plain white rock with the name and dates scored roughly, as if by the blade of a knife.

Two strands of barbed wire and a wooden gate enclosed the cemetery. "I'm glad to see it's fenced," the engineer said.

"I'll flag all four corners so it will be plainly visible to the machine operators." Blake pulled two red bandannas from his jacket pocket and tore them in half.

He set to work while Lou Benson stood with Marik in the pasture, his quiet eyes scanning the little graveyard and its newest addition. "A family cemetery is a sacred thing," he said. "You have my word we won't violate it. The road can make its turn at least fifty feet from there."

Marik pictured the big machines scraping the earth only fifty feet away and her breath felt tight. But the windmills had saved the ranch from bankruptcy, and once construction was finished, the ridge would be quiet again. With the new road in, she'd be able to drive to the cemetery instead of walking a quarter mile over rough ground.

When the engineer returned, red banners waved from the wooden posts at each corner of the graveyard. For a moment, all three of them observed the area in silence. Then they hiked back up the ridge to stake out the new windmills.

Early Monday morning, four yellow behemoths arrived at the private gate to the wind farm. Marik stood on the front porch and watched them roll onto her property and disappear from view behind the outbuildings. They reappeared along the gravel road and lumbered up the hill like motorized dragons. It should have been exciting—and it was—but there was a certain sadness attached to carving up the land.

She turned away and went indoors.

That week she listened to the growl and scrape of the colossal machines, and the irritating *beep-beep-beep* when they shifted into Reverse. Their steady rumble accompanied her as she unloaded sacks of feed from the back of the truck, followed her to the north pasture when she patched the barbed-wire fence. The noise of the machines blocked out birdsong and cattle calls, the sound of the wind and the windmills.

Even so, she imagined she could hear Burt Gurdman's invectives over a mile away. Lou Benson told her that this time they would post an armed guard overnight on the ridge to prevent vandalism to the machinery.

When Marik mowed the grass airstrip by the river, she killed the tractor engine and sat for a few minutes watching the big earthmovers on the ridge to the north. Horizontal lines sliced the side of the hill, defining the new road. Mounds of white gravel awaited, twinkling like snowy peaks in the sunlight. If construction was stopped, GPP&L had wasted a lot of time and money.

The day before the town meeting, the Pacheeta newspaper carried a story quoting Gurdman's criticism of the wind farm—including the possibility of harmful electrical rays emitted by the transmission of their generated power. There was a reference to "potential dangers to wildlife," but no mention of the dead eagle. Maybe no one at the meeting would know about it. She'd still heard nothing from either Ranger Ward or Jace Rainwater.

She did hear from Casey Scott.

"Got that background check," he told her on the phone. "This guy Rainwater's so clean he makes me nervous. No arrests, no disgruntled ex-employers, not even a speeding ticket. His degree from TCU is legit, and with a three-point-five grade average."

"His references gave me the same story," she said.

"He's living separate from his wife, but apparently spends a lot of time with his son. The kid's in special classes."

"What kind of special classes?"

"The schools don't give out that information. But if it's relevant, I can find out."

"No. It's not relevant." But it might explain Rainwater's concern about his son coming to visit.

"One other thing might be of interest," Scott said. "I saw our friend Daisy Gardner here in Redhorse the day before yesterday."

At the mention of Daisy, Marik felt a little pinch inside her ribs. "Daisy gets around."

"Seemed a little out of her area for a weekday, so I followed her a while, just out of curiosity. She ended up at Will Rogers Elementary School on the west side of town."

"Probably following up on one of her cases."

"Yeah, maybe. But she didn't go in. She was taking pictures, from way back with a long lens. I know you said to drop our original project, but I thought I'd pass that along. No charge."

Marik signed off. Redhorse was in a different county, but there was no telling how far Daisy's surrogate children were scattered. She hadn't heard from her for nearly a week, and that was probably a good thing. Let the tension dissolve, if it would.

In the afternoon she worked in her studio with the windows open, the rumble of machinery floating in on a warm breeze. She had started the painting for Betty Jane Searcy, and the larger version of the river scene was shaping up nicely, too. She'd managed to capture the cool morning light, and the feminine figure appeared among cottonwood trunks at the painting's edge with no conscious bidding. Lost in her work, she barely heard her cell phone ringing somewhere in the house. By the time she found it on the kitchen table, there was a voice mail from Jace Rainwater.

"I'm on the road and the reception's iffy here," he said. "But I wanted to let you know…" A dead space obliterated something. She caught the word *eagle,* then "I'll bring the results to the meeting tomorrow."

The rest of what he said was lost in static. When she called back, a phone-company recording said the number was temporarily unavailable.

That night and again the next morning, she tried Rainwater's number in vain. If she'd understood the gist of his message, he had the necropsy results. But why would he drive all the way to Silk for the community meeting? No matter what the results showed, if nobody in town knew about the eagle, she darned sure didn't want Rainwater to bring it up.

Chapter Seven

The Methodist Fellowship Hall was already half-full when Marik arrived. She hadn't been able to reach either Jace Rainwater or Ranger Ward by phone, and neither of them was seated with the thirty or so citizens scattered among rows of folding chairs on the linoleum floor. Earl Searcy sat behind a table at the front of the room with one of the council members. Two empty chairs awaited other councillors.

Marik recognized most of the crowd from the backs of their heads: Betty Jane Searcy, of course; Deputy Sheriff Bill Ferguson; and five or six neighboring farmers and ranchers, some with their wives and some without. Daisy Gardner and her tote bag lounged halfway from the back on a side aisle. Toward the front, rigid as cardboard cutouts, sat Burt and Lena Gurdman. Burt's ball cap was pulled low on his head.

Marik saw the scene in sepia tones like an old Western movie—*Ambush at Dry Gulch*. She had an urge to turn around and go home. But Daisy was waving her over, moving the tote from a chair she'd been saving. Marik hesitated a moment, but gratitude for having a friend in the room overruled any hard feelings from their last encounter. She walked down the side aisle to join Daisy.

Daisy was cradling a plastic cup and a small bag of Doritos on her lap. She'd probably come straight from work with no time for dinner. "There's coffee over there by the kitchen," she said when Marik sat.

"I'm hopped up enough, thanks. Have you seen anything of Great Plains Power & Light?"

"Not yet, but it's a little early." People were still filing in at the back. Daisy sipped her coffee and eyed Marik with a slight frown. "How have you been?"

"Fine. Why?"

"You look tired. And I haven't heard from you since I raked you over the coals the other day." Her eyebrows lifted, testing Marik's reaction. When there was none, Daisy moved on. "I heard they've started work on the rest of the windmills. A preemptive strike?"

Marik's smile twisted. "Yeah. I guess."

"Nothing like pissing off the enemy before battle." Daisy crunched a corn chip, her eyes surveying the room. "Ah. That guy looks like a power-company drone, doesn't he?"

A sandy-haired man in slacks and a polo shirt had stepped just inside the door, assessing the assemblage through wire-rimmed glasses. He carried a folder of paperwork. Marik recognized the emblem of GPP&L on his green shirt.

"Well, that's two of us, at least," she said.

"I'll bet you've got more support than you think." Daisy offered the cellophane bag. "Dorito?"

Marik shook her head. One of the other council members had taken his seat, and it looked like the third, the only woman, would be absent. Mayor Searcy pounded his gavel with absolutely no effect. People around here didn't see each other that often, and they were enjoying the chance to visit.

The mayor pounded again. Marik cast a glance over her shoulder and saw Ranger Ward step into the hall, followed by a lanky form it took her a moment to recognize without his hat. Jace Rainwater. The two sat down together on the back row, their attention focused on the gavel-rapping from the front of the room. She watched for a moment longer but couldn't catch the eye of either man.

"Let's come to order," Earl shouted. "We have a full agenda and we don't want to be here all night."

The mumble of voices gradually waned. The mayor waved a paper in the air. "Does everybody have a copy of the items for discussion?"

Nobody did. The mayor glanced at his wife and Betty Jane retrieved the agendas from the back table. White papers fluttered down the rows. They hadn't even stopped rustling before Burt Gurdman popped up from his chair.

His weathered face was slightly grizzled, and a stubby fringe of black hair stuck out beneath the edge of the tight-fitting cap. "I have something to say about that wind farm!" he said loudly.

As a young man Burt might have been handsome, but with advancing age his prominent nose had begun to curve toward his chin like a talon, especially when he frowned. And Marik had never seen him without the frown.

Mayor Searcy cut him off. "You'll get your turn, Burt. But that's the third item on the agenda, and we're going to take up the matter of a police chief first." He called on one of the council members, who stood up and began speaking. Gurdman remained standing for a moment, clearly irritated, but finally sat down.

The discussion went on for several minutes. "What's a police chief gonna do, patrol the three paved streets in town?" somebody asked.

A straw vote defeated the question of a police chief.

After that, with the crowd in a placatory mood, the proposal to extend rural water lines to a dozen homes east of town was favorably received.

Burt Gurdman stood up again.

"All right, Burt. Hold your horses a minute while I introduce the discussion," Earl Searcy said. He consulted his notes. "Construction of phase two of the Killdeer Ridge Wind Farm is ready to begin. In fact, I understand preliminary work has *already* begun." He looked over his glasses at the GPP&L guy, who nodded. "This was approved by the council more than a year ago and did not require a general vote because it's on private property. But recent complaints about the project have come to our attention and we wanted some input from the community. As most of you know, Burt and Lena Gurdman's farm borders Killdeer Ridge Ranch, owned by Marik Youngblood. Burt will speak first, then we'll hear from Great Plains Power & Light, and Marik, and anybody else who has something pertinent to contribute." He looked over his glasses at Gurdman. "Go ahead, Burt."

Burt stepped from his seat and faced the group. Marik saw Lena's back stiffen beneath her print dress.

"My cattle and farm are in danger from those damn wind towers, and so are the rest of you, whether you know it or not." He held up a copy of the newspaper article and reiterated his claim that the towers emitted "electrical rays" with unknown effects. He jabbed a finger in the general direction of Marik's ranch. "That beef she's raising could be contaminated. And did you know every one of those windmills has a computer inside it? They could be watching all of us, for all we know, keeping track of what we do, reporting to the government. Or some *other* government!"

Several people in the audience groaned, and Marik heard a snicker.

"It won't be funny if one of your kids turns up with brain cancer!" Gurdman snapped, his face turning darker.

A large woman near the back spoke up. "Those big windmills do kinda look like space aliens. But once you got forty-five space aliens already, what's a few more?"

Laughter rippled through the crowd. People started muttering, making their own jokes, and Marik relaxed in her seat. Maybe she wouldn't have to say a word.

But Gurdman wasn't finished. "Okay, Ella Scoggins," he yelled toward the woman who'd spoken. "If you're not afraid of cancer, ask Marik Youngblood about the dead eagle she found underneath one of those windmills." The room fell quiet. "You're a tree hugger! Bet you didn't know those windmills killed a bald eagle—our national bird!"

As if he gives a shit about the national bird, Marik thought.

All eyes turned toward her, and her face steamed. Unless Kim at the wildlife department office liked to gossip, there was only one way Gurdman could know about the eagle.

She glanced toward the back where Ranger Ward and Rainwater sat, but it was the power company guy who stood up. "I represent Great Plains Power & Light," he said. "I hadn't heard about this, but I can tell you the likelihood of an eagle flying into those blades is extremely slim."

"Then how do you explain that dead bird right under one of them?" Gurdman said. "With its wing broken!"

A hum like an alto chorus of bees rose among the crowd. They looked toward the GPP&L guy for an explanation.

The power company man was at a loss. "My company would like to examine the bird," he said, stammering slightly. "Do you know what happened to the carcass?"

Ranger Ward stood up, wearing the uniform that everyone recognized. "Miss Youngblood brought the eagle to the Department of Wildlife Conservation office in Pacheeta. We sent it off to be examined for cause of death. I've brought someone who can explain those results."

When Jace stood up, even Burt Gurdman fell silent. A new face in town was always interesting, not to mention a ruggedly striking face attached to a six-foot-four frame. There was subdued movement in the room, like the rustling of feathers.

"My name's Jace Rainwater," he said, and tipped a non-existent hat. "A necropsy on the dead eagle was performed by a veterinarian for the U.S. Fish and Wildlife Service. He found the eagle's injuries were not consistent with flying into a stationary object. The wing bone would have been broken at a different angle. His guess—which he can't prove, of course—is that the wing was broken by several strong blows from the top with a blunt object. Like a board or a baseball bat."

A gasp went up from the group. Bodies shifted in chairs, and there were mumblings of indignation. "So what killed it?" somebody asked.

"Diazinon poisoning," he said. "It had eaten meat laced with a heavy concentration of Diazinon. Eagles will eat available carrion, and they don't have much sense of smell."

"You don't use Diazinon to poison varmints," a man said. "You spray it for fleas and ticks. Or we used to, before it was outlawed."

"Exactly." Rainwater allowed them a moment to draw their own conclusions. He raised his voice above the mumbling. "That's why the vet thinks the meat was intentionally tainted."

Lena Gurdman had remained facing forward during this whole exchange. Now she turned quickly to face the stranger at the back of the room, her features sharp as a garden hoe. Marik saw fear and outrage in her eyes.

Burt tugged on the brim of his cap. "Are you accusing me of something, mister?"

Earl Searcy had been elected largely for his peacemaking skills. He rapped his gavel and earned his votes. "Nobody's making accusations. Hell, half the men in the room still have some Diazinon sitting around in a shed somewhere. I know I do."

"Me, too," somebody else put in. "But I damn sure don't use it to poison eagles."

Most of the citizens turned back toward the front, unsure who was to blame for what.

The power company man recovered from his temporary paralysis. "I'd like to point out one more thing," he said. "When the tax money GPP&L pays on the wind farm starts rolling into the county coffers, you might have plenty of money to hire your new police chief." It was obviously the message he had come to deliver before the eagle business derailed him. He smiled weakly and sat down.

"Well, there you are," Mayor Searcy said and rapped his gavel on the table. "Our business being concluded, this meeting is hereby adjourned." He and the other council members made for the door before anyone could object.

Some folks gathered around the coffeepot for further discussion and others filed outside, joking and chatting among themselves. Nobody spoke to Burt and Lena Gurdman, who sat like fence posts in their chairs. Marik almost felt sorry for Lena.

Marik moved outside with the others, feeling as if she'd dodged lightning. On the sidewalk, Ranger Ward and Jace

Rainwater were waiting for her. She frowned at them and spoke softly, so they had to lean close to hear.

"It would be nice," she growled, "if somebody let me in on these things and saved me an ulcer."

Ward laughed and stood with his hands locked behind him like a soldier at ease. "Sorry about that. I just found out myself a few hours ago. And we still wouldn't have known if Jace didn't have a friend with FWS who put a rush on the results."

"What some people will do to land a job," she said, and looked at Rainwater. "You're hired."

Rainwater's face opened and Marik finally smiled. Ward pumped his hand, congratulating him, and then Rainwater shook Marik's hand and Marik shook Ward's hand and they all laughed. Ranger Ward said good-night and walked away toward his truck.

Marik realized Daisy was beside her, waiting to be introduced to her new foreman. She obliged, hoping Daisy wouldn't start her own interview of Rainwater tonight.

"I'll talk to you later," Marik told her. "Thanks for coming."

Daisy took the hint. She started to leave but stopped when two stiff figures appeared in the doorway of the church hall. "Uh-oh," she said.

Marik glanced up into the spiteful eyes of Burt Gurdman. It was dark now, but the ruddy color of Gurdman's face was easily visible in the parking-lot lights. He was gripping his wife's arm as if she might get away.

His voice carried across the space between them. "I guess

you think you've won, missy. You and your damned wind-mills, tearing up the land."

Conversation among the other townsfolk stopped imme-diately. Gurdman took two paces toward Marik, towing Lena. "I wouldn't be so self-righteous if I was you. Let him who's without sin cast the first stone!"

The medicinal smell of his breath hung in the air between them. Marik's mouth opened, but his comment was so absurd she didn't know what to say.

Burt raised his voice another notch. "Maybe the whole town ought to hear the truth about Marik Youngblood. Ask her what happened to her bastard child!"

For a few seconds the air went absolutely still. Marik couldn't breathe.

Then Burt pushed his wife past the astonished stragglers and thrust her toward their beat-up truck. No one on the sidewalk said a word as the Gurdmans climbed inside. Burt backed up and roared away, his tires spitting gravel toward a statue of the Virgin Mary reaching out her white hand.

The townsfolk began to buzz among themselves, but Marik was transfixed by a glimpse of Lena Gurdman's ghostly face looking back through the pickup's smudged window.

Chapter Eight

Lena sat rigid on the truck seat beside her husband and prayed for a wreck that would kill them both.

She liked her chances. Burt was driving like a madman, cursing, stomping the brakes halfway around a corner. The tires skittered sideways and the cracked vinyl of the armrest dug into Lena's palm. She pictured the truck spinning out of control, saw them leaping the grader ditch in slow motion and smashing head-on into the trunk of a hackberry tree. Her heart beat like a hammer against her breastbone. One of these times she would surely explode, dead of a heart attack at forty.

Better sooner than later, if it was sudden. Lena knew a thing or two about suffering, and she wanted no part of that. She had a low threshold for pain. She prayed the pickup would crash before they got home, before Burt's anger turned toward her. And before she had to face the cancer she was certain flowered right this minute in her womb, eating her up from the inside out, just like her mother.

But prayers were never answered. She knew that from experience. Burt said God was another of her stupid fantasies, and that's one time he was right. Mama was a super-Christian, calling on the Lord for every little thing, and what good did it do her? She'd spent her life agonizing on why the innocent suffered, then died a lingering, painful death of her own.

To Lena it was obvious. The innocent suffered because the world was a giant accident without sympathy or conscience. She figured death would be a black moment, like a light snapping out, and then eternal nothing. She saw no downside to that, as long as it didn't involve a lot of pain.

The pickup hit a pothole and her head nearly struck the ceiling. Burt broke out with a new stream of curses. She braced her feet apart on the gritty floorboard, seeing again the moment at the town meeting when that stranger stood up and told about a poisoned eagle. She had watched Burt's neck turn muddy as a riverbank, and little pieces of unwanted memory clicked into place.

A few weeks back, Burt took to disappearing for a couple of hours every evening without saying a word. Usually it was right before supper and she'd had to keep his food warm, with the gravy skinning over and turning thick. He came back from wherever he'd been smelling oily and sharp, with a look on his face that kept her from questioning him.

One evening he'd backed the truck into the barn and shut the doors.

That was the night he got up from bed at midnight and put on his pants. His dark shape rocked the mattress as he shoved on his boots.

"Where you going?" she said.

"Go back to sleep. I won't be gone long." She heard the truck start up and drive away.

She'd imagined all kinds of crazy things, but he was back within an hour. After that night he didn't make any more unexplained trips and she forgot about it. Lena was good at forgetting; she'd had to do a lot of it in her marriage.

But the minute the tall stranger at the town meeting said *Diazinon,* she could smell that peculiar stink again, and she knew. Burt must have poisoned a carcass down by the river where the eagles fed. When the bird got sick enough, he'd finished it off and planted it up on the ridge in the middle of the night.

She imagined him raising a board high above his head, bashing the defenseless bird over and over, and the oatmeal cookies she'd eaten at the meeting rose in her throat.

Folks around here loved the bald eagles that wintered along the river. They even called the high-school football team the Silk Mountain Eagles. Burt had counted on community outrage over the dead eagle to stop the Youngblood woman from getting the rest of her windmills. Not only had his plan failed, somebody figured out what he'd done. Maybe they couldn't prove it, but everybody in that meeting knew he was the eagle killer, not the windmills. Now he was in a black rage, and that was bad luck for her.

The pickup slid around another corner and for an instant Lena thought her prayer was answered after all. The tires hit loose shale at the road's edge and the back end fishtailed violently and slid into the grader ditch. Only the seat belt kept her from slamming against Burt's stony shoulder. But the ditch was shallow, and instead of slowing up, Burt gunned the engine. The tires bit and the truck plunged forward and straightened out on the road.

Burt swore louder, but not about the close call. He was still swearing about the wind farm and Marik Youngblood.

When Marik's father ran that ranch, he was just as broke as anybody else. He even stopped by their farm once in a while. But now, with those big, spooky windmills, the Youngblood woman was like those rich kids at school who always got what they wanted, and who could make other kids miserable just by ignoring them. Marik hadn't said one word at the town meeting, yet people lined up to take her side.

When Marik first came back to the ranch after J.B. was killed, Lena had looked forward to having a woman neighbor. She'd spent a whole day washing and ironing her curtains. She'd baked lemon cookies and put them in the freezer in case Marik stopped by for coffee. The ten or twelve years' difference in their ages didn't mean much now that Marik was grown. The two of them had some things in common, whether Marik knew it or not. Lena had thought she might talk to Marik about that.

But Miss Rich-blood was too busy making money to be neighborly. Lena had seen one of her paintings in the bank when Burt went in to negotiate a loan for the new tractor. She wondered how much money Marik got for a painting like that. It was a big landscape, with soft colors that made Lena feel sad and hopeful all at once. It was beautiful and mysterious and signed with just one name— *Marik*. Lena had looked at the painting a long time and known that Marik Youngblood would never come over for coffee.

Burt wheeled into their driveway and slammed to a halt by the house, gasoline sloshing in the half-empty tank. Another of Lena's prayers denied.

When Burt was this worked up, his anger could last for hours. She'd told herself, and him, that if he ever hit her she'd be gone. But she didn't know where to draw the line about *words*. His tirades invariably circled around to include her stupidity, her clumsiness. She knew she wasn't smart, and with her considerable height and bone structure, she'd never been graceful. But his words still hurt, especially when he said she was lazy. That was a plain lie; she worked like a soldier around that farm. She could plow a straight line or dig postholes like a man and still come in at dark and put a hot meal on the table. Even if she wasn't feeling well, which was most of the time.

Burt barged out of the truck and stalked into the house without waiting for her. The silence was lovely. She sat still and let her heartbeat return to normal. Maybe she could stay here in the quiet darkness all night, listen to the hoot owls and doze sitting up. But in less than a minute Burt leaned out the aluminum storm door and yelled.

"What the hell are you doin' settin' out there? Get in here where you belong!"

Guess he needed an audience.

That's all she was good for, wasn't it. That and hard work. She never went anywhere by herself anymore, after he got mad about some article in a women's magazine she'd bought with the groceries. Now he kept the pickup keys in his pocket and drove her to town himself. The day she'd finally realized she was a prisoner in her own home, she had taken Burt's battered screwdriver and hid it beneath the laundry hamper.

It was his favorite tool that he used for everything from jimmying swollen doors to ruining the ice-maker in her refrigerator. He would never look under the hamper, but it was a place the screwdriver might have got kicked by accident. It gave her a great deal of satisfaction when he searched and ranted and demanded that she help him look for it. After a week, when he gave it up as lost, she'd sneaked the screwdriver under the seat of his pickup where it would eventually roll out as if it had been there all along.

The next week she had made small tears in his boxer underwear.

But tonight there was no relief in sight. The door of the truck creaked open and she closed it carefully and walked to the house, past the spindly pansies that never seemed to grow no matter how much she watered them. She crossed the living room as quietly as she could and headed for the bedroom, but she didn't make it.

"Brew up some coffee," he barked. "No way I'll be able to sleep now."

"Caffeine'll make it worse," she pointed out on her way to the kitchen, but luckily he ignored her. She'd grown up learning to hold her own against an older brother, and sometimes her quick tongue got her in trouble. It was a habit she needed to break, for her own good.

Lena put a coffee filter and grounds in the Mr. Coffee machine and poured water into the back. She switched it on and stood by the cabinet to wait, hoping Burt would stay in the living room. Instead, he followed her into the kitchen and started pacing.

"Damn meeting was rigged," he said for the third time, his voice drowning out the gurgle of the coffeemaker. "Earl Searcy must be in cahoots with the power company."

She had to dodge him to get his cup and the sugar bowl out of the cabinet. Her father used to pace the kitchen like that, mostly when he was worried about hail getting the wheat crop, or drought, or greenbugs, or a half-dozen other ways their year's income could be threatened. When she was a girl she'd sworn she wouldn't marry a farmer, would never put herself at the mercy of nature for her daily bread. As if she had choices. She was a plain girl, perfectly suited for farm-work and making babies, her daddy said. He couldn't wait to marry her off to the first suitor and let her brother inherit the farm.

"Dumb bastards can't see danger when it's right over their heads," Burt stormed. "Wait'll their livestock turns up deformed."

When she went to get milk from the refrigerator he bumped into her and pushed her roughly out of his way. "Rich get richer and the rest of us get screwed. Somebody needs to take that Youngblood woman down a peg or two."

Without meaning to, Lena spoke her thought, out loud. "You shouldn't have threatened her like that where everybody could hear. If anything else happens at that wind farm, everybody'll know it was you."

He gave her a black look. "Just make the damn coffee. See if you can do it right. That crap you gave me this morning tasted awful."

Maybe it was the arsenic, she thought archly, but thank goodness that didn't come out aloud. Burt wouldn't put up with sarcasm.

She put milk and sugar in his coffee mug and robbed coffee from the pot before it was finished brewing.

"Maybe they'd like to have sugar in the gas tanks of those expensive machines again," he said, his lips stretched thin. "That stopped 'em for more'n a week last time."

She set the cup on the table at his place. "You'll get yourself arrested," she said, "and for what? You're not going to win against her and the power company."

Burt stopped pacing. His eyes dilated like a cat's in the dark, no irises left.

"What I *don't* need is you telling me what to do. What the hell do you know about anything?"

"I know you killed that eagle."

She recognized her mistake as soon as she said it. But she still might have been all right if she hadn't glanced up and accidentally met his eyes. Burt was like a feral dog; he took offense if you looked him in the eye.

The back of his hand sounded like a gunshot when it hit her cheekbone.

The force knocked her sideways and she couldn't untangle her feet. When she fell, her mouth struck the edge of the walnut hutch that had been her mother's. Pain blazed through her lip.

He stood over her, his fists clenched. She wondered without caring whether he was going to kick her. She wouldn't have felt it, her lip hurt so bad.

His voice was deadly quiet. "And I'm telling you, you don't know a gawd-damned thing."

Warm blood dripped from her chin. She could barely see him through the haze of pain. Something dark flickered in the back of her mind, a forgotten memory. Something she didn't want to remember.

Maybe he'll kill me, she thought. Maybe that was God's answer to her prayer, like a sick joke.

But Burt turned and left the house, grabbing his cap and boots on the way out. The aluminum storm door rattled shut behind him.

Lena lay on the floor until she heard the truck leaving. Then she pulled herself to her feet and stanched the blood with two paper napkins. Her head roared like a tornado.

She found her way down the hall, steadying herself with one hand on the wall. Where her fingers touched the wallpaper, they left faded red stains like watercolor roses.

In her bedroom—*their* bedroom, which had no lock on

the door—she closed herself in. She wet an old washcloth and cleaned the blood from her face, gently, as her mother might have done. Then she leaned toward the mirror and examined her split lip. When she bared her teeth, she saw a small chip off her right front incisor. A red bruise was forming on her cheekbone.

She looked at her flushed face, the premature wrinkles around blue-gray eyes that looked like her father's. Daddy was in a nursing home now, completely out of his mind. Even if he wasn't, he'd probably side with Burt instead of her.

I said I'd leave him if he hit me, and now he has.

But Mama's dead and I have no place to go.

Lena watched her lip swell up until she looked like one of those primitive tribeswomen on the National Geographic channel. But at least the swelling covered the chip on her front tooth.

No place to go.

She had no money of her own. Her brother and sister-in-law hated her, and the feeling was mutual.

Lena felt the cancer taking little bites from her intestines. She wished again that the truck would have spun off the road and killed them both. But it hadn't, and she had to deal with that before Burt came back, if he did.

Moving quickly, she carried her clothes, her toiletries and shoes, down the hall to the spare bedroom. Then she used Burt's screwdriver to install a padlock on the inside of the door.

After midnight, lying awake in the strangeness of a different bed, she heard him come home and her body tensed.

She heard his footsteps clumping on the wooden floors, the toilet flushing. But he didn't come looking for her, and finally the slice of light under her door flicked out. Even when the house went silent, she was afraid to go to sleep.

Chapter Nine

Lena's wedding day had confirmed to her the callousness of the male race. She had come into the parish hall after the ceremony, where a few friends of the family were gathered for cake and punch. She was still wearing the white linen dress and lace jacket she and her mother had made for her wedding. The dress was a practical, street-length sheath she could wear to church later on, but it was the prettiest dress she'd ever owned. She was barely eighteen, but that afternoon she felt womanly. By tomorrow, she would no longer be a virgin.

Her father stood among a cluster of men in one corner, with his back to the room. He was the center of attention on his daughter's wedding day and making the most of it. His voice was the kind that carried even when it shouldn't. Mama said he must have learned to whisper in a sawmill.

Her older brother was there, too, self-important in his ill-fitting brown suit. As Lena walked past the men she heard her father's unmistakable baritone.

"Yeah, I'm a lucky man," he said. "Burt Gurdman could have done better."

Her brother laughed loudest of anybody.

Lena's feet had tripped on the words. She wasn't accustomed to wearing high-heeled shoes, and they slipped on the waxed floor. She careened forward, catching hold of the refreshment table as she went down. The punch bowl sloshed.

Her mother and aunt rushed to help her. But the men turned away in disdain. Not one man came to help her up or ask if she was all right. Not even Burt.

The women had brushed her off and dithered over her. But she'd still had to stand behind the table and cut the cake, her white dress ruined by a stain of red Hawaiian punch. After all these years, the taste of white frosting still cloyed on her tongue.

Now Daddy was a pitiful shell of the robust man he'd once been. After her mother died, Alzheimer's had leached away his mind. But Lena hadn't forgiven him. Marik Youngblood's father would have protected her from a man ten years older, a driver on a traveling combine crew who had eyes for his daughter. J. B. Youngblood would have run him off the place and told him never to come back. He doted on his girls; Marik got to go to art school at a university. Lena's father, by contrast, couldn't wait for her to marry and move out.

She was fourteen the summer she met Burt Gurdman, too young to know better. When she took lunch to the field for the harvest crew, she'd felt Burt's eyes watching her. Nobody had ever looked at her with that kind of interest, and she felt a heat rise within her that had nothing to do with the June sun. Once in a while, when she felt brave, she met his dark eyes and smiled.

He came again the next summer, too. And when harvest season was over, Burt Gurdman showed up one day at their door. Nobody in the family could figure out why he'd come. But her mother invited him to stay for supper, and afterward he asked if Lena could sit out on the porch swing with him. Lena was embarrassed by the shock she'd seen on her family's faces, even her mother's. Later her brother said Burt must be a pedophile, and that was the only time she heard her father tell Eldon to shut up. Daddy liked Burt from the beginning, maybe because they were so much alike.

Burt came calling often after that. He rarely had money for a movie, so her mother would invite him for supper and afterward he and Lena would sit on the porch by themselves. She was a sophomore in high school, but he talked to her like she was a grown woman and she was flattered. She'd never had a boyfriend before. And Burt was no boy; he was already a man.

He talked about his dream of owning his farm free and clear, raising wheat and cattle and chickens, maybe a few hogs. He wanted sons who would work with him and carry on the family name. His dreams were small but they were possible, unlike her fantasies of business school, an urban apartment shared with girlfriends and a designer dog, chartreuse parakeets in a wicker cage. No one suspected Lena of such ideas. Even her mother was taken aback when Lena confided in her. Mama didn't say anything, just shook her head.

Business school was a pipe dream. Burt Gurdman was real.

She was sixteen when he proposed. Daddy would have let him marry her right then, but Mama insisted she finish high school first. They got married the day after she graduated.

Sex turned out to be more of a chore than the romantic fantasy she'd dreamed about. Even so, Lena was happy in the early years of their marriage. They were poor as pond water, but they were a team. They worked side by side, sunup to sundown, planning for the day they could pay off the mortgage on the farm and make improvements to the house.

It was hard to tell if Burt was happy. If he had any emotions, he kept them to himself. It was just his way. After their wedding night, he never again said he loved her, as if once should be all that was required. He took for granted that the man was always boss, and Lena excused that, too, because she was used to it.

But no matter how hard they worked, they couldn't seem to get ahead. Hail got the wheat crop; a late freeze took the oats. A permanent frown etched itself on Burt's forehead. Instead of paying off the mortgage, they had to borrow more. Maybe it was because he felt like a failure that he began to criticize. When a coyote stole one of the chickens, it was Lena's fault for not shutting them up before dark. If the corner posts leaned, she hadn't held them straight enough while he tamped them down. When she miscarried, it was her fault that she couldn't give him sons.

The morning after the town meeting, Lena made Burt's breakfast as always and neither of them said a word while he ate his eggs. He didn't acknowledge her swollen lip or apologize for what he'd done. He said nothing about her moving into the spare bedroom. But at least he didn't bitch about the coffee.

When he went outdoors, Lena set up the ironing board in the dining room where she could see out the front window while she worked. What choice did she have except to go about her chores as if nothing had happened? If you ignored awful things long enough, sometimes they went away, like a bad dream. She had done that before. She consoled herself that she'd taken his best shot and was still standing.

She was halfway through the basketful of clothes when a copper-colored pickup drove in and parked in front of the house. She watched Deputy Sheriff Bill Ferguson get out and put on his hat. Another man got out from the other side, and she recognized the wildlife ranger who'd showed up at the meeting last night.

Here to look for Diazinon, probably. That would piss Burt off for sure.

She saw Burt drop hay into the pen beside the barn where Borax the mule tilted one furry ear toward the strangers. Then Burt sauntered toward the two men, as unconcerned as you please. Lena turned off her iron and quietly stepped out onto the porch so she could hear. She stayed under the shadow of the overhang, trying not to draw attention.

"I could make you get a warrant," she heard Burt say. "But I won't. Go ahead and look anywhere you want."

Which meant he'd already got rid of the big bottle of tick poison that had sat on a shelf in the barn for years, right next to the weed killer and the bloat medicine. Burt was a saver, even stuff he'd never use. The inside of the barn looked like a junkyard, but she was supposed to keep the house spotless.

The deputy nodded, and Lena figured he knew Burt had dumped the tick poison. But he was doing his job, going through the motions. Maybe he thought his visit would serve as a warning so Burt wouldn't do something like that again.

For a minute Lena imagined what would happen if the deputy actually found the Diazinon. Or a bloody board Burt might have used to break the eagle's wing. Did they actually arrest people for killing an eagle? It would be good enough for him. Maybe God didn't exist, but sometimes Mother Nature got even all by herself.

What if she went outside and showed the deputy her split lip, told him her husband had hit her? He'd probably just look away, embarrassed like the neighbor men at her wedding, and not do a damn thing. Men always stuck together. And after the deputy went away, there was no telling what Burt might do.

Lena went back inside and watched out the window. The deputy and the ranger went into the barn, then the shed where Burt kept the pickup. They even looked in the little well house. She wanted to yell out the window to look in the stock pond behind the barn, but of course she didn't.

Burt trailed behind them, scowling, but she could see he was feeling cocky. They wouldn't find any Diazinon, nor any bloody club. Not an eagle feather anywhere. Burt wasn't dumb. In fact, he was downright cagey. She had the feeling he *wanted* Marik Youngblood to know he'd planted the dead eagle, like a threat. For the life of her she couldn't figure why he was so dead set against that wind farm. It was more than the money; it was like he was afraid. Maybe he really thought those big windmills gave off toxic rays.

When the ranger and the deputy had looked everywhere, they got back in the copper-colored truck and drove away. Lena went back to her ironing, but she was so tired and sore today it was a struggle to stand over his steaming shirts until she was finished. The heat rising from the ironing board made her swollen lip throb.

Burt didn't come inside until lunchtime. They sat at the kitchen table in silence, eating bacon-and-egg sandwiches. Lena had to take the bacon out of hers because she had trouble biting and chewing.

"Did you see our visitors this morning?" he said finally, still ignoring her bruised face.

Lena nodded.

"Looking for Diazinon." His mouth twisted. "I haven't had any of that stuff for years."

Liar.

Burt sat there grinning like a dead pig in the sun. He needed taking down a notch, and the sheriff wasn't going to do it, that was obvious.

When Burt went back outdoors, Lena went to the phone in the kitchen. She stood where she could see out the side door to make sure Burt wasn't coming back toward the house.

Her finger quivered as she punched in Marik Young-blood's phone number. She heard it ring once, and her breath came short. If Marik answered, she would tell her Burt was responsible for the sugar in those gas tanks, and that he did poison that eagle just to cause her trouble.

The phone rang a second time.

But Marik already knew what he'd done, didn't she? What difference would it make to her that Lena knew it, too?

Lena thought again of the big landscape painting in the bank, the way she'd looked at it and known Marik would never come to visit. She hung up the phone.

Chapter Ten

Jace Rainwater slid into the routine at Killdeer Ridge Ranch like a familiar foot in a well-worn boot. The first week he inventoried the cattle and set up records on a spreadsheet that included birth dates, sire and pasture locations of all the new calves. He did this on his own laptop and made a copy on CD for Marik. She looked at the disk in her hand and realized how antiquated and naive she'd been about book-keeping. Like Monte before her, she'd kept track of the cattle with the aid of a pencil and a pocket-size notebook.

Jace made permanent repairs to the north-pasture fence that she'd temporarily patched, and he fixed a leak in the barn roof. Soon he had assumed all her morning chores except for her ritual drive to the windmills. She was free to spend more time in her art studio.

Theoretically she appreciated those extra hours. In practice, she spent a lot of time looking out the north window toward the ranch yard, listening to the distant growl and beep of the dirt movers on the ridge. She watched Rainwater hacking down weeds between the outbuildings, hammering new nails into the loose boards of the horses' corral. With the weather warming, he had moved Bully outdoors where the calf could eat fresh grass and get more exercise. Marik felt a little pang of jealousy when Jace entered the gate with the nipple bucket and Bully scampered to meet him.

She had no talent for leisure. She had worked ten-hour days since Monte left, and now she felt useless.

Get over it, she told herself, turning from her studio window back to the easel. *Throw yourself into your art the way you always wanted to.*

Paint something wonderful, dammit.

But soon she found herself at the window again, clocking the efficient way Jace went about his work, so that without hurrying he accomplished the routine chores in less time than it had taken her. When those were finished, he found other jobs that needed doing. One afternoon he brought both tractors out of the barn, the big green John Deere and the little orange Case that she had used to mow the runway. J.B. had used Big Green to sow wheat and haul round bales of alfalfa hay from the field, but the tractor sat idle after he died. Rainwater laid out her father's tools on a burlap sack and used them to service both machines. It gave her a funny feeling to see him handling her father's wrenches and vise-grip pliers.

First the John Deere's deep-throated rattle and then the higher-pitched popping of the Case floated into the house, obscuring for an afternoon the sound of machinery on the ridge. It made her feel primitive and iconic—the woman of the house going about her quiet chores while menfolk did their masculine work outdoors.

Good grief, I've devolved three generations. To hell with that.

She wondered if she could capture her contradictory emotions in a painting and began to play around with sketches of a pioneerlike woman. Before long she realized the sketch was her vision of the ghost lady of Silk Mountain. It wasn't what she'd set out to portray—or maybe it was. Maybe that love-hate relationship toward the land and the men who tamed it was exactly what Leasie felt the day she cleaned her house and climbed Silk Mountain to end her life.

Marik was zoning out, sketching like mad, when the phone in the studio rang. Hardly anyone called on the listed ranch number anymore. She put down her sketch pad and answered crisply, "Killdeer Ridge Ranch." Trying to convince herself she still ran the place?

"Hello, Marik."

The masculine voice, smooth as an anchorman's, sounded vaguely familiar. It irritated her when people she seldom talked to expected her to recognize them in two words. "Yes?"

"I saw you on the airstrip the other day when I flew over."

And still it didn't register. She tried to place the voice

among the members of Flying Farmers who'd been her dad's friends. Nothing fit.

Then suddenly she knew. "Devon?"

She could hear the smile in his voice. "I guess I was flattering myself to think you'd know me immediately."

"A little." Her heartbeat lurched and that irritated her, too, but she softened the edge in her voice. "That was you in the little Piper? I never knew you to fly a low-wing."

"I still don't. It belongs to a colleague. He wanted me to try it out, so we went for a joyride while I was back home. I was going to land and say hello, but the strip looked a little rough."

He still called the state *home,* she noticed, though he'd lived in D.C. for at least five years. Congressman Devon Dulaney. Until he'd learned about J.B.'s accident six months after the fact, she hadn't talked to him since he moved east. Then he'd phoned, contrite because he wasn't there for her father's funeral. He'd also sent an extravagant arrangement of flowers that scented the entire house.

"The runway's out of service," she said, and didn't mention that she'd mowed it after seeing the little plane buzz over. "What brings you to Oklahoma?"

"Actually I'm back in D.C. now. I was home a few days to attend a couple of dinners and visit my parents."

His parents were the only rich people she'd ever met that she actually liked. Maybe because they shared her love of art, they'd always treated her as an equal. "How are Mike and Sally?"

"Mom had a little flare-up with her heart," he said, "but

it wasn't too serious. They put in a stent and she's on medication. Both of them are in pretty good shape actually. They walk every day."

"It's good they still have each other. Not everybody's that lucky."

"I know. But they're only in their sixties. The new forty, you know."

"Right." She waited for him to say why he'd called.

"I just wondered how you were getting along," he said. "With the ranch. You know, without your dad."

She perched on a paint-spattered wooden stool, suddenly tired. "It was rough sometimes."

"And still is, I imagine."

There was graphite dust on her fingertips. She rubbed them on her jeans. "But I've hired a foreman, and despite my cantankerous neighbors, phase two of the wind farm is under construction."

"So you plan to stay on at the ranch?"

"I guess so. Thanks to GPP&L." The wind farm was in his district and the sort of local project a politician loved to tout to other legislators. To be fair, though, Devon was a sincere proponent of wind energy.

"You always loved the place," he said. "I hope you're happy there."

"Hmm." The ranch was too isolated for Devon's gregarious nature. At one time they had discussed that fact in great detail. "You either love it or you don't," she said, exactly what she'd told him back then.

Devon seemed to run out of something to say, a minor

phenomenon. For several beats she listened to the hiss of the long-distance line. She thought of saying, *How is Eden?* But that seemed intrusive; she'd never met his wife.

"Are you still painting?" he asked

"Yes. Quite a bit lately, since I have more time."

"I'm glad to hear that," he said, his voice energetic again. "I'd like get one of your Oklahoma landscapes for my office. Do you have a brochure or something? A Web site?"

"Neither. I really ought to do the Web site thing, I guess."

"Be sure to let me know when you do. Did I give you my e-mail last time we talked?"

"I think so, yes." And his office number, and his cell.

"Okay then." He paused. "Take care of yourself, Marik. You know you can call me if I could help in any way. Use the cell number so you don't have to go through an assistant."

"I appreciate that," she said. "It's good of you to call."

She hung up and sat still for a moment, listening to the pulse in her ears.

A spring afternoon in her sophomore year…a rally on the South Oval of campus, for some cause she couldn't remember. A dark-haired grad student spoke from a platform improvised from beer kegs and plywood, and mobilized his audience in support of his views. She didn't hear a word he said. He was quite possibly the sexiest-looking guy she'd ever seen, and they had made love for the first time the night before. Crazy, uninhibited sex that bore no resemblance to the sweet fumblings of a former boyfriend from her hometown.

The wind was warm and smelled of flowers. It was all she could do not to jump onto the platform with him and tell everyone what a spectacular lover he was, and that he'd chosen her as his partner. Maybe give them a demonstration. She felt wild and young and horny as a rabbit, her skin migrating like velvet beneath a carnal hand.

The memory gave her shivers. Hormonal memoirs of the impossibly young.

The room seemed suddenly too warm. She opened the neck of her blouse and went back to her drawing table, thumbing through the sketches. Nothing pleased her now; everything seemed boring and flat. She slid them into a drawer and pushed it shut firmly, ending a reminiscence that could come to no good.

That week Jace asked for Saturday and Sunday off so he could drive to Amarillo and see his son. A ranch foreman's job was seven days a week, and hardly nine-to-five. It was only fair that he take a weekend off here and there.

Early Saturday morning she was awakened by the sound of his truck starting up and rolling down the driveway. In a way it was good to have the place to herself again, but she also felt the eerie aloneness return. She was glad, a little later, when the rumble of the backhoes started up on Killdeer Ridge. The familiar noise kept her company.

Marik had already reclaimed Bully's morning feeding, and today the entire docket of chores was all hers. She took her time. Lime-colored leaves covered the elms, and her father's daffodils were blooming in the rock garden beside the house.

Jace had things in such good shape that by noon she was back in her studio, chicken-salad sandwich on a plate, diet cola in an ice-filled glass. She was accustomed now to painting every day, and she could see the discipline reflected in her work. She'd begun to relax, her brushstrokes looser and more confident. The river scene was finished and hanging on her gallery wall in the studio. She stood before the painting and knew Devon would buy it in a heartbeat, at whatever price she named. But she liked it right where it was.

Wearing her father's old shirt that served as a painting smock, she squeezed paint onto her palette and mixed colors. Then she perched on a stool in front of the easel, where the ghost lady of Silk Mountain balanced on the lip of a terra-cotta ledge with the wind in her hair.

It was early in the afternoon when the yellow dinosaurs on the ridge fell silent. Marik stopped a moment and looked at the window, quiet ringing in her ears. *Huh. That's unusual.* She shrugged it off and went on working. Fifteen minutes later, she heard a vehicle in the driveway.

She met Lou Benson on the front porch. His blue eyes looked clouded as he touched the brim of his hard hat. "Afternoon, Ms. Youngblood."

She had suggested several times that he call her Marik, but he didn't seem able to do it. "Come on in, Lou," she said.

He glanced at his feet. "My boots are too dirty," he said. "I came to see if you could ride up to the ridge with me. We've uncovered something you need to see."

Marik frowned. "Sure. But what is it?"

Lou hesitated. "It's bones. I'm not sure what kind. One of the guys on the crew used to work in an emergency room, and he thinks they're human."

Marik stiffened and he read the look on her face. "We didn't hit the cemetery, I swear. These bones were fifty feet away from there, at the edge of the new road."

"Nobody's buried up there outside the cemetery," she said, stripping off the painting smock and tossing it aside. "It must be animal bones." She followed him toward his pickup.

"I sure hope you're right." He grimaced. "Because the bones are small. Real small."

Small bones, she thought as Benson's pickup jounced over the cattle guard at the gate. But she asked no questions, saving her concern until she saw what they'd found and where they'd found it. Lou was quiet, too, as they drove up the winding road. A lion of a March wind blew scraps of cloud across the sky, and the windmill blades plied the air like backstroke swimmers.

The discovery site was just where Lou had said, on the slope close to the family graveyard but too far away for any of the remains to have migrated there. All work had come to a halt. Three men in hard hats hovered around the location, one of them crouched over, looking at something on the ground. The other workmen had gathered farther away beside their machines, smoking.

Donning the hard hat Benson gave her, Marik approached the three men with a queasy feeling in her stomach. There had to be an innocent explanation; this was not a place where human bones would be.

The crouching man rose and all three took a step back. They watched her face as she leaned down toward three white bones, two of them about five inches long, one even shorter, that lay just beyond a rim of graded dirt. Whatever else had been attached to the bones was missing.

They looked like miniature leg bones. Too small for a newborn calf. Perhaps the size of a small coyote or dog.

"I think the grader picked them up from over there," one of the men said, pointing.

She and Benson walked to the spot he indicated, knelt and examined the raked dirt. Not three feet away she saw a fragment of white showing through the red soil.

"Anybody have a shovel?" she said.

They shook their heads. These guys moved dirt on too large a scale for hand tools.

Marik began to dig with her hands.

"Maybe we should wait," Benson said. "Call somebody official?" When she didn't answer, he said, "I've got some gloves in the truck."

But her hands had exposed more of the white surface, and Benson didn't move. She brushed away dirt. This bone wasn't shaped like the others. It was broader and rounded slightly like the side of a bowl, but smaller. Barely larger than a teacup.

"Oh God," she whispered.

She ran her fingers around white edges. A sinking feeling started in the back of her throat and kept on descending without hitting bottom. Her fingernails clogged with dirt, brushing away soil until there was no more denying. "Oh God oh God…"

On the ground before her lay the miniature skull of a human infant.

Chapter Eleven

Coincidentally, or maybe not so coincidentally, Burt Gurdman got his wish. Construction of the new wind turbines came to a halt. GPP&L also shut down the existing windmills for safety reasons while the Oklahoma State Bureau of Investigation descended on the ranch and marked off an excavation site with yellow plastic ribbon.

Marik sat on the hood of Red Ryder and watched agents in tan coveralls remove dirt with trowels and whisk brooms and miniature shovels. The wind knotted her hair and sent dust devils across the work site. The agents worked until nightfall on Saturday and posted an officer to guard the ridge overnight. She lay awake and imagined the officer up there alone, with the wind and the stars and a baby's bones.

The OSBI agents started again early the next morning.

They sifted through a fifty-by-fifty-foot area a few inches at a time. When they were finished late Sunday afternoon, an almost complete skeleton lay pieced together on a cloth, like the remnants of J.B.'s dismembered Cessna.

Marik looked down at the baby's outline, painfully small and fragile. Whose child was this? How could it be here on the ranch without her knowing?

A physician from the medical examiner's regional office arrived from Pacheeta to examine the bones. The OSBI lab in Oklahoma City would ask a forensic anthropologist for the official determination, but off the record Dr. Guthrie theorized that the baby was a girl, barely more than newborn. He couldn't tell whether or not the bones had been moved. Marik was standing close enough to overhear when the doctor drew his hand through thinning gray hair and made a private comment to the OSBI agent in charge.

"The child must have been buried fairly deep originally, because there's no animal damage evident," he said. "If I had to guess, I'd say the bones have been underground at least five to ten years."

Marik stopped breathing.

Lou Benson saw her face and guided her to sit on a mound of excavated dirt. He brought her a bottle of water from the cooler in his truck. She discarded the hard hat and drank, wiping water from her chin with the back of her hand.

"Sorry," she said. "This is just so awful. How on earth did a baby end up here?"

Lou crouched beside her, his weathered face creasing

around his eyes. "Maybe some teenage girl couldn't handle motherhood. Who knows." He fingered the icon that hung around his neck. "I'd like to get a pastor out here to say a prayer, give the remains some kind of blessing."

Marik nodded. "Let's try Reverend Blakely at the United Methodist Church in Silk. He might be able to get here quickly."

"I've met Reverend Blakely," Benson said. "A good man."

He drew a cell phone from his pocket and walked away a short distance to make the call.

Marik sat on the dirt mound, feeling wrung out. She'd lain awake most of the previous night thinking that if someone was determined to stop progress on the wind farm, planting unidentified human remains on the work site was an ingenious stroke. How could anyone prove who'd put them there? Would Burt Gurdman go that far? By morning she had convinced herself that he would. But the doctor's estimate of the age of the bones shattered her certainty and raised another awful possibility.

If the doctor's guess was correct, this baby was born close to the same time as her daughter. Was that coincidence? Had J.B. known a baby was here? If so, why had he never told her? She thought about Daisy Gardner's adamant refusal to let her know where her daughter was.

Had her father lied to her by omission? Was Daisy lying to her now?

The idea was too sickening to absorb. But she had to know. No matter what the fallout, she had to know for sure whether this abandoned baby was her child.

Benson approached again. "Reverend Blakely is on his way. I'll ask the OSBI boss to wait for him before they move anything," he said.

Marik nodded and watched him walk across the site toward CSA Jacobs, the lead investigator. Jacobs was also on his cell phone and Benson had to wait until he hung up. What would people do without their modern technology?

And there was her answer. Modern technology.

She took a long drink of the bottled water, picked up her hat and walked doggedly around the excavated site. The OSBI agent was talking to one of his team when she approached.

"CSA Jacobs?"

"Yes, ma'am."

"Will your lab do a DNA test on the bones?"

"Yes. That's routine nowadays to help make an identification. DNA is hard to obtain from an infant if the teeth and bones aren't fully formed yet. But it might be possible from bone marrow."

"I'd like you to take a sample from me for comparison," Marik said. "So we can know if this baby…might have belonged in our family cemetery."

He nodded. "We'd have got around to asking you eventually. Without anything for comparison, DNA results can't tell us much." He turned to the other agent. "Sandra, will you get a DNA swab from the truck, please?"

Sandra nodded and walked away, returning in a moment to scrape the inside of Marik's cheek with the swab. Sandra's hair and eyes were rich brown, and one slightly crooked front tooth had turned gray.

Marik watched her seal the swab into its clear tube. "How long do results take?"

"Could be six to eight weeks, sometimes longer. The lab's always backed up." Sandra smiled. "It's not like on TV."

Marik nodded. "Will you please let me know the results?"

Sandra looked to her boss.

"Sure," he said. "I'll call you when we have something."

Reverend Blakely arrived in a shale-encrusted compact car. Lou Benson gave him a hard hat, which he looked at with something like alarm before fitting it on his head. Marik, Lou and the OSBI staff gathered around the fragmented bones. They stood in silence while the pastor opened a well-used Bible and read.

His voice was rich and comforting, and it carried across the slope. "'Take heed that ye despise not one of these little ones, for I say unto you, that in heaven their angels do always behold the face of my Father… Even so it is not the will of your Father which is in heaven, that one of these little ones should perish.'"

An orange sun grazed the horizon, and Marik felt its heat lodged in her throat. She saw tears in Lou Benson's eyes, and somehow that made her feel better.

The reverend offered a brief prayer and several of the assembled men echoed his amen. He closed his Bible and sighed. Even as the pastor drove away, the bones were being bagged separately in plastic and packed into a foam carton.

Everybody went home, including Marik, and the yellow ribbon was left to ripple in the wind. There would be no construction on Killdeer Ridge tomorrow. And maybe for many tomorrows after that.

That evening Marik left an urgent message on Daisy Gardner's voice mail. At 10:00 p.m. she still hadn't heard back. Daisy often went out of town for her job—but not on Sunday night.

Too keyed up to sleep, she carried a mug of decaf to the glider on the front porch. The ranch was dark and quiet, a relief from the commotion of the past two days. Night sounds rose around her like a dirge. The ridge had been violated, the gouged earth forced to give up a sacred secret.

Her muscles tensed when headlights flashed toward her on the driveway. Then she realized it was Jace, back from Amarillo. His long-axled pickup pulled in beside the foreman's cottage and doused its lights. She watched his lanky shape step down and retrieve something bulky, probably a duffel bag, from the passenger seat.

Marik thought of a line from an old John Wayne Western—Mattie Ross to Rooster Cogburn: *Leave it to you to get another tall horse.* An oversize truck was the modern cowboy's tall horse.

Jace went inside the house and lights came on. It was a three-hour drive from the center of the Texas Panhandle. He would probably hit the sack to be ready for early chores. She set the glider in motion again and puzzled over the fact that she felt more relaxed now, knowing he was home.

In a few minutes he came out again and walked toward her house. The night was cloudless and lit by a three-quarter moon. Thirty feet from where she sat, Jace realized she was there on the porch and he waved.

"I saw your light and figured you were still up," he said.

"What's going on with the windmills? They're all shut down."

His awareness surprised her. Her own ears were attuned to the windmills, but she wouldn't have expected him to notice their stillness in the dark.

"You missed all the excitement," she said. "If you're sure you want to hear about it tonight, pull up a chair. I just made a pot of decaf."

"Sounds good. Keep your seat and I'll help myself."

"Mugs are in the cabinet above the coffeepot."

It felt odd to sit on her porch while a man she hardly knew made himself at home in her kitchen. Not a bad feeling, just odd.

In less than a minute he came out of the house and spread himself into one of the Adirondack chairs. She should have knocked the dust off that chair. Too late now.

"Okay. What's up?" he said.

She explained the discovery of the bones on the ridge that weekend.

"A baby," he said. "Jeeminy Christmas."

"I have no idea who she was." She hoped that was true. "It seems awfully diabolical even for Burt Gurdman, but you have to wonder if he resents the wind farm enough to rob a grave somewhere and plant the bones on my property." She thought of Burt's accusation: *Ask her what happened to her bastard child.*

Jace shook his head. "His wife must be as weird as he is. I heard somebody at the town meeting say that she hardly ever leaves her house."

"I think I've seen Lena two times in my life, and one of them was the other night." She sipped her coffee but it had gone cold. "Of course, if the bones have been up there for years, that has nothing to do with the wind farm. And I might be learning some family history I never wanted to know." Her stomach jittered. Why hadn't Daisy called back?

"Anyway, the turbines are supposed to come back online tomorrow," she said. "But who knows how long before construction can start up again. If it ever does."

"GPP&L won't give up easily," Jace said. "They have too much invested."

"I hope you're right. If I have to regurgitate the lease money on those last twenty-five towers, the ranch will be in trouble again."

They were quiet then, listening to the night, thick with frog-song and the hoot of an owl.

"Hear that?" Marik said.

"Which one?"

"There—that one."

"A whippoorwill."

"Yes. The first whippoorwill of the season."

They listened again for the haunting, three-noted call. "When we lived in West Texas," he said, his voice wistful and slow, "we had them year-round. And rain crows, which are really black-billed cuckoos. Dad said his grandfather actually thought the rain crow's call brought the rain, and at harvest time he'd shoot them on sight."

"Superstition precedes science. My great-grandfather believed a white buffalo was an omen of good fortune."

"Hmm. It would have been good fortune enough just to *see* one," he said. And a second later, "Especially if you weren't drinking."

Marik laughed. If Monte were sitting here tonight, he would approve of Jace Rainwater. And that was the happiest thought she'd had for the whole depressing weekend.

"How's your son doing?" she asked.

Her question fell into silence. Finally she heard him take a deep breath. "Zane's okay, I guess. He's in a new school that's supposed to be good. But he doesn't like going there."

She thought of her middle-school students, how hard it was on some of them to be the new kid in school. "Maybe he'll find a buddy soon, and that will help. Kids are pretty resilient."

"Zane isn't." Another pause. "My son has autism."

For a moment she couldn't think what to say.

"Damn," she said finally. "That's rough."

"Yeah, it is," he said. Then, he stood, ending further discussion of his son. "I'd better hit the sack. Thanks for the coffee." He handed her his cup and clomped down the steps. "Good night."

"Night."

Marik watched his loose-gaited walk down the path to his cottage. Jace had finally trusted her enough to tell her about his son. It explained a lot about the wall of privacy he'd erected around his family. He was obviously still wrestling with the unfairness of his son's difficulties.

Just like Daisy said, the good guys were always married.
She tossed the cold remnants of her coffee over the railing
and went inside.

Daisy Gardner called at 7:00 a.m. "You sound groggy.
Up and at 'em, girl."

"Rough weekend," Marik said. In fact she was still in her
pajamas, waiting by the coffeepot while it groaned and
steamed.

"You can't do the bop in the sack," Daisy quoted. It was
something J.B. used to say. Her dad and Daisy shared the
annoying trait of being perky in the mornings.

"Sorry I didn't call last night," Daisy said. "I worked in
my flower bed all day and didn't think to look for messages
when I came in. What's going on?"

Marik robbed a cup of premature coffee. "The construction workers found human bones up on the ridge."

"Oh, no. The cemetery?"

"No. Outside the cemetery. They're the bones of a baby."

"My Lord."

"And you don't know anything about this?"

"Me? How would I have heard?"

"I mean about where the bones came from. The doctor
from Pacheeta guessed they'd been buried five to ten years."

"Wait a minute. What are you getting at?"

Marik's throat tightened. "Daisy, was that my daughter
up on the ridge?"

"Your daughter! That's ridiculous."

"Is it? I wasn't very stable after she was born. Maybe it was easier to tell me she was thriving with her adoptive parents than to tell me she died."

"Don't be paranoid. That is not your baby they found."

"Prove it. If my daughter's alive, tell me where she is."

Daisy hung up.

Chapter Twelve

Lena stood in the chicken yard and shielded her eyes from the sun. Something was happening up on Killdeer Ridge. The big machines that she'd heard grinding away, day after day, had suddenly stopped.

She'd noticed it around midday on Saturday. By evening other vehicles were coming and going, but from here she couldn't tell who they were or what they were doing. Even on Sunday, cars and pickups crawled along the white roads on the crown of the ridge.

Burt had noticed it, too. He didn't say anything, but he was edgy as a politician's accountant. All day she'd seen him stop his work every few minutes and look up toward the windmills, scowling. In the house he paced from the kitchen to the living room and back again, from one east-facing window to the next. She couldn't get her housework done for tripping over him.

She didn't ask Burt what he thought was going on. After he'd hit her, she didn't speak to him unless she had to.

Lena squinted into the sun and saw a black vehicle wind down the switchback and disappear on the other side of the ridge. If Marik Youngblood was a regular neighbor, Lena could just call her and ask what all the commotion was. But that wouldn't do, would it. Thanks to Burt's malicious pranks and Marik's snooty airs, Lena couldn't phone her nearest neighbor just to talk.

She remembered the first time she'd seen Marik Youngblood, shortly after she and Burt got married. J.B. had stopped by to offer his congratulations and to welcome his neighbor's new bride. Lena was touched by the courtesy. J.B. was a slow-talking, friendly man, and he'd brought Marik with him. She was a little girl then and already motherless. She looked like a tomboy in her jean shorts and boyish striped T-shirt, her blond hair in need of combing. Her legs were tan and thin with a scab on one knee. Lena thought how pretty she'd look in a ruffled dress and some patent-leather sandals, but Lena never had that kind of girl clothes, either.

Marik had hung on her daddy's hand, never getting a step away from him. Lena looked at the girl's somber face and wanted to give her something that would make her smile. But she had nothing to offer. She remembered the way J.B. ruffled Marik's hair and hugged her against his leg when they went back to their truck.

Lena had waved to them as they drove away, thinking how awful it would be for a girl to grow up without her mother. Lena was close to her own mother and missed seeing her every day. She couldn't imagine knowing she'd never see Mama again. For the first time it had occurred to Lena that her mother was likely to die before her. Someday she'd be motherless, too, like little Marik Youngblood.

It happened sooner than she could have expected. The winter cancer struck Lena's mother, her father hadn't called to tell her until her mother was nearly bedridden. Mama hadn't wanted to worry her, he said. Lena's gruff, burly father sounded broken on the phone.

Lena had packed a bag without asking Burt's permission and gone to stay with Mama until she died. She cooked soft foods that didn't upset her mother's stomach; she changed her clothes and laundered the bedding. She sat beside Mama's bed and read aloud chapters of the Bible that Mama requested. Mama got weaker and paler, but she never complained or lost her sweet smile.

Lena's father stayed drunk most of those weeks, unable to watch his wife suffer. Usually he was only a binge drinker, coming home loud and rowdy every so often. Lena had watched her mother deal with it for years in her gentle, Christian way. Mama never criticized him openly. She simply withdrew from her husband until he was sober. And the next day when Daddy would do some chore she'd been wanting done or bring her a treat from the store, Mama would thank him and lay her palm against his cheek. Lena knew she'd never be as good a woman as her mother.

Thankfully, her brother, Eldon, mostly stayed away while their mother died. Mama and Daddy had moved to town by then, and Eldon lived on the family farm with his snotty wife. He would call their father and ask how things were going, and use the farmwork as an excuse for not coming by. He was too selfish and too much a coward to sit with Mama and talk.

Lena had never got along with her older brother. Growing up, his size made it easy for him to bully her. He delighted in getting her in trouble or hurt, and if she cried he laughed at her. She used to beg Mama for a little sister so they could gang up on Eldon.

When she was seven, Eldon had convinced her that if she tied a blanket around her shoulders like a cape and jumped off the chicken house, she could fly like a super hero. He told her he'd done it dozens of times and he raved about how much fun it was to fly. He tied the blanket for her and boosted her up. She'd been scared looking down from the edge of the tin roof, but Eldon stood below, calling her a coward and a sissy. He said she had no guts and nobody would ever marry her.

She was lucky she'd sprained her ankles instead of breaking them. At Mama's insistence, their father punished Eldon by making him clean out the chicken house alone. Raking out the ammonia-smelling chickenshit, feathers clinging to his sweaty face, he'd growled at Lena that he'd get even with her. But that time she got him first. She punctured the tires on his bicycle and when he came looking for her, she hid around the corner of the barn with the ax. She couldn't run on her swollen feet. She still remembered her brother's howl of pain and the bright blood soaking through his shoe. She'd damn near cut off his big toe.

Lena had stayed at her mother's bedside for three weeks. With her father in a stupor, his memory already starting to slip, Lena had Mama all to herself except for God. When the pain got too bad, her mother prayed, and Lena bowed her head and pretended to pray with her. Mostly she accused God of being heartless and unjust.

Finally the doctor upped the morphine dosage and let her mother slip away. Burt drove up for the funeral, and took Lena home.

That night, even though she was an emotional wreck, Burt demanded sex. He was rough with her, and it seemed more like punishment than passion. He was angry because she'd left him alone so long. And because she hadn't asked him before she went. Despite his established pattern of brooding and criticisms, Lena had never thought of leaving him until that night.

Long after his breath sawed steadily beside her, she had lain awake with tears on her face, mourning her mother and her loveless marriage. She had lost her only friend. Loneliness rose up like a howling ghost.

Finally Lena had slept, and in the morning things didn't seem as bad. Lena knew her mother would never advise her to leave her husband. She should stay and endure, work things out. That's what women did.

That was the week Burt found her copy of *New Woman* magazine and took away her keys to the truck.

★ ★ ★

Near noon Lena stopped watching the traffic on the ridge and went inside to fix lunch. She made bologna sandwiches and potato salad and iced tea.

Burt came in and washed his hands in the kitchen sink. She hated that. She'd asked him not to do it a hundred times when they were first married. By now she'd given up.

Burt chomped a bite out of his sandwich, put it down on the plate and looked inside. "Where's the sliced tomatoes?"

"All gone. So's the lettuce and most of the milk."

Burt harrumphed but he finished his sandwich, then shoved back his chair. "Got to go down to the co-op this afternoon and get chicken feed. You got a list made for the groceries?"

She knew what he really wanted was to ask around in town, see if anybody knew what was going on up by the windmills. She took the grocery list down from the bulletin board by the kitchen phone and dropped it on the table beside his cap. Not asking to go with him today. She didn't want to ride beside him in the truck.

"Might get a different brand of coffee," she said without looking at him. "Something you like better."

He took the list and shoved it into his pocket. Not even asking if she'd like to ride along and pick out the groceries herself. Just like he'd never apologized for her bruised eye, still yellowish-purple underneath, or the chip that was gone from her tooth.

Lena switched on the TV while she washed their plates

and set them in the drain rack. Burt went in and changed his shirt and came back out. He left without saying another word.

Bastard. Tearing holes in his boxers wasn't enough to make her feel better anymore.

She heard the truck tires crackle on the driveway. At the front window, she watched the dust funnel behind his truck grow smaller and smaller on the shale road. When it disappeared, she turned off the TV and went back to the kitchen.

Rummaging through the cabinets, she found two empty plastic bottles and filled one of them with water. She carried the bottles out the front door and across the yard. The wind smelled of new grass and a warm sun pressed down on her shoulders. The scab on her lip burned like a brand but her stomach felt just fine.

In the pen beside the barn, the mule looked at her with sleepy black eyes.

"How're you doing, Borax?" she said. "I'll come back in a minute and bring you an apple. Would you like that?"

Borax was a female, or as much of one as a mule could be. That gave the two of them kinship. She and Borax had to stick together.

In the musty-smelling barn, Lena stopped to let her eyes adjust. On the wall just inside the barn doors, Burt had built a set of shelves from two-by-fours. Sure enough, the big jug of Diazinon was gone. She saw that he had wiped the dust rings from the shelf where it once sat. The bloat medicine and the green bottle of weed killer were still there.

She opened the dirt-caked top of the weed killer and sniffed. The chemical didn't smell nearly as strong as the tick poison. In fact, it didn't have much smell at all.

Carefully, she poured the weed killer into the empty water bottle. She was pleased to see the liquid was clear. She replaced the chemical with water, tightened the cap and set the green bottle back on the shelf.

In the house she made a masking-tape label that said "bleach" and pressed it onto the plastic bottle containing the clear liquid. She stored the bottle beneath the kitchen sink. Then she took an apple from the crisper, cut it in half and kept her promise to Borax.

The next morning at breakfast Lena prepared Burt's coffee cup with special care, adding an extra spoon of sugar and a single drop of vanilla, for aroma.

Burt came in and sat down. He began to wolf down his pancakes.

"That's the new coffee you bought," she told him. "See if you like it better."

He took a big slurp and made a face, but he couldn't say it was awful, could he, since he'd picked it out himself.

Chapter Thirteen

Daisy pulled a stack of five-by-seven photos from her tote bag and dealt them out like tarot cards on Marik's kitchen table. The subject of each photo was a blond-haired little girl. They were taken on a school playground.

"I'm showing you these against my better judgment," she said. "But since you've decided I'm a liar, here they are. I will *not* tell you where she lives."

Marik let her eyes slide over the pictures. She stuffed her hands beneath her thighs on the chair, as if touching the photos might burn her.

The images looked soft, perhaps taken from a distance and enlarged. The girl's face was smooth and rounded, caught on the cusp between babyhood and pre-teen. She was playing, not looking at the camera. She had a small mouth and chin, and the shade of dark blond hair that would turn brown as she grew up. Like Marik's hair. In the background, the blurry shapes of other children moved among swing sets and a jungle gym.

There was nothing in the pictures to distinguish the playground from any other. But thanks to the cowboy P.I., Marik had no doubt when and where the photos were taken. Her only doubts were whether this was actually her child.

She examined each picture, waiting for something familiar, some kind of recognition. It didn't happen.

"This could be any little girl," she said. The blood rushing through her ears was louder than her voice.

"What did you think, she'd look just like you?" Daisy laid the last photo on the table. "Maybe she looks like her father."

Marik shook her head slowly. "Not really."

Eye color was impossible to tell from the photos, but they didn't look dark. Was this the child she'd carried for nine months, labored to deliver and agonized about giving up? She found it hard to breathe.

She searched one image after another and saw what might have been the trace of a dimple on a rounded cheek. Marik didn't have dimples and neither did the baby's father. But J.B. did, big friendly creases that she always wished she'd inherited. The thought of J.B.'s granddaughter carrying his dimples scalded her eyes.

She cleared her throat. "May I keep these?"

"You may not. I don't want your investigator friend trying to trace down the location."

Too late.

"I haven't changed my mind about your contacting her or her family," Daisy said. "I took these to prove she's thriving. If you truly care about her welfare, you'll leave her alone."

Marik felt like a wind-tower blade, nine tons heavy, turning and turning. "You should have been a mother. You do a first-class guilt trip."

"I try. It comes in handy in my line of work." Daisy looked at the empty coffeepot and stood up. "Would you like some coffee, Daisy? Why thanks, I'd love some. But don't get up, I'll make it myself."

Marik stared at the photos while Daisy made herself at home in the kitchen. After J.B.'s plane crash, Daisy had taken off work and stayed with her every day, from early until late, managing phone calls and out-of-town company, freezing casseroles after the funeral. When Anna and her husband flew back to California, it was Daisy who helped Marik sort through J.B.'s things. They had folded plaid shirts into boxes for Goodwill, wept together over his empty boots. How could Marik doubt her?

But there it was—the baby's bones up on the ridge, the unfamiliar face in the photos.

"Can I at least know her name?" Marik asked.

"No. I'm sorry."

The coffeepot made a sound like a wounded rooster. "Do you ever clean this thing?" Daisy said. "You're supposed to run vinegar through it once a month."

Marik had called her daughter Eva. It was an old name,

a name that knew things. Perhaps now she was Amy or Tiffany, something airy and young.

"Don't try sneaking one of those out," Daisy warned, her back turned as she took a cup from the cabinet. "I've counted them."

The photos destroyed the fantasy that Marik might someday recognize her daughter in a crowd, instinctively feel the maternal link. The loss of that illusion left her hollow.

Daisy brought her mug of coffee to the table and sat down. She was dressed for work, Monday at the office. Only two other women worked there, and they were on flextime. No one would gripe at the area supervisor for coming in late.

"So. How's the new foreman working out?" she said. As if they could just move on to other subjects.

Marik shrugged, her eyes still fixed on the photos. "He's fine. But he's not Monte."

Daisy smiled. "Nobody is. The world could only handle one Monte." She sipped her coffee. "Tell me about these bones they found on the ridge."

Marik told her briefly, distracted by an urge to get outdoors and be alone, to let the wind blow through her. She slid the photos into a stack and pushed them away.

"About what Burt Gurdman said the other night," Daisy said, looking at her closely. "Lots of women have babies outside of marriage, even around Silk. You don't need to be embarrassed."

"I'm not embarrassed about having a baby," Marik said.

"I never was. But I'm ashamed that I gave away a human being. Like...a *plant,* or a book."

Daisy shook her head. "It was the bravest thing you could have done."

They'd had this discussion before. Finally Daisy sighed and slipped the photos into her tote bag. "I'd better get to work."

She set her cup in the kitchen sink and turned back to Marik, resting her backside against the cabinet. "You know I'm here, Marik. Whatever you need, except for this one thing. Keep me posted?"

"Sure," Marik said. "Thanks."

She was still seeing the image of a little girl beside the swings, strands of hair lifting like spiderwebs against the light. Was it really Eva? How far would Daisy go to protect her from knowing that something awful happened to her baby? She heard Daisy's car drive away and couldn't move, her body limp.

If the child in the photos was her daughter, she knew where to find her.

Red Ryder waited in the shadows of the barn. She had put the old pickup at Jace's disposal for ranch chores, but he usually preferred to drive his own truck. She climbed inside, adjusted the bench seat closer to the steering wheel and settled into her father's shape in the hollowed-out cushion. The truck started up on the first try; Jace must have tuned it up.

Halfway up the gravel road to the windmills, she realized

the right-side window—which had been stuck partly open for years—was rolled up. She mashed the brake and leaned across the seat. The window cranked down and up smoothly. The cab looked cleaner, too. Luckily there were still grass-hopper guts on the windshield or she'd think it was a stolen vehicle.

On Killdeer Ridge, all but two of the forty-five wind-mills turned leisurely circles against the sky. The comput-ers were probably resetting the pair that were still. Marik parked in her usual spot where she could see the country-side for miles around. She got out and sat on the warm hood of the truck.

Will Rogers Elementary in Redhorse.

"If you truly care about her welfare, you'll leave her alone."

But her doubts would never rest unless she met this child in person. Maybe not even then.

On one of the bottom pastures by the river, Jace's pickup was circling slowly among the cattle, checking for new calves or animals that might need attention. The wind erased the sound of his vehicle before it reached her. Halfway down the ridge the huge dirt movers sat silent, their mammoth tires caked with clay. Yellow ribbon still fluttered around a reddish-brown square of freshly dug ground. And beyond that, barely visible in the grass, four spots of red marked the corners of the graveyard. Nothing else moved, not even the resident killdeer. It was quiet as a battlefield where everyone had died.

Too quiet. A watchman ought to be here.

She pulled the cell phone from her pocket and dialed Lou Benson. "Any news?"

"We've asked for an injunction from the court that will allow us to resume construction by next week," Lou told her. "I'm not sure we even need a court order, but GPP&L likes to stay on the good side of the law. With the court's approval, there'll be no question."

"Let me know if it goes through, will you?" Marik said. "And Lou, given the circumstances, I really think you should post a guard up here again."

"Nobody's there?"

"Just me and the wind. Somebody could vandalize your machines or screw around with the area where they dug up the bones."

"I thought the local law was going to post somebody."

She forgave him that overestimate; he hadn't spent much time in Silk.

"I'll call GPP&L and ask them to send out a security guy," Lou said.

Marik drove back to the house, still unsettled and jittery. On the answering machine in the studio, a red number two was blinking. She pushed the button and slipped on her painting shirt while she listened.

The voice was feminine, with a soft southern accent. "Miss Youngblood, this is June May. I own a small art gallery in Lawton. Someone told me about your painting in the bank at Silk and I stopped by to see it the other day. I'd really like to see more of your work. Could you please phone me at Wild Things Gallery during business hours…"

Marik pushed Replay and jotted down the phone number, wondering if *June May* went through life feeling backward. She was smiling about that when the second recording started—a small hiccup, like a catch in a female voice, then two seconds of silence before someone hung up. Huh. *The second hang-up in two weeks.*

She left a message at June May's gallery, then stuck the phone number on the bulletin board and prepared her paints. It was flattering to think that a gallery owner was interested in her work. Lawton might not be Santa Fe, but it was Oklahoma's third-largest city and a respectable start. Maybe she'd invite Ms. May to the ranch to see the paintings in her studio.

She had set aside the ghost-lady painting to let it dry and to gain some distance so she could assess what else it might need. Today she addressed the composition sketched out on her easel. The giant windmills towered against a cloud-banked sky, while in the foreground, white-faced cattle grazed in peace. The focal point was an old-fashioned windmill—the kind that settled the West, according to Jace—pumping water into a stock tank. Marik liked the juxtaposition of old and new, the coexistence of rural simplicity and modern technology. But it was hard to concentrate on painting with the image of a blond-haired child branded on her eyes.

At noon she stopped work and made two ham sandwiches and a green salad. Jace was a big eater, so she heated up baked-potato soup. Having lunch together was an easy way to communicate about the daily ranch work. When it was almost ready, she dialed his cell phone.

He showed up within ten minutes, washed up and joined her at the kitchen table.

"Smells great," he said, and dug in.

She told him about the phone call to Lou Benson. "He sounded pretty confident that the court would give approval to resume construction soon."

"That's good news."

When they'd finished, she stacked the plates. "I'm going to town this afternoon. Need anything?"

He looked at her earnestly. "Would you mind? I'm nearly out of grub and I'd rather castrate calves than shop for groceries."

"Let's hope you're better at it, too." She handed him a notepad and pen. "Write down what you need."

The grocery store in Silk was small and overpriced, but she preferred to patronize the local store instead of making the drive to Pacheeta. Coming out of the market with her cart full of brown sacks, she nearly rolled over the foot of a small boy who had set up shop on the sidewalk. Beside him sat a cardboard box populated with three fur balls.

She stopped the cart and smiled at the boy. "Whatcha got there?"

"Daddy says we can't keep them. We already have two dogs." His nose was sprinkled with freckles, and his round blue eyes looked sad.

Two of the puppies were asleep, but the third one stood on its hind legs at the edge of the box and wagged a greeting. Its paws and muzzle were snow white, the chunky body mostly brown, and it had a black mask around its eyes like Zorro, another of her dad's Western heroes.

Marik bent down and rubbed the pup's head. A wet spot

appeared immediately on the newspaper in the box. "What kind are they?" she said.

"Two girls and a boy. That one's a girl."

"No, I meant what kind of dog."

He shrugged. "I dunno. Part shepherd, I think. Only twenty dollars and they've had their shots."

The pups were long-haired, with ears just long enough to flop over on the ends, and extraordinarily big feet. They would be large, woolly dogs.

Marik loved large, woolly dogs. She wondered if the girl in Daisy's photos had a dog of her own.

She picked up the girl puppy and snuggled it against her. It was already chunky, obviously well fed. She reached for her billfold.

"She's their leader," the little boy said, stroking the two pups left in the box. "They sure will be lonesome without their sister."

Marik hadn't driven a mile out of town before Zorro managed to get out of the box and climb onto her lap. The pup turned two cramped circles between Marik and the steering wheel before settling down with her head on Marik's thigh. The other two puppies slept piled together in the box on the passenger seat.

Three puppies. Ye gods. Did she need to mother something that badly?

You're compensating, you big dope. That's fairly pathetic.

But she had kept a little doggie family together, and that made her smile.

Marik stroked the broad little head on her lap. "You're

going to love the ranch," she told the pup. "It's a great place for a dog."

The puppy's ears felt like velvet slipping through her fingers. When Zorro gave an enormous sigh and fell asleep, Marik's nose burned. The dog could have peed on her lap and she wouldn't have cared.

Chapter Fourteen

Jace reached into the cardboard box and picked up one of the puppies. "You got *three?*" He held the pup on his forearm like a loaf of bread and massaged its head. The dog salivated with pleasure.

She shrugged. "We have plenty of room."

"We?"

"I thought we could fence off an area by the house that includes the carport," she said. "I never use the carport anyway. They can stay out of the rain there until I get a doghouse."

"You get the materials, I'll build the pen."

"Not a pen. A nice big yard, where they can exercise until they're big enough to run loose."

"You might need an extra barn," he said. "Look at the size of these feet. So you're calling a *girl* dog Zorro?"

"Okay, Zorroette. Zorro for short."

He pointed to the male dog. "So who's he, Hopalong Cassidy?"

Marik grinned. "Hopalong. I like that. And the other girl can be Calamity Jane. C.J. for short."

"Good grief." He went back to work.

Zorro and C.J. liked to race through the house pulling the blanket Marik had put in their cardboard box. Hoppy chewed the box, leaving soggy brown tidbits all over the floor. Somehow Marik had thought puppies slept more than this.

On her morning drive to the windmills, she dared not leave the pups in the house alone, so they rode along. Red Ryder's cab looked like a Three Stooges movie. She laughed all the way to the ridge. Getting the dogs was the best decision she'd made since hiring Jace.

On the ridge, though, she found nothing amusing. There was still no watchman on duty. She left a blunt message on Lou Benson's voice mail. She was preaching to the deacon, but Lou wanted his machinery protected and she knew he would call the company again. GPP&L would pay more attention to his complaints than to hers.

She decided to call the OSBI agent who'd given her his card, too, and ask when that yellow tape could come down. It gave her the creeps, as if the ridge had been the scene of some awful crime.

The Pacheeta hardware store delivered fence materials, and she held the wrought-iron panels straight while Jace attached them to posts and the dogs wrestled in the grass over a pair of knotted socks. They seemed overjoyed with their new digs, sniffing out rabbit scents in the corners, barking at Lady and Gent when the horses came to the corral for water.

That afternoon, temperatures rose to unseasonable heights, and the breeze was heavy with humidity. A burst of thunder just as Marik opened the kitchen door brought her little charges tumbling indoors. C.J. trembled at her feet, begging to be picked up. Hopalong made a beeline up the stairs to his favorite sleeping spot under her bed. But Zorro stood with her at the living-room windows, front paws on the sill, and watched the storm.

Marik tousled her spotted ears. "You're fearless, are you? I hope that doesn't get you in trouble some day."

On Monday she left the puppies alone in their yard for the first time. Jace had located a group of stocker calves he thought she should buy. If the ranch was ever going to be profitable, it was a good place to start.

Jace waited outside the gate while she set out extra puppy food and arranged the blanket in their box. "They'll be fine," he said, amused by her fussing. "They have each other for company."

"I know," she said. But still she felt like a deserter as they drove away in Jace's white truck.

It was two and a half hours to the Oklahoma City Stock-yards. She rode shotgun and bought the gas.

The Oklahoma City Stockyards looked and smelled just as she remembered from trips with her father. The stock-yards was a world unto itself, a city within a city.

Jace parked in a gravel lot next to a paint-deprived red pickup with three rangy hounds lounging in the back. He spoke to them as he walked past. "How's it going, guys?" The dogs regarded them with languid, pink-rimmed eyes.

Together Marik and Jace mounted the wooden steps to the catwalk that ran above forty acres of cattle pens. Below their feet, restless livestock milled and bawled, their ears pricked forward.

Jace located the pens where a specific group of stockers was warehoused until the sale. He and Marik leaned over the railing to inspect the calves. The animals had sturdy bone structure and their hair coat was thick and healthy.

"They look good," she said. "Plenty of milk from their mamas."

Jace nodded. "The man from the commission company said they have four hundred head available altogether. If we could get a hundred of these at a decent price, I'd sure do it."

"So would I," she said. "Let's get into the arena before they run these through."

With her line of credit at Pacheeta F&M Bank verified, Marik and Jace entered the auction arena. Rows of padded seats on concrete risers surrounded the semicircular ring where cattle were driven in one door and out the other side. In the hub of the ring, on a raised platform, sat the auctioneer and his helpers. Men in jeans and ball caps or cowboy hats filled most of the arena's chairs, but there were women, too, and a few children, learning the family business early. Ceiling fans stirred the smell of dirt and cattle.

Everyone's attention was fixed on a dozen panicked calves now up for auction. Marik listened hard, tuning her ear to the rapid-fire chatter of the auctioneer.

Thousands of dollars changed hands in less than a minute. Luckily, the stockers they were interested in didn't come up for a while, and Marik had time to gather her wits and get into the rhythm of the bidding. By noon, she owned ninety-five good-looking bull calves and felt as jazzed up as an Olympic champion. She'd also spent more than thirty thousand dollars. They settled up with the clerk and made arrangements for a truck to deliver the calves later in the week.

They rode home with the windows half down and an April wind whipping through the cab. Redbuds bloomed along the creeks, and thickets of sandplum swelled in greenish-white clouds along fence lines. Marik slouched back and propped one knee on the dashboard. She had enjoyed teaching art to schoolkids, but it never gave her the thrill she'd felt today. She must have been smiling, because Jace glanced over and smiled back.

The buzz of contentment was still with her when they drove through the cedar archway to the ranch. Jace rolled the truck to a stop in front of his house. Marik thanked him for driving and walked up the driveway. On the ridge, the sun hung between two windmills, gently turning. It had been a long day and she was tired, but it was a good tired.

The puppies set up a ruckus when they saw her. Two of them stood on their hind legs at the fence and wagged a greeting as she drew close.

"Hey, guys!" she called. "I'm glad to see you, too. Where's Zorro?"

She entered the yard and bent over the gyrating puppies, scratching their backs and avoiding the playful puppy teeth. But Zorro was nowhere in the yard. She stepped underneath the shadow of the carport and looked inside the box. Zorro wasn't there.

Marik stood up and surveyed the grassy yard. There were no holes dug under the perimeter of the fence, no place in the pen for Zorro to hide or get under the house. The gate was still latched, and there was no way a puppy that small could have gotten over the chest-high fence. How could Zorro be gone?

"Zorro!" Her eyes scanned the circular gravel driveway and the barns, the empty corral. "Zor-ro! Here, Zorro!"

Only an echo came back from the barn.

Then she saw it—a footprint in the rain-softened dirt at the mouth of the carport, inside the fence.

It was a man's footprint, much larger than hers, and fresh. Jace had not come inside the pen this morning after the rain. She crouched over the shoe print. It had a round toe and a waffle sole, like a farmer's boot. The kind Burt Gurdman wore.

Marik swore, her breath coming fast and hard. There was no other explanation. First the vandalism, then the eagle, and now this. Had he come here to threaten her again and taken Zorro because she wasn't home?

If he's harmed an innocent puppy…

She slammed through the kitchen door and across the

living room, took the stairs two at a time up to her bedroom. She threw open the closet door and from the top shelf took down her shotgun. Jammed two shells into the chambers and cracked it shut.

The dogs had followed her inside. She shooed them back outdoors and trotted across the gravel to the barn. She hung the shotgun in the rack behind Red Ryder's seat and ground the starter.

Jace was coming out of his house when she drove past. He'd probably heard her calling for Zorro. She didn't stop. He would try to talk her out of confronting Gurdman and she didn't want to waste time. An image of what might have happened to Zorro flickered through her mind and the thought made her ill.

On the main road, she turned on the headlights. The sun was still up on the other side of Killdeer Ridge, but here shadows covered the road. The Gurdman farm lay adjacent to the ridge on the west, but it was four miles by road. She drove north to the first crossroads and turned west, red dust boiling up behind the truck, then back south at the second section line.

When she pulled up to the Gurdmans' white frame house, the blue light of a television flickered through the curtains. Sparse grass grew around the house, and a row of straggly pansies clung to survival beside the front porch. Mottled chickens wandered in front of the yawning doorway to a large round-top barn. In a pen beside the barn, a lop-eared mule watched her with benign eyes.

Marik had been here only once before, with J.B., shortly

after the Gurdmans bought the place. She was eight years old at the time; maybe the place had looked this sad then and it just hadn't registered. But she clearly remembered thinking that Lena looked too young for a husband who was born old.

She killed the engine. The curtains in a front window shifted, revealing nothing but a slice of darkness. She thought of Lena's stiff back at the town meeting, Burt's grip on her arm as he'd pulled her toward their truck. Marik stepped out onto hard-packed dirt and caught a faint aroma drifting from the house—*meat loaf, potatoes.* Lena was cooking supper.

Marik's anger deflated. She had no proof that Burt had been at her house. She should have called the sheriff and told him her suspicions instead of coming over here with a shotgun.

But by then, it might be too late for Zorro.

She left the shotgun in the truck and started up the walk toward the house. In her peripheral vision she caught movement and turned back.

Burt Gurdman had emerged from the shadowy interior of the barn. He was carrying a five-gallon bucket and wearing round-toed waffle stompers.

When Gurdman saw her, he set the bucket down and stepped in front of it. He crossed his arms and spread his feet, framed by the darkness of the barn door. She thought of a line from Robert Frost about his farmer neighbor: *Like an old stone savage, armed.*

Gurdman waited.

"Burt," she said, and walked forward.

His eyes were flat and hard. "What are you doing here?" If he knew why she'd come, his face was an expert liar.

"My dog is missing. A puppy."

"Maybe it got run over up on the highway." The black eyes narrowed. "Bad things happen if you're not careful."

Her chest cinched. "Was that another threat, Burt?"

He didn't answer.

"I need to look inside your barn."

He set his legs farther apart. "The hell you do. Your dog ain't here."

She looked at his feet. "Those shoes have a waffle sole? There was a shoe print in the dogs' pen."

"Get the hell off my property."

Was she imagining a red smear on his pants leg? What was in the bucket he'd set behind him?

At that moment a white pickup turned into the driveway and skidded to a stop beside hers. Jace got out fast and came up beside her.

"This your new *boy?*" Gurdman said, making it sound dirty. "Now the *both* of you can get the hell off my property."

Marik heard the distinctive sound of a rifle bullet ratcheting into a chamber. She turned just enough to see Lena Gurdman on the porch, an apron tied around her waist. The long-barreled rifle in her hands was leveled at Marik and Jace.

The skin on Marik's back shivered. She'd never in her life had a gun pointed at her, and the feeling changed everything. *I could die here,* she thought. *And never know my daughter.* Whatever sympathy she might have had for Lena pinched out like a flame.

Gurdman's mouth twitched. "Saw in the newspaper where they'd found a baby's bones up on the ridge," he said. "Is that where your bastard child ended up? But you just kept *digging,* so you could get all that money."

Her fists clenched and unclenched. How could Burt Gurdman possibly know she'd had a child?

Should have got the shotgun out of the truck.

Jace's hand closed on her arm. "Come on," he said softly. "Let's go."

"If you've done something to my dog," she said to Gurdman, her voice loud in the quiet farmyard, "I'll get you for it. One way or another. She's just an innocent puppy!"

"You're breakin' my heart," Gurdman said. "Lena! If they're not out of here in twenty seconds, put a hole in that nice truck her boy's drivin'. Right through the windshield."

Lena held the rifle level and said nothing. Her face was as blank as milk.

Jace pulled Marik away. "Come on," he said quietly. "These people are nuts. Let the sheriff handle it."

He pushed her into Red Ryder's cab and stood by the door until she turned the key in the ignition. Her hands were claws on the steering wheel, her chest beating like wings. Jace got into his truck and motioned her ahead of him out the driveway.

She drove, expecting the rifle's explosion behind her, the

shatter of glass. But all she heard was the drone of Red Ryder's engine.

He won't get away with this. If the sheriff won't do something, I swear to God I'll shoot the son of a bitch myself.

Chapter Fifteen

It was a dangerous moment for Lena to accept that she hated her husband.

The realization came to her while she was standing on the porch with a loaded rifle aimed at Marik Youngblood, and Burt took the opportunity to run his mouth.

"Saw in the newspaper where they'd found a baby's bones up on the ridge," he said. "Is that where your bastard child ended up? But you just kept *digging…*"

The harsh way he'd said *digging* sent a razor-edged pain through Lena's rib cage. The light turned white around her, blotting out everything like an overexposed photograph. She thought she'd gone blind. For several seconds she couldn't breathe, while the truth she'd denied for years crystallized into a hard, sure knowledge. She understood why Burt had fought so hard against that wind farm, the secret he was trying to hide. Her stomach rolled.

When her vision came back, color slowly bleeding into the farmyard again, a wave of nausea came with it. She thought of the bones they'd dug up on Killdeer Ridge, not a mile from her house. Lena shifted the tip of the rifle ever so slightly and aligned the sights on her husband's head.

Her finger twitched on the trigger. But she was a coward, just like her brother accused her when they were kids.

Lena's aim slid back to Marik Youngblood's spine. She hoped none of them could see the tip of the rifle trembling. She hated Marik, too. Any woman who could willingly give up her baby must be evil at the bone. Lena held her aim, her heart floundering like a wounded animal, and waited to see what would happen.

But nothing did. The ranch hand said something to Marik and put his hand on her arm. In less than a minute the confrontation was over. Marik and the hired man drove away in separate trucks, and Lena was left facing Burt's scowl across the barnyard.

Even from this distance she could see the high color in Burt's face. The memory of his fist ran through her jaw like an electric shock that ended in her chipped tooth. Maybe he had really expected her to shoot the ranch hand's truck.

Burt surprised her. "You did good," he said, expressionless. Then he picked up his bucket and went back toward the barn.

She hated the flutter of pleasure that arose from his approval.

Coward.

Lena went back into the house and took the meat loaf and baked potatoes from the oven. No telling how long it would be before Burt came in to eat. Her hands shook inside the oven mitts and she cautioned herself to hang on tightly as she set the hot dishes on the stove top. Her breath came in short bursts through her open mouth.

The creamed peas had come to a boil and stuck to the bottom of the pan. She stirred them loose lightly, so the brown flecks of scorched milk wouldn't spoil the white sauce, and poured the peas into a bowl. She covered it with foil and set it, too, on the stove top. Then she sank into a chair at the table and wilted.

She could still feel the coldness of the rifle in her hands. She closed her eyes and heard the lurch of her heartbeat in her ears.

How long had she hated him? Months? Always?

But she knew the answer. Out there on the porch she had relived the exact night the hatred started. She hadn't been able to think about it for years. Some things were better not remembered, or you'd go crazy. She cursed herself for not leaving him then, when she still had enough gumption to be on her own.

The sound of the barn door rumbling shut drifted through the front screen. Lena got up and set his plate and silverware on the table. Burt would be coming in now. She put on a pot of strong coffee and prepared his cup with particular care.

He drank it and ate his dinner without saying a word. He didn't even ask why she wasn't eating.

★ ★ ★

She should have put Benadryl in the coffee, too. Because that night after she had dressed for bed and slipped into the respite of cool sheets, Burt pounded on her locked bedroom door.

"Open up, Lena, before I knock this door off its hinges."

She sat still in the bed, crushing a pillow against the burn in her stomach.

"You're my *wife,* goddammit!"

When she mustered the courage to speak, her voice sounded like a child's. "I'm having my period," she said.

"Don't lie to me. Open the damn door!"

She counted five seconds before his boot slammed into the door. Her body jerked. She bit down on the corner of the pillow.

When he kicked the door again, the wood around the hinges splintered. The third time, the hinges gave way and the door fell sideways in slow motion. It swung recklessly by the twisted padlock, still fastened.

She wondered if he would hit her, but he contented himself with a different kind of violence. While he rutted on top of her like a wild pig, Lena gripped the bedding in her fists and watched a shadow bloom on the bedroom ceiling. The shadow was shaped like a dog's head. She wondered if he really had stolen a puppy from the Youngblood ranch, and if so, what he'd done with it. Her head bumped against the headboard, and on the ceiling she saw a vision of Burt bashing the poisoned eagle, crushing the bones in its dark, graceful wing. She hoped it was dead before the bashing, and quickly behind that thought she pictured the baby bones she'd read about in the Pacheeta newspaper, uncovered by the big machines on Killdeer Ridge. She closed her eyes but the image of the bones remained and tears ran down her temples.

Coward. Coward. Coward.

The next morning Burt started up the tractor and drove out to windrow the wheat on the layout ground so he could get the government subsidy for not harvesting. He'd told her to pack him a sandwich, which meant he'd be gone most of the day. Watching him leave, Lena said a prayer of thanks to her nonexistent God. She had laced Burt's morning coffee with so much weed killer she was certain he'd smell it, and her heart had pounded all through breakfast. But he didn't seem to notice; his sense of smell had been damaged by a sinus infection years ago.

Now he was gone and she could breathe again. Maybe he'd get stomach cramps and fall off beneath the tractor wheels. One of her parents' neighbors had died that way, plowed himself right under.

Then again, maybe the weed killer was so old it had lost all its potency, like her daddy.

When the dishes were done, she tuned the TV to her morning game show, but halfway through she dozed off in the chair, sore and exhausted. It was past noon when she put on her old sneakers and went out to feed Borax and the chickens.

The ground was still damp from the recent rain, and the TV weatherman said they were in for violent weather again tonight. Already a dark mass of clouds gathered on the western horizon.

She poured a scoop of oats into an old dishpan for Borax, and the mule mumbled its thanks. Burt wouldn't give Borax oats when there was green grass in the pen, but Lena sneaked her a treat now and then. Borax never missed a chance to nip at Burt, either, but she'd never offered to bite Lena.

The chickens, though, Burt treated like royalty, buying the best feed so they'd produce more eggs. Whatever they produced above what Lena used for cooking, Burt could sell in town.

He'd left the barn open when he drove the tractor out, and Lena went inside to get the chicken feed. She took the lid off the big tin garbage can that held the feed, flinching at the soreness between her legs when she leaned over. Maybe she'd get an infection and go to the hospital, where women in white uniforms would take care of her, bring her meals to the bed. Maybe she'd never come home.

Lena looked around for a bucket to scoop up the feed. Three plastic buckets sat underneath Burt's junky work-bench. The top of the bench was littered with rusty tools and odd lengths of twisted wire, everything covered with oily grime and dust. When she reached for the bucket, a red object among the clutter caught her eye. It was some kind of leather strap that looked new. Lena picked it up and fingered a buckle on one end, five holes in the other. A row of metal studs ran down its length like decorations. Caught in one of the studs she found a thin tuft of blackish-brown hair.

She lifted the strap to her nose and sniffed. It smelled like leather and puppy. She was holding a new dog collar in her hand.

She wasn't aware of collapsing, but suddenly she was sitting on the dirt floor of the barn, her legs splayed in front of her. The dog collar dangled from her limp hand and the vision from her bedroom ceiling filled the dim barn like a movie theater: she saw Burt's arms rising and falling above the wounded eagle, lifting and smashing. She felt herself beneath him again, her face turned away, eyes open, fists gripping the sheet. She felt her head pounding against the headboard, heard his grunting as he bashed and bashed against her, and his face morphed into something subhuman. Then she saw a clear image of a tiny baby's face, contorted with fever and crying.

She leaned over and threw up her breakfast. After that, everything went dark.

Lena awoke on the barn floor, smelling hay and dirt and bile. She pushed herself to a sitting position and scooted away from the place where she'd thrown up. She was dizzy, and her mouth tasted sour and dry.

When her head stopped pounding she made herself stand, though her knees wanted to melt and take her down again. She still hadn't fed the chickens or gathered the eggs, and they were her responsibility.

She kicked dirt over her lost breakfast, but the smell was on her clothes and threatened to make her heave again. She took off her skirt and then her blouse and tossed them away.

In her bra and half slip and dusty sneakers, she leaned against the workbench to catch her breath.

The red dog collar lay at her feet. She picked it up, looked at it a long moment and fastened it around her neck.

Clouds boiled up behind the house and the wind shivered her skin. Lena watched her white legs in the clunky shoes while she poured feed into the chicken troughs and scattered the rest across the beaten ground. Speckled hens scurried to peck at the feed. She thought of the ghost woman of Silk Mountain. Legends began with something true that got embellished over the years. Lena imagined a young farm wife out here alone with the extremes of weather and the unrelenting wind. Probably living in a dirt soddy. Maybe her husband was a monster, or just a dull-witted oaf who never talked to her. And there was no way out. Nowhere to run.

She pictured the young wife climbing up the tiered rocks in her petticoats, red shale mixing with the blood on her scraped knees and hands, until she stood at the very top and looked out over nothing. Nothing but miles and miles of miles and miles, and that's what her life was, with no escape.

Some people said suicide was cowardly. They were wrong. Lena knew it took a great deal of courage to jump.

She teetered on that edge. She might have found a way to jump right then, but once again Burt interfered. She heard a sound and saw the tractor percolating back up the road without the mower behind it, and Burt hunched down over the steering wheel, holding his gut like he was in pain.

Chapter Sixteen

Thunderheads massed in the southwest, shaking the sky with pulses of lightning. Tornado alerts blanketed the state. The weatherman on Marik's radio announced with ill-concealed pleasure that things were setting up for the storm of the decade.

She had been in her studio since noon with little to show for it. When the lights blinked out, she was grateful for an excuse to stop painting. She went to the windows and watched the sky darken. If Zorro was still alive, was she out in the storm alone? The idea clotted in her throat. She had called Deputy Sheriff Bill Ferguson that morning and told him about her stolen puppy and the shoe print that made her suspect Burt Gurdman. Ferguson wasn't the sharpest spade in the shed, and apparently he wasn't a dog person, either.

"Is the dog valuable?" He sounded like he was stifling a yawn.

Her voice rose slightly. "She is to me."

"I'll get out that way later in the week," he drawled. "But I can't keep searching Burt's place without a warrant. He let us do it last time but I doubt he'll be that cooperative again."

"Then get a warrant."

"With all due respect, Miss Youngblood, the judge isn't going to issue a search warrant because you don't get along with your neighbor."

"Hey! Bite me," she'd snapped, and hung up. If a chimpanzee ran against Bill Ferguson in the next election, she'd stump for the monkey.

Thunder rattled the windows. Marik brought C.J. and Hopalog inside and they assumed their positions—Hoppy beneath the bed upstairs, C.J. curled on her lap on the sofa. The electricity had flickered back on, so she tuned the TV to local weather. There was video of an ominous wall cloud lowering near Pacheeta. On radar, two more angry storms ticked steadily across the Texas Panhandle toward Silk Mountain. It looked like it was going to be a long night. Marik thought again of Zorro.

Hail pounded the roof like stampeding cattle. Marik gathered her flashlight and portable radio in case the power went out again. She microwaved popcorn and sliced an apple into the bowl, then she and C.J. curled up in the living room, braced for round two of the storm. She considered phoning Jace, but he knew about the storm cellar behind the carport. He would look out for himself.

For half an hour horizontal rain lashed the windows and the network channels carried nothing but weather warnings. Three funnel clouds were tracking across the state, one of them near Silk. Residents were advised to take shelter.

Then the lights went out.

Lightning cracked like a rifle shot close to the house. C.J. whined and even Hopalong came slinking down the stairs and joined them. Marik hated the spidery storm cellar. She refused to go down there unless a twister was close enough to smell it. Barring a capricious change of direction, this one ought to pass east of the ranch. She hoped the Searcys were below ground.

She lit three candles and peered out the window toward Silk, but it was totally dark now. Lightning revealed the shattered mulberry tree, but everything else was wrapped in rain. She listened for the freight-train rumble of a tornado; heard only thunder and wind. Long minutes later, the radio reported that the tornado had touched down in an open field and finally dissipated. Someone had lost a barn, but there were no known injuries.

The third-string storm appeared to be weakening. The power was still out when Marik made her way upstairs to bed.

But the weather wasn't finished disturbing her sleep. An hour before dawn, she was awakened by an unnatural silence. The wind had stopped. She listened to the darkness, but heard not a creak nor a sigh, not a whisper. It was like someone had sucked out her breath.

She got up and opened a window. The night was moonless

and dark as a lake. She leaned her forehead against the screen and inhaled the cooler air outside. The lace curtains hung limp at her shoulders. On the horizon, the spiny back of Killdeer Ridge mounded like a sleeping dinosaur, the windmills as still as white skeletons. The hush was spooky, as if the earth had stopped turning. Foreboding spidered down her arms.

Something out there was *wrong*.

She wondered if on Silk Mountain tonight, the ghost of Leasie Youngblood was walking.

The branch of a tree shivered—perhaps the restless stirring of a bird. The movement was enough to let her breathe again, and a memory unfolded: a night like this when she was very small, the scent of fresh sheets on her parents' bed. She had come to her mother, crying.

"What's wrong, honey?"

"I had a bad dream. I'm afraid I'm going to die."

Her mother smelled like soap and flowers when she hugged her. "But there's nothing wrong with you, sweetie. You're perfectly healthy. People don't die unless something is wrong." Mama lifted the sheet to let her climb in. "You've just got the night crawlers."

Marik giggled, thinking of the night-crawler worms her dad used for fishing. She stayed the rest of the night in her mother's soft protection.

This windless night had given her the night crawlers.

Sleep was out of the question. She slipped on a jogging suit and walked barefoot down the stairs, through the silent house to the front porch. The damp boards felt cool and familiar to her feet and the clean scent of ozone prickled her nose.

In the northern sky, Ursa Major flickered through a humid haze. She stood on the porch and breathed deeply, waiting for dawn.

At sunrise Jace came out of his house and walked toward the barns to start his chores. Bully watched him through the board fence of the corral, and Marik watched from her seat on the glider. The stocker calves were due for delivery today. This morning Jace was going to finish repairs to the fence around the pasture they planned to use. It might have been her imagination, but he seemed to be keeping an eye out for Zorro.

After breakfast she fed Bully and decided to shower before driving to the windmills. She was drying her hair when the phone rang.

"I hope I didn't phone too early," June May said. "I wanted to call before the gallery opened and we got busy."

June sounded young and enthusiastic. She bragged on Marik's painting in the bank and eagerly accepted an invitation to come to the ranch on Saturday to see more of her work. Marik told herself she should clean house before then, but it probably wouldn't happen.

By the time Marik approached the gate to the windmills, she was two hours later than usual. The gate was already open. Probably the GPP&L caretaker was checking on the turbines after the storm. Even if they'd had a watchman up there last night, the tornado alerts would have sent him scampering home.

The wind was calm, having squandered its breath on

violence. Halfway up the curving road, she saw two pickups parked on the ridge beneath the listless turbines. One was the white truck she'd expected, with the GPP&L logo on the door. The other was the bronze vehicle of the county sheriff's office. Maybe Deputy Ferguson had responded to her call about Zorro after all. But why up here?

She parked beside the other vehicles and looked down the ridge. The yellow OSBI tape had blown loose and trailed limply across the new roadbed. Rain puddles checkered the exposed shale. Deputy Ferguson and the power-company man were standing near Windmill 22, both of them on their cell phones. When she got out and walked down the rise toward them, she saw a third man sitting on the ground against the base of the windmill, arms slack at his sides, a brown cap over his face.

Ferguson saw her and pocketed his phone. He watched her approach, frowning curiously as if waiting for some reaction.

"What's going on?" she said.

He studied her face. "I was just trying to call your house. That's Burt Gurdman over there by the windmill."

"What's he doing up here?"

"Not much," Ferguson said. "He's dead."

Marik looked from his face to the man slumped against the tower, and back again. "Is that a bad joke of some kind?"

"No, ma'am."

The air went out of her. "Holy shit."

She shielded her eyes from the sun and looked down the

hill at Burt's body. Now she noted the unnatural slump of his posture, the way his legs splayed out with the waffle soles of his boots toe-up. "Was his cap like that when you found him?"

"No. Cap belongs to the power-company fellow. Burt's eyes are still open and I covered his face," Ferguson said.

Marik grimaced. "Can you tell how he died?"

"There's a bloody contusion on the back of his head. I can't move him until the sheriff and M.E. get here." Ferguson spread his feet and crossed his arms. "Were you up here yesterday evening before the storms?"

"No. I was home all afternoon."

"Anybody with you?"

Marik scowled. "Just the two puppies he didn't steal. You think he's been up here since before the storm?"

"Looks like it. Body's drenched, and when I drove in, the only tracks were from the GPP&L truck. Rain would have washed away anything before that."

"If he came up here to vandalize stuff, maybe lightning got him."

Ferguson shrugged. "Doesn't look like lightning to me. Looks like somebody beat the hell out of him."

Marik shook her head again. "This is unbelievable."

"Sheriff Dean will want to talk to you. Why don't you wait in your truck." He sucked his teeth. "Hope you know a good lawyer."

"I don't need a lawyer," she said, frowning. "Burt probably got hit by lightning, or else fell off one of those big machines and hit his head."

"Right."

The deputy walked away and she watched him a few seconds before turning back the way she'd come. When she got back to Red Ryder, she called Jace's cell phone.

"Mornin'," he said.

"Morning. We've got trouble up here on the ridge, and I'm outnumbered. Can you come up?"

"What kind of trouble?"

"Burt Gurdman's dead body."

For the second time in a month, Killdeer Ridge swarmed with lawmen. The sheriff's office was out in full force, and Dr. Guthrie made a return appearance on behalf of the medical examiner's office. The OSBI agent who'd been there before showed up to assist, but the county sheriff was in charge. They were treating it like a crime scene, and Marik sensed bad things to come.

She and Jace stood as close as they were allowed and heard the sheriff say the rain had obliterated any clues that might have explained how Gurdman got there and why. There were no tire tracks, and no footprints except those of the GPP&L worker who found him.

The worker, whom she'd met once before, wasn't allowed to leave the scene yet, either. He ambled over to talk with her.

"You didn't notice anything unusual when you drove in?" she asked him.

He shook his head. "Afraid not. That's what the sheriff asked me, too. To tell the truth, I was talking to my wife on the cell phone and not paying much attention. She's pregnant. Morning sickness, you know." He shrugged. "I'd already seen that all the windmills were running, which is pretty much what I came to find out. That was some storm." He ran a stubby hand over his hair and replaced his hard hat. "Was he the guy who vandalized the dirt machines last time and planted that eagle up here?"

"One and the same." Even though she couldn't prove it.

"Jeez. Looks bad for you, huh." He wandered off toward his truck.

"I wish people would stop saying that," Marik said.

Jace smiled without humor. "The lawyer idea probably wasn't a bad one."

She looked at him. "*Et tu*, Brutus?"

"I know you didn't kill him," he said, "but you've got motive, witnesses who heard him threaten you at the town meeting, and Mrs. Gurdman, who'll say you came over to their place accusing him of stealing your dog. If lightning didn't get him, who would you suspect?"

"Swell."

"I can tell them I didn't see you leave the place yesterday afternoon, but I don't know how much good that will do since I work for you."

"Maybe they'll think I hired you to do him in."

"There's a happy thought."

Marik sighed. "Sometimes I wish this town did have bona fide police. Ferguson calls me *Miss Youngblood*, but he was calling Burt by his first name. *'I can't keep searching Burt's house.'* Like they were old drinking buddies."

Jace raised his eyebrows. "You might want to soft-pedal the attitude when the real sheriff talks to you."

"Yeah, yeah."

They cooled their heels for another hour before Sheriff Dean approached. He was a beefy man, about fifty, with sharp gray eyes encased in weathered wrinkles. He tipped his hat and introduced himself to her and Jace. "Miss Youngblood, we're setting up a temporary office in Silk where the barbershop used to be. It's a vacant storefront."

Marik nodded. It was right next to Daisy's office.

"I'd appreciate it if you'd come down there at three this afternoon and give me your statement," the sheriff said.

"You don't want it now?"

"Right now I have to call on Mrs. Gurdman." His jaw tightened. "She doesn't know yet. Besides, I'd like to get your statement on tape. So we don't misrepresent anything you say."

Her neck prickled. "Sheriff? Do I need to bring a lawyer?"

Sheriff Dean shrugged. "Strictly up to you," he said, his expression bland. "We're just gathering information at this point, trying to establish some facts. We'll know more after an autopsy, but it's my educated guess that Burt Gurdman was murdered."

Chapter Seventeen

Gray scum coated the two white sinks still attached to a back wall in the abandoned barbershop. Dust moats thickened the midafternoon light that angled through smeared windows. Marik regretted that Daisy's car wasn't parked outside the office next door. She'd have felt better with Daisy's no-nonsense presence nearby, even on the other side of a brick wall.

Sheriff Dean had borrowed a utility table and six folding chairs from the Methodist church. His real office was in Pacheeta. On top of the table lay the tools of his trade: a notebook and pen, a police radio and a low-tech tape recorder. The sheriff sat on one side and waved Marik toward the chair across from him. Deputy Ferguson was there, too, leaning against the wall with his arms folded.

Beside him, a coffeepot and a tower of plastic cups balanced on the seat of a chair pulled up to an electrical outlet.

Marik sat, and Jace took the chair next to her. He had arranged for the driver of the cattle truck to call him before it arrived. "I think you ought to have somebody with you," he'd told her with an expression that didn't make her feel a bit better about her situation. She had no idea where to find a lawyer on such short notice.

When Marik was settled, the sheriff pushed a button on the tape machine and it made a whispering noise. "May I have your permission to tape this interview?" he said distinctly.

She shrugged. "Sure."

"Please state your name, and where you live."

Marik did.

"You, too," he said to Jace. When Jace had complied, the sheriff addressed Marik again. "We don't know yet what time Mr. Gurdman died, so let's account for your time from noon yesterday until eight this morning, when the GPP&L man arrived at the windmills."

Marik nodded. "Around noon, Jace and I had lunch in my kitchen. When he went back to work, I went into my studio."

"You're a painter," the sheriff said, and she nodded again. "You'll need to answer aloud," he said.

"Yes."

"Your studio is in your home?"

"Yes. I worked there all afternoon until the lightning started, around four-thirty or so. I brought the two dogs inside and waited out the storm. Went to bed close to midnight, and I was still home at eight this morning." She didn't mention her night crawlers, or the eerie stillness just before dawn. Was Burt Gurdman on the ridge then?

"You never left the house?"

"No."

"What did you have for dinner?"

She looked at him, frowning. "Umm...popcorn and apples."

"That's got to be the truth. Who could make it up?" The sheriff laughed and Marik relaxed a little.

He wrote something in his notebook and looked at Jace. "Where were you yesterday?"

Jace looked surprised and uncrossed his long legs. "Working on the fences in the pasture by the barn. If Marik had driven in or out in the afternoon, I'd have seen her. Or anybody else."

"And nobody did?"

"Nobody."

"What about the evening? After dark?"

"It was storming by then. I went to my own house, ate dinner." He glanced at the tape recorder. "Canned chili. Went to bed around nine when the electricity went off."

"You slept through the tornado warnings?" The sheriff raised his eyebrows.

"I guess so, yeah."

"So you weren't watching the driveway after five o'clock."

Jace frowned. "Not specifically."

"And the noise of the storm might have covered up the sound of a vehicle."

"Maybe. But I'd have noticed headlights. Before nine, anyway."

The sheriff turned back to Marik. "What about you? Can you verify where Mr. Rainwater was during the afternoon and evening?"

Her eyes widened. "Uh…" Jace gave her an alarmed glance. "I saw him working the fences in the afternoon. My studio windows face the driveway and barns. I would know if he'd left in his truck."

"But after dark?"

Marik shrugged and the sheriff made more notes. The tape recorder whirred.

"Tell me about your relationship with your neighbors, the Gurdmans."

Marik took a deep breath. "We didn't get along, as I'm sure you've heard. Burt opposed the wind farm, vigorously. During construction of the first phase, somebody vandalized the big dirt movers, but they didn't catch anybody doing it. Then recently I found a dead eagle beneath one of the windmills, like it had run into the blades. But it turned out the eagle had been poisoned and planted up there."

"How do you know that?"

"We had a necropsy done on the eagle. The vet found Diazinon, and he thought its wing had been broken intentionally."

"Who do you think was responsible for that?"

"I think it was Burt."

"Did you confront him about it?"

"No. It all came out in the town meeting. Deputy Ferguson went out to Burt's place the next day and looked around. You'd have to ask him what he found."

"Not a thing," Ferguson chipped in. "No Diazinon, no eagle feathers. Of course, that doesn't prove anything either way."

"It's my understanding Mr. Gurdman made some sort of threat to you after that meeting," the sheriff said.

He'd done his homework. "I guess you could call it that," she said.

"What did he say?"

"That maybe everybody should know the truth about me."

The sheriff's gaze stayed level. "Do you know what he meant by that?"

She took a deep breath and examined her hands, knit together on the table. "He said I'd had a bastard child and maybe people would like to know what happened to her."

"And is that true?"

She looked at him sharply. "No child is a bastard. Only men like Burt Gurdman."

Then, more softly, "I once had a baby that I gave up for adoption."

Sheriff Dean nodded and noted something on his tablet and Jace looked down at his boots.

Before the sheriff could ask anything else, the door opened. They all looked up, and there in the doorway stood Lena Gurdman.

Sheriff Dean pushed a button and stopped the tape. He stood. "Come in, Mrs. Gurdman. I think you know everybody here."

"Holy shit," Marik said under her breath.

It was obvious that Sheriff Dean was expecting Lena, intending to get all the principals in the same room and see if somebody blurted out the truth. The technique probably worked for most of the cases he dealt with in Silk County.

When Lena recognized Marik, she froze. She was a tall woman, rawboned but thin, and looked even taller silhouetted in the doorway with the light behind her. She wore a shapeless cotton dress and leather sandals, with the white feet and tanned ankles of someone who wore sneakers to do her chores.

Marik stood up and met watery blue eyes. "Hello, Lena. I'm very sorry about Burt."

Lena's mouth trembled, then tightened. "No, you're not." Her voice was hoarse and bitter. "You killed him and we both know it."

Marik's mouth opened but Sheriff Dean was quick to intervene. "Nobody knows what happened yet, Mrs. Gurdman." He stepped toward Lena and gently motioned toward a chair farthest from Marik. "But we're going to find out. Please sit down here. Can Deputy Ferguson get you some coffee?"

Lena looked at the half-full Mr. Coffee pot as if it were a snake. "No! I don't want any coffee." One hand wadded a fold of her loose skirt, the other gripped the handles of a well-used leather purse Marik recognized. She had donated that handbag to a church rummage sale last year.

Lena still made no move to sit down. "I haven't been well, you know."

The sheriff nodded sympathetically. "How about some water?"

"Yes. Okay. Some water."

The sheriff nodded at Ferguson, who looked pained at the request. He picked a white cup off the plastic tower and left through the front door. Apparently the water in the old barbershop was turned off or not fit for drinking.

Lena moved to the chair and sat, scooting it back from the table where Marik had resumed her seat. Sheriff Dean took his place at the table again and pushed the button on the recorder.

"Mrs. Gurdman, I'm going to tape-record our conversation so we don't misquote anybody. Is that okay with you?"

Lena frowned at the machine, but she nodded.

"Aloud, please," he said.

"Okay," Lena said.

"You've already told me that you last saw Burt just before the storm hit yesterday afternoon. Then he went out, and you didn't realize he hadn't come home all night until this morning. Is that correct?"

"Yes. I…have my own bedroom."

"Why are you accusing Miss Youngblood of his death?"

Lena looked at Marik with a heat that pushed Marik back in her chair. "They hated each other, that's why."

Marik thought of denying that she hated Burt Gurdman. But that was quite possibly a lie, and she was too surprised by the rough, thin quality of Lena Gurdman's voice. She tried to remember if she'd ever heard it before today. Lena hadn't spoken at the town meeting, nor while she was standing on her front porch wielding a rifle. It sounded like a forced whisper, a voice that was seldom used.

"Hate's a pretty strong word," the sheriff was saying, his face impassive. "Why do you say they hated each other?"

Lena's eyes shifted to the wall above Sheriff Dean's head, then to her rough hands, clenched together in her lap. "Burt was against that wind farm," she said. "He said it was because those things were dangerous, but really it was the money. They could have put a few of those windmills on our land, let us make some money, too. Instead, she'll get rich and we're left to scratch out a living like chickens."

Deputy Ferguson came back in and set a cup of water in front of Lena. She picked it up and they all watched as she drank the entire cupful without stopping.

When she set the cup down, the sheriff said, "So Burt resented Miss Youngblood. But what makes you say she hated him?"

Lena made an odd sound through her nose. "Why wouldn't she? Last year Burt put sugar in the gas tanks of those big dirt machines. Held up construction for weeks. And he poisoned that eagle, too. Everybody knows it. Then the other night she came over to our place and accused him of stealing her dog."

"Did he take Miss Youngblood's dog?"

Lena's voice stumbled. "I…I don't know anything about that." She began to click the tip of one fingernail with another. The nails looked broken, or chewed. "I never saw any dog."

The sheriff's voice softened. "Were you aware of what he'd done to the eagle before that town meeting, Mrs. Gurdman?"

Her head dropped lower. "No. I had no idea. I don't hold with hurting innocent animals."

Sheriff Dean cleared his throat. "What evening was it that Miss Youngblood and Mr. Rainwater came to your place?"

Lena looked up. "His name's Rainwater?"

The sheriff nodded.

"Night before last, I think…I've sort of lost track of time."

"I understand. It's been a terrible day for you. Miss Youngblood, was it night before last?"

"Yes," Marik said.

"Mrs. Gurdman, tell me what happened that evening. Then we'll let Miss Youngblood tell her side of things."

Lena shot a quick glare at Marik. "She came over there with a shotgun in the rack of her truck, and said her dog had disappeared and she wanted to look in our barn. Burt wouldn't let her. I heard them yelling so I got Burt's rifle and came out on the porch."

"Was Miss Youngblood aiming her shotgun at Burt?"

Lena hesitated. "No. She left it in the pickup. Then that fellow there drove up in his own truck and he kind of talked her into leaving. Burt told me if they didn't leave in twenty seconds to shoot out his window. But I didn't."

Sheriff Dean watched her. "Anything else?"

Lena looked at the sheriff, her eyes fierce and bloodshot. "She threatened him before she left. She said if Burt had done something with her puppy, she'd get him for it, one way or another. That's what she said. *One way or another.*"

Sheriff Dean made a note on the yellow pad. "All right. Miss Youngblood," the sheriff said. "Is there anything you want to add to Mrs. Gurdman's version of what happened?"

Marik blew out a breath. "Not really. Except that I haven't seen Burt since, and I didn't kill him."

Lena lifted her chin. "He went up there last night to vandalize those machines again. I know he did, because he came to the kitchen and got my new sack of sugar, and he took it with him. She must have caught him at it and... killed him!"

"We found a broken sack of sugar up on the ridge," Deputy Ferguson put in.

"Thank you, Deputy," Sheriff Dean said. "But we're not interviewing *you.*"

He shrugged. "Sorry."

Marik's skin prickled. She could see how it looked—the bad blood between them, the body on her land, no way to confirm she hadn't left her house last evening during the storm.

The sheriff was quiet for a moment, reviewing his notes. She shifted in her chair, hoping the interview was over, but the sheriff spoke again.

"When Mr. Gurdman left home yesterday afternoon," he asked Lena, "did he drive his pickup?"

She hesitated. "I guess not. The truck was in the shed

this morning. It's only about a mile overland from our place up to the windmills."

Jace's cell phone trilled. "Sorry," he said quickly and moved away from the table. They couldn't avoid hearing him in the quiet room. "Okay," he said. "Thanks. I'll be there ahead of you." He turned to Marik. "It's the cattle truck. I've got to go."

"Before you do," Sheriff Dean said, "one more question. I believe you were at the town meeting last month when Mr. Gurdman threatened to tell people about Miss Youngblood's child. Correct?"

"Yes," Jace said.

"Did he mention that again the evening you went to the Gurdman's farm?"

Jace glanced at Marik, but said nothing.

"What did he say?" the sheriff said. "Please be as specific as you can."

"It was personal. I'd rather not answer that."

"You're in this up to your ears, Mr. Rainwater. I'd advise you not to withhold information."

Jace shifted his cell phone from one hand to the other. His voice dropped lower. "He referred to the bones they found on Killdeer Ridge a few weeks ago. He asked if that's where her baby ended up."

Sheriff Dean nodded. He leaned forward and shut off the tape. "We're done here, for now. Nobody is to leave the county until this matter's resolved. Understood?"

Marik was the first one out the door.

Jace caught up with her beside her car. "I'm sorry," he said.

She didn't look at him. "We'd better get out to the ranch and meet that cattle truck."

She climbed behind the wheel and drove fast, her mind pinballing from logic to full-blown paranoia. The prospect of being charged with a felony was a lot like major surgery—it didn't sound all that frightening when it happened to somebody else. When it happened to you, it was terrifying. And right now it looked inevitable that she would be charged with murder.

The only lawyer she knew was a man in Lawton who'd handled her father's estate. He was semiretired and didn't do criminal law, but maybe he knew of someone. She wondered how it worked. Would they actually arrest her, take her to jail? Her mouth went dry, and she cranked the air-conditioning, aiming the vents at her face. Then rolled down the windows for good measure.

Everything looked really bad, but it was all circumstantial. There couldn't be any physical evidence that connected her to Burt Gurdman's body.

Unless someone had planted it, like the eagle.

Could mousy Lena Gurdman have followed her husband to the ridge and—what? Bashed him in the head? From what she'd seen, that was hard to believe. Burt was stronger, quicker. And undoubtedly meaner.

Who else might want Burt dead and Marik blamed?

Deputy Ferguson?

Jace Rainwater?

Marik felt sick. Jace had seemed too good from the beginning, but what possible motive could he have for this?

She was wrong even to think it. She needed to talk to somebody with a cool head—somebody she knew was on her side.

Daisy answered her cell on the third ring. "Where are you?" Marik said.

"East of Pacheeta about twenty miles, coming back from a home visit. I was wondering if I'd ever hear from you again."

"I need to talk to you."

"Uh-oh."

"It's not about that. Burt Gurdman's dead. They found him up by the windmills and the sheriff thinks he was murdered."

"My God. And there you sit with all the motive anybody would need."

"Exactly. And Lena Gurdman is accusing me."

"Hang in there. I'll be at the ranch in half an hour."

The cattle truck arrived before Daisy. Marik held the pasture gate while the truck backed in. It felt good to do something normal, something physical. There was barely room in the barnyard for the driver to maneuver the rear end of the possum-belly trailer through the pasture gate, its big tires leaving ruts in the wet ground.

At the back of the trailer, Jace lined up the portable chute and urged the calves down the ramp, not rushing them. Marik watched the calves trot into the pasture, blinking their big eyes, their hair kinked from the damp ride. They stood in a tight bunch at first, but when the truck moved out of the pasture and Jace closed the gate, some of the calves headed toward the back of the field to a small pond that was brimful with rain. They looked skittish but otherwise in good shape.

Being around cattle was like meditation. She looked at their broad, quiet faces and liquid eyes, breathed in their earthy smell and felt centered again. This was real. The possibility of being charged with murder was a Quentin Tarantino movie.

Daisy's little Honda squeezed past the semi in the driveway while Marik was signing papers for the truck driver. She kept her receipts and left the rest to Jace. He was walking among the herd, checking them over as Marik and Daisy went into the house.

Daisy gave her a sideways glance, frowning. "How are you doing?"

"Better than when I called you. But I still could use a drink."

"Who couldn't."

They sat at the oak table with a bottle of red wine. Marik described the scene at the ridge that morning, then Sheriff Dean's interview in the dusty storefront and Lena Gurdman's accusation. Daisy was a practiced listener, and she said all the right things. Marik could see her mind working.

The wine spread through her limbs like sunlight. She slouched in the chair and stretched out her legs. "If they do charge me, I'm going to need a lawyer fast. Do you know an attorney who's had experience with something like this?"

"I've dealt with two who practice criminal law in Pacheeta," Daisy said. "One looks like a disciple of Charles Manson, and the other, if I'm not mistaken, played high-school football with Burt Gurdman."

"Swell. What about in Redhorse, or Lawton?"

"Honey, you need more than a lawyer. You need some-body who can exert pressure on the sheriff's office and make sure they do their job. It's time to call in your markers. Didn't you tell me you know our congressman?"

A warmth more than wine rose to her face. "I didn't think of Devon. He is an attorney."

"The state-employee scuttlebutt says he's a straight arrow."

"I don't know what good he could do me from Wash-ington, D.C., or if he's still licensed in Oklahoma."

"A well-placed phone call from D.C. could do a *lot* of good, if he's willing. How well do you know him?"

She looked at her empty wineglass. *Well enough that he recently offered to help me any way he could.*

"He was in law school when I was at OU," she said, thinking of the last time she'd seen Devon Dulaney on TV, the politic smile, the eyes that missed nothing. He had owned that quiet confidence long before he ran for office. "And I know his family."

Daisy shrugged. "There you go. Don't wait until you're hauled in for arraignment before you tell him what's going on. Call him tonight."

"Hmm."

She had no doubt that Devon could—and would—use

his influence to help her. But there were risks involved in making contact with Devon Dulaney again. She'd have to weigh those risks against the advantage of having a popular politician in her corner. He might not be content to advise her from a distance. She definitely did not want him to show up in person.

Chapter Eighteen

At nine o'clock the next evening she capitulated. All day the prospect of being formally charged with murder had stalked her; she envisioned a local prosecutor with delusions of grander job opportunities who wanted to use her case as a rung on his career ladder. Even worse, all hope of personal privacy would be gone; her decision to give up her baby for adoption would be masticated in every church hall and beauty salon. Next to that sick feeling, the risk of contacting Devon Dulaney gradually paled.

She thumbed Devon's number into her cell phone.

Ten o'clock D.C. time. She pictured him at a fund-raising dinner, talking policy with rich old men in black tuxedos, possum-haired wives in designer gowns that revealed too much crepey skin. His phone would be set on Mute and he'd find her message later, another supplicant from his home district.

Or perhaps tonight he was working in his home office—dark wood and Persian rugs, shelves lined with law books he hadn't opened in years, a room decorated by Eden. In a newspaper photo, Eden had looked beautiful and imperially slim, with tight skin over high cheekbones, a woman who would never sweat. She had a degree in interior design but had never worked for a living. The model Washington wife.

All these thoughts in the space of three rings. And then his melted voice on the line. "Marik? This is a surprise."

His cell had identified her.

"Hello, Devon. Am I calling too late?"

"Not at all. I'm home by myself watching cable news."

"Ah. The comedy channel."

"Exactly."

When Devon had precisely one drink—it used to be scotch and soda on the rocks—his laugh sounded like sex. It sounded that way now.

"It's good to hear from you," he said. "Is everything all right?"

A natural question since she'd never before phoned him in Washington. On the rare occasions they'd talked, Devon had called her. She took a deep breath. "I need your advice." Why couldn't she say *help?* "Remember I mentioned a neighbor who was giving me grief about the wind farm?"

"Yes. Is he still complaining?"

"Worse than that. They found his body up on the ridge.

Possibly bludgeoned to death. I'm quite likely to be charged for his murder."

"Good God." She heard his voice change, could feel him frowning. "How could they think that?"

"Plenty of motive. His body on my property. No verifiable alibi. Then there's his widow, who's telling people I did it."

"What can I do to help?"

"I need to find a good criminal attorney who won't end up owning my ranch when this mess is over."

"I'd do it myself, pro bono, but you need somebody local and with more trial experience. A couple of names come to mind. Let me do some checking and I'll get you a name and number by tomorrow."

"Thanks. Tell me if I'm out of line here, but do you think you could also phone the county sheriff and just express your concern for a thorough investigation? That might keep him from rushing to file charges."

"You've got it. Silk County—that would be Leon Bell, right?"

"Not anymore. There's a new sheriff in town," she said drily. She gave him the name and phone number.

"Try not to worry," he said. "I'll keep track of this until it goes away."

She had seen his confidence work magic before—in sports, in politics, in making love. The tightness in her chest loosened. "I appreciate this. I wouldn't ask you if I weren't really concerned."

"I know that too well. You didn't even call me when your father died."

"Like you called me when you decided to get married?"

Caught, he hesitated. "I sent an invitation."

"Not the same."

Another pause. "You're right. Not the same."

Then he shifted gears without a clutch. "The House goes into recess this coming week. I could rearrange a few meetings and fly out there, caucus with your attorney and the sheriff in person."

"That's not necessary," she said quickly. "I'm sure a couple of phone calls will do the trick." She lightened her voice, brushing away his suggestion. "I'll owe you a painting for your office after this."

"That's a deal. I'll phone you tomorrow about the attorney. And Marik? I'm glad you called me."

When she hung up, the house felt cavernous.

Choices and accidents. So many ways life might turn out differently.

She'd first met Devon Dulancy at an airport—a place of permanent transition, where people defied gravity in favor of flying. It was a small city airport not far from the university campus, the spring of her sophomore year. On a break from studying for midterms, she'd rented time with a flight instructor for a quick refresher. It was her dad's idea. She hadn't had time to fly in nearly a year and he wanted her to stay current on her certificate.

The day was sunny and breezy, and piloting the unfamiliar plane heightened her senses and her adrenaline. They made three passes around the airport, doing touch-and-gos, the instructor's voice calm in her headset. Then she brought it in for landing. When they climbed out of the cockpit, the instructor's next client was waiting on the tarmac.

She'd seen the guy before, on campus, and pegged him as a grad student. His eyes were espresso brown.

"Nice landing," he said. "How many hours have you logged?" His face was too handsome; he didn't look real.

"Quite a few," she said. "I've had my license since I was seventeen."

"Show-off." His smile showed perfect white teeth. "I'm still working on mine."

"That *was* a good landing, Marik," the instructor said. "Come fly with me anytime." He signed her logbook and turned to the new guy. "Ready, Devon?"

But Devon was still smiling at her. "I'm Devon Dulaney," he said, and held out his hand.

"Marik Youngblood."

"Maybe I should get *you* to give me lessons."

The instructor rolled his eyes. "Get in the plane, hot-shot."

Marik gave him a thumbs-up as they walked away.

The next day, he phoned her dorm room and they met for pizza. Sitting across from him in a red vinyl booth, the college crowd noisy around them, she discovered tiny flecks of blue and green light in those dark brown irises. And a penetrating intelligence she'd rarely encountered. They talked about flying and then their majors; Devon was first-year law. They both knew the conversation was a cover for an electric attraction. They circled around it like a hot wire, wondering how to pick it up without getting burned. That Friday when she went home for spring break, fantasies of Devon Dulaney followed her to the ranch and hurried her return to campus.

They saw each other two more months before he took her to his little house off campus and made love to her. By then anticipation created a holocaust. Maybe he'd known all along that it would. He was older, more experienced. Besides her high school boyfriend, she'd dated only a few young men at the university, none seriously.

After that they went to his place often, making love on cool sheets in his darkened bedroom, on the sagging sofa covered with a faux-leopard throw; on a kitchen table that creaked in rhythm until they finally broke out laughing. She had no clue that Devon came from money. Even his Buick Regal wasn't new.

Their favorite place for making love was a cane-backed chair on his front porch. After dark, with wind surging in overgrown cedars, they were hidden in the shadows beneath the overhang. Their voices hushed, their desire heightened by the delicious danger of headlights flashing down the quiet street.

Devon had no roommate. He said another person coming and going would distract from his studies. He did not ask her to spend the night. He studied rigorously, determined not just to pass the bar exam on his first try but to graduate at the top of his class. It was her first glimpse at the iceberg tip of his ambition, and she admired it. They didn't need to discuss the future; she was enchanted with the now.

That summer when she went home to the ranch, Devon had come for a weekend visit. He won J.B. over with an intense curiosity about the cattle business. Marik watched them and wondered if Devon was working her father; he'd never seemed that interested in ranching before. Monte was even more suspicious, picking up on Devon's political ambitions immediately.

"That young feller plans to run for office. Mark my words," Monte said. He distrusted politicians as a general principle, even if they weren't in office yet.

Shortly before Christmas his last year of law school, Devon took her to meet his parents at the family home. By then she knew his family was wealthy and influential, but she wasn't prepared for the grandeur of that two-story, columned mansion. Devon said his father had ridden the crest of the 1980s oil boom and was smart enough to get out before the bust. The elder Dulaney had invested his profits in insurance companies that made high-interest loans, but he'd kept his energy holdings in a small, well-managed oil company that made a comeback in the 1990s.

Devon apparently got his shrewdness from his dad and good looks from his mother. Sally Dulaney was a club woman who did charity work, an existence totally foreign to Marik and a little appalling. But Sally Dulaney was not a stereotype. She was warm and interesting, with naturally graying hair and a smile that lit up her brown eyes. She shared Marik's passion for art, not as an artist herself but as a collector.

On that first visit, Marik sat in the sunroom with Sally, drinking raspberry iced tea from a crystal tumbler. Sally talked candidly about her family, as if they'd known each other for years. Devon had two sisters, both older. One had a history of depression and was a constant worry to her parents. The other had married a schoolteacher, given them two grandchildren and taught elementary school to help make ends meet. Sally Dulaney was devoted to them all.

Marik learned that Devon had been president of the student council and honor society at his high school. He played baseball because other sports took up too much time. She knew he was a dedicated runner and played par golf when he had time.

As they talked, snippets of a spirited conversation between Devon and his father drifted in from the study. Sally said the two were close, except when it came to politics.

"Devon's afflicted with a social conscience," Sally said, smiling, "and Bill accuses him of being a Democrat in conservative clothing."

As an undergrad, Devon had been president of the Young Republicans on the OU campus. Sally said he'd been offered an internship in Washington, D.C., with a distinguished senator who was a family friend. He would leave as soon as his course work was finished.

Devon had not told Marik this.

"Your mother says you're moving to D.C. next summer," she said on the drive back, her eyes focused on the highway, a sensation in her stomach that felt unpleasantly like jealousy.

"I'd intended to go to D.C., yes," he said. "But now it looks like I won't be going after all. Dad has another idea."

Bill Dulaney had told him that shortly after the first of the year, a state legislator from their district was giving up his seat for health reasons. Devon's father wanted him to file for the special election; there was a good chance he could run unopposed. He could become the youngest member in the state house of representatives.

She was torn between gratitude to his father for keeping him here and alarm at the man's control of Devon's future. *Instant career, quick and dirty.* She managed to keep her voice neutral. "Do you always do what your father wants you to?"

Devon shrugged, watching the road. "He says it's my decision, of course. But he offered to finance the campaign, and it's an unbelievable opportunity. The state legislature is a perfect stepping stone to the U.S. Congress."

The idea was so far from her frame of reference that she almost laughed. But with sudden realization, she saw that for people like the Dulaneys, it wasn't far-fetched at all. With Devon's skills and his father's money, no dream was out of reach.

It was a full-frontal glimpse of the size of his ambition, and size mattered. A warning sounded in her head. She wondered how much—or who—Devon might be willing to sacrifice to achieve his goals.

By spring, she had her answer.

Chapter Nineteen

At mid-morning, Marik walked in the pasture among the new calves, getting them used to her presence and checking for signs of travel stress. The grass was shin deep, thriving on recent rains. Jace had taken the small tractor to mow the runway and the roadsides. The wind was full of birdsong and the occasional lowing of the new calves. She almost missed the tingle of her cell phone in her pocket.

"His name is Keenan McCowan," Devon said. "I went to law school with him. He's a bit of a free spirit but very bright, ethical, and he's handled several high-profile criminal cases. I explained the situation and he's expecting your call."

She repeated the phone number twice and dialed it as soon as Devon hung up.

Keenan McCowan sounded calm and professional. He

lived in Oklahoma City but offered to meet her halfway, at the law office of his friend in Redhorse.

"I'd be glad to," she said, "but I'm under orders not to leave the county."

"Doesn't apply," he said. "You're meeting with your attorney. I'll advise the sheriff."

She memorized the address and agreed to be there at 10:00 a.m. Monday. "What if Sheriff Dean files charges before then?"

"On a Saturday or Sunday? Highly unlikely. But we'll take an aggressive approach. I'll give him a call today, let him know you have representation and tell him we intend to cooperate in any way possible to aid his investigation."

She liked his style. As usual, Devon had done well. She wondered how much it was going to cost her.

That afternoon June May, owner of the Wild Things Gallery, came to the ranch. Marik remembered she was coming barely in time to clean up the kitchen and adjust the lighting on her wall of paintings in the studio. *The Ghost Lady of Silk Mountain* sat on an easel by the windows.

Ms. May was tiny, with vivid blue eyes and long, butter-scotch hair twisted up carelessly with a tortoiseshell clamp. She arrived fifteen minutes early and came to the door apologizing and breathless.

"I wasn't sure how long it would take to get here from Lawton. What a beautiful old house! This is a real working ranch, isn't it?"

Marik laughed. "Yes, and there's a chance I smell like cattle. Please come in."

In her fashion jeans and layered tunic, June May looked like a teenager. But she told Marik that she'd owned the gallery for six years and had named it for the children's book by Maurice Sendak, *Where the Wild Things Are*. Either June didn't know anything about the recent trouble on Killdeer Ridge, or she was polite enough not to mention it. She accepted an iced tea and Marik led her into the studio.

June spent a long time examining each piece on Marik's display wall, asking questions about color and technique. It was an ego-boosting experience. Except for her art professors, Marik had never had anyone knowledgeable express so much interest in her work. June praised the river landscape with Silk Mountain in the background, and actually gasped when her eyes fell on the painting of cattle grazing beneath the wind turbines and the old-fashioned windmill. Marik tried not to grin like a simpleton.

"If those pieces aren't promised," June said, "I feel sure they would sell at Wild Things. And I love the mysterious, hidden figure. That gives you a signature, a trademark. Collectors love that."

"I didn't intend it as a commercial gimmick."

"Of course you didn't. But there's a business side to art, and there's nothing wrong with— Oh my God! What's this?" She had turned away from the display wall and glimpsed the painting on the easel.

"The Ghost Lady of Silk Mountain," Marik said.

"Of course. I've heard the legend."

"It's ninety percent finished, I think. I just don't know yet what that last ten percent is."

June May stepped closer to the canvas. She brushed a strand of hair from her freckled cheek and studied the painting with narrowed eyes, her lips pressed together. "Hmm," she said. She sidestepped to avoid a glare from the window and studied some more. "Have you thought of simply deepening the shadows among the rocks? To make them a bit more ominous. This is the moment before she jumped, right? Emphasizing the chiaroscuro might really reinforce that emotion."

Marik looked from June's rapt face to the painting. "That's a good idea. I kept thinking I need to add something, but maybe not. Just more contrast between the harsh sunlight and deep shadows."

"I can't wait to see it again when you're finished. That painting could be absolutely amazing. I'll bet you could sell several hundred prints."

"Really? I've never tried prints."

"We work with a Dallas print company that's marvelous. But that's getting ahead of the horse. Let's talk about the gallery business."

"I'm pretty naive in that regard."

"Why don't you come down to Lawton and visit Wild Things, look over the other work we represent. If you're satisfied with what we're doing, we can discuss terms. I would love to add you to our list of artists." She glanced around the studio again. "You have enough quality work here that we could launch you with a one-woman show. Maybe borrow that piece from the bank for display, too."

"I'd love to see your gallery, but I'm not sure how soon I'll be able to get away." *Or leave the county.*

"Whenever you can," June said. "Do call me first, so I can be there when you visit." She finished her drink and gathered her bag and car keys. "Thanks for a lovely afternoon."

When June had gone, Marik went back to her studio and tried to look at her work with new eyes. Could June see things that Marik was too close to see?

She spent all of Sunday in her studio. By evening she had reworked the ghost-lady painting, and June was right. Deepening the shadows emphasized the desperate step the ghost lady was about to take.

What woman hadn't felt close to that edge?

On Monday morning she set out for Redhorse with two computer-generated maps, a meal-on-the-go bar and her thermal mug of coffee. It was a two-hour drive. She had no trouble finding the address McCowan had given her for Landis and Smith, LLC, attorneys-at-law. Six vehicles occupied the parking lot: a silver BMW, a banana-yellow pickup, three chromed-up SUVs and a red Mustang convertible. She tried to guess which might belong to Keenan McCowan. Probably the Beamer.

He was waiting for her in the conference room, where the glossy tabletop reflected an upside-down cappuccino in a Starbucks cup. She wished he'd brought one for her.

"Marik? Hi, I'm Keenan." He stood and offered his hand.

McCowan was average height, average looking and average build, the kind of man no witness could describe after a crime—except for one shocking detail. His head was covered with finger-length curls that looked like a brunette wig for Shirley Temple. Was this what Devon meant by "free spirit"? She was too taken aback to speak.

He must have been used to ignoring that reaction. When they shook hands his smile was friendly and showed perfect teeth. "Have a seat. Can I get you something to drink?"

"Thank you. Maybe something curly. I mean cold! Diet cola?"

"No problem. I'll be right back."

She changed her guess to the banana-yellow pickup.

But his briefcase was ostrich leather, obviously expensive, and the suit jacket hanging on the back of a chair hadn't come from JCPenney. Still, how could a jury get past that hair?

He returned with a can of soda and a cup of ice. "Devon sure thinks a lot of you," he said, sitting down across from her. "If I don't make you happy he'll nail my hide to the barn." He smiled.

"All it takes to make me happy is not to get charged with murder. Just for the record, I did not kill Burt Gurdman."

"I believe you. And even if I didn't, I'd give you my absolute best efforts." He readied his legal pad and pen. "To do that, I need you to tell me everything there is to know about your dealings with Mr. Gurdman. The uncensored version, and from the beginning."

The meeting lasted two hours, during which she forgot all about McCowan's weird hair. She liked the way his mind worked; he was extremely intuitive, and quick.

"The best thing that could happen," he told her, "is for the sheriff to find out who did kill Gurdman, or at least another likely suspect, right away. Do you know anything about Gurdman's past? Enemies? Gambling debts, stuff like that?"

Marik shook her head. "Not a clue."

"The spouse is always a good prospect. What about Mrs. Gurdman?"

"If I were his wife, I might have had to kill him, but Lena seems completely dependent. I don't know if she'll be able to function on her own."

"I'll see what I can find out about Gurdman's background." He smiled. "I love playing detective."

He put down his pen and sat back. "I've told the sheriff that any questions he has for you should be directed through me. I don't think we'll hear anything from him until after the autopsy is completed. That gives us a week minimum, probably longer, to point Sheriff Dean toward the bad guy. If you think of anything else that might help, let me know."

When Marik stepped out of the office building, the April sun felt more like summer than spring. Heat waves wrinkled up around the remaining vehicles in the parking lot.

Keenan McCowan was definitely the Mustang convertible.

It was past noon and she was starving. She took the protein bar from her purse and unwrapped it while the air-conditioning blasted and she studied the second map she'd brought along. When she'd oriented herself, she retraced her route to a main thoroughfare and headed across town.

She'd been anxious about meeting with McCowan, but that was nothing compared with the skitter of nerves when she approached Will Rogers Elementary School. Her timing was perfect; the schoolyard was full of children at recess after lunch.

She slowed on a shady street north of the school grounds and coasted to a stop. From this angle, the playground looked the same as the one in Daisy's photos. She took a fistful of brochures from the glove compartment—her cover story in case someone noticed her—and got out, closing the door quietly.

The shouts and laughter of children drifted to her at the chain-link fence surrounding the playground. She stood in the shade of ragged elm trees, their limbs partially amputated by last winter's ice storm. A group of children with round, babyish faces swarmed around the swings. First graders, no doubt. Older girls played hopscotch on a concrete slab, and clamorous little boys kicked a soccer ball around a grassy, open area at the opposite corner. It made her think of her teaching days, and she smiled.

There were dark-haired children of Hispanic and Native American heritage, a few African-American children and brunettes, and a jillion blondes. Then she noticed a child sitting with her back against the brick building, reading a book. She looked about the same age, with the same hair color as the girl in Daisy's photos. But from here Marik couldn't be sure. Daisy had used a zoom lens.

"May I help you?"

The voice was forceful and suspicious. It belonged to a

large, dark-skinned woman in a navy pantsuit who stood just inside the fence beside her. Her arms were crossed and she wasn't smiling.

Marik did smile, disarmingly she hoped. "I came to see the principal and stopped a minute to watch the kids playing. I used to teach art in a middle school and I miss the children."

"I'm the principal," the woman said. "We already have an art teacher."

A horn sounded across the playground, and the smallest children—first and second graders, probably—swarmed toward the doors. The rest kept on playing.

"I'm not applying for a job," Marik said. "I just wanted to leave these for the teachers. I own that ranch out by Silk where GPP&L put in the big wind turbines." She offered the brochures over the fence.

The child with the book was still reading. Didn't she have any friends to play with? Marik's throat tightened.

"We don't like strangers watching the kids," the principal said, and she was frowning again.

"Of course. I apologize." She forced herself to meet the woman's eyes. "My name's Marik Youngblood. The brochure explains how wind energy works, and tells about the Killdeer Ridge project."

The principal opened one of the brochures. "I read about the wind farm. That's a good thing for Oklahoma."

"I think so, too. If your teachers would be interested in doing a unit on green energy, I'd be happy to serve as a resource person."

The woman nodded. "Convert the tiny taxpayers. Not a bad idea. I'll share these with my teachers."

"There's a contact number for the power company's PR person on the brochure," Marik said, moving away. "I'm sure they'd be glad to supply some materials."

As she escaped to her car, the principal called out. "Next time, come in the front entrance and sign in at the office."

Marik signaled an acknowledgment without looking back. She pulled away from the curb, her palms sweaty on the wheel. Did you ever outgrow the fear of being in trouble with the principal?

Another school bell rang and Marik saw the little reader get up and brush off her clothes. When the girl glanced in her direction, it was all Marik could do not to wave.

Had she just caught a glimpse of her daughter?

Chapter Twenty

The day of cutting and branding, the Searcy brothers arrived at 7:00 a.m. and brought word that their mom had volunteered to cater lunch. Neighbors like the Searcys more than made up for the crazy Gurdmans. Marik had heard nothing more from either the sheriff or her attorney.

As the day warmed, the feet of man and beast beat the soft dirt in the cattle pens to a slimy pulp. The air grew rank with the smells of seared hide and cow dung. Marik worked with Jace on opposite sides of the squeeze chute. He guided a calf into the chute from the holding pen, and Marik closed him in. When the calf was secure, she leaned over the railing and drove a vaccine-filled needle into its shoulder. Jace cropped off the budding horns of the Herefords—the Angus calves had no horns—and smeared salve on the stumps. Then he clamped on an ear tag. Jace was methodical and relaxed at his work, and he never raised his voice. He had none of the jittery haste Monte used to have when working cattle.

Marik released the calf into the arms of the Searcy brothers. One of them specialized in castrating, the other in branding. The Searcys' teamwork was amazing to watch. In short order, each new steer was free to join his neutered peers in the pasture. By late afternoon only half a dozen calves remained in the holding pen.

Amidst the bawling and shouting and hoofbeats, Marik's ear caught the distinctive thrum of a lightplane engine. She perched on the top railing and squinted toward the sky south of the windmills, above the river. In the angled sunlight, a cross-shaped silhouette circled above the grass airstrip.

She refilled the syringe while another calf was herded into the chute. The airplane circled again, this time flying low over the runway. The pilot was checking out the condition of the grass strip. Then the plane ranged out across the river, banked a wide turn and started its approach. She hadn't the slightest doubt who the pilot was.

"That plane's going to land," she told Jace. "I'd better get over there."

"No problem." Beneath the wide brim of his hat, a glint of mischief showed in his eyes. "Girls usually do quit the job early."

She smiled. "It's not because I'm female. It's because I'm the boss."

She set the vaccine where he could reach it and hoisted

her leg over the wooden railing. The plane had disappeared behind the ridge when she pulled off her gloves and headed toward the house. She thought of going inside to clean up but instead crawled behind the wheel of Red Ryder in her dusty jeans and manure-stained boots. If company was going to drop in unannounced, this was what he could expect. Her one concession was to pull the bandanna off her head and shake the dust out of her ponytail.

By the time she got to the landing strip, the plane was on the ground and taxiing back up the runway toward the empty hangar. She parked beside the building and stood watching, anxious to see the pilot of the plane, wishing fervently he had not come.

The aircraft was a Cessna Skylane, an elegant little four-seater with dark blue and metallic-gray stripes. If her dad had seen that plane, he'd have mortgaged the ranch to buy one.

The Cessna stopped on the asphalt pad in front of the hangar and the engine quieted to an idle. Sun glazed the cockpit windshield, obscuring the face behind the glass. She motioned toward the hangar and saw the flash of a hand in response. The plane revved up again and buzzed beneath the corrugated tin roof.

Her father had built the hangar like a pole barn, open on both ends. Its peaked roof was long and narrow, and there were tie-downs for two planes cast into the concrete floor—one space for Queenie and one for a guest. J.B. always planned for company.

When the plane's engine cut off, there was something lonely in the resulting silence. Wind swept through the hangar, and a crow cawed from the trees along the river. The eagles were gone now, flown north to Canada for the summer. Right now Marik wished she'd gone with them. She braced her shoulders and entered the deep shade of the hangar.

The left-side door of the cockpit opened and Devon Dulaney stepped down. He was bareheaded and looked fit in his casual slacks and knit shirt, leather loafers that cost as much as a stocker calf and would last longer. She wondered if he still ran every morning. Maybe he worked out in a private gym for VIPs.

Devon was one of those men who grew more attractive as they matured, and he'd been unjustly handsome when he was in law school. She walked toward him with her faded T-shirt and unmade face, thinking, *There is no God*.

"Hello, Devon."

Luckily he wouldn't expect her to hug him. He met her eyes and took the hand she offered in both of his. It wasn't quite enough, and he leaned to kiss her cheek. His scent and the gentle scrape of stubble on her face brought a visceral memory.

She stepped back. "Not too close. We've been working cattle all day."

His teeth shone white in the shady building. "I thought I detected some cowgirl perfume." Fine lines crimped around his eyes, the only visible brand from two terms of crafting legislation for an ungrateful nation. "You look great, regardless," he said.

"Now you're talking like a politician."

He glanced at the tie-downs on the hangar floor. "Should I tether my horse?"

"Depends. How long are you planning to stay?"

In answer, he retrieved a leather duffel from the backseat of the Cessna. "As long as I need to."

"Then we'd better tie her down. This is tornado season."

She ducked beneath the left-side wing and anchored it with a double half-hitch of the rope attached to a steel ring in the floor. It felt good to be tending to an airplane again. Devon tied the other wing and the tail and they kicked chocks beneath the wheels. He picked up the duffel and they walked out of the hangar.

As long as he needs to. Who gets to decide that?

When he saw Red Ryder, he laughed. "Is that your dad's old truck? I swear that thing was old when I visited you for the weekend, must have been nine or ten years ago."

"Yeah, that's Red Ryder. My foreman tuned it up or it might be dead by now."

Devon glanced into the truck bed and opted to put his duffel up front by his feet. They jounced over the tire tracks running through matted pasture grass. She could have brought the SUV, which was considerably cleaner. For some perverse reason, she was showing him her roughest side, as if she was determined to offend him. Or to prove she was right years ago, that they were too different to stay together. But if Devon was turned off by the earthiness of ranching, or of her, he would never show it.

"You didn't get my message, did you?" he said.

"What message?"

"I called early this morning before I left D.C. to let you know I was flying in."

"Ah. I've been working outdoors since early this morning. I left my cell in the house so I wouldn't lose it."

"'In the mud and the blood and the beer'?"

It was a line from an old country song. She smiled. "Two out of three, anyway." They crossed the cattle guard and turned onto the shale road.

"I apologize for not giving you more notice," he said. "I wasn't sure I could come until late yesterday."

"You really didn't need to make the effort. I think McCowan has things well in hand."

"I'm sure he does. But I was glad for an excuse to get away for a few days."

She glanced over at his profile. He was looking across the fields and the wide sky, and his expression seemed almost sad.

"Is something wrong, Devon?"

He looked at her. "What, with me? No. Everything's peachy." He smiled and the wistfulness was gone. "So, you have a new foreman, huh?"

"Yes. Monte packed up and bailed out. But I got lucky with his replacement. Jace is a good hand." She turned onto the paved road toward the house.

"I'm always surprised by how green it is here," Devon said. "It's beautiful."

She cleared her throat. "How's Eden?"

"She's fine. She's Eden." He shrugged. "She has a busy life, much of it separate from mine, and that's probably a good thing for her."

"Did you tell her you were going to visit an old girl-friend?" She said it lightly and smiled.

He looked at her with a puzzled expression. "I never thought of you as a girlfriend."

She lifted her eyebrows. "Thanks a lot. What would you call it? We weren't exactly platonic."

"You were the woman I intended to marry." He said it simply, and he didn't smile.

In the few moments she met his eyes, Red Ryder drifted left of center. She corrected the truck's path and shook her head. "Geez, Devon. Your memory's selective. I recall a whole list of reasons marriage wouldn't work for us."

"Maybe you're right. I can only remember the part where I asked you to share my life and you said no."

That's just it. It was your life, not mine.

Marik pulled beneath the log entrance to the driveway and stopped the truck. "This is not going well," she said grimly. "Maybe you shouldn't have come."

He didn't respond immediately. "I needed to come, Marik. We were friends once, no matter what else. And I don't have many people I trust enough to call a friend."

She looked at him and weariness sat down on her shoulders. The years between them had vanished and they were back where they'd parted. But tonight there would be no makeup sex, no hormonal rush to compensate for a different kind of compatibility that was missing. If Devon had come here to work something out in his own mind, it was the worst possible time.

But now he was here, and she couldn't dismiss the

wounded look in his eyes. It was an expression she recognized, an aching for something lost. Even if it was something you'd never had.

She let up on the brake and the truck rolled forward. "You can freshen up and get settled while I pay the Searcy boys. It looks like they're finished." Her voice sounded tired even to her.

She gave Devon her father's room, the master suite on the ground floor at the back of the house. When J.B. died, she'd never considered moving into his space, though the bedroom was larger than hers and had a sitting area where her father's rolltop desk still stood. It made a perfect guest suite.

She left him there and closed the door to her studio on her way back through the house. She wasn't ready for him to see her paintings. When a stranger like June May looked at her work, it didn't seem personal. But Devon knew her. It would be like standing before him naked.

In the barnyard, Jace and the Searcys were swapping stories about the day's work, their faces masked with dirt. She wrote checks to the brothers and thanked them for their help. When they'd gone, she told Jace a U.S. congressman would be staying a few days at the ranch.

He was unimpressed. "Let me know if you want me to take over your chores," he said. "Just don't ask me to babysit."

Her mouth twitched. "I was thinking he could trail you around while you worked." He gave her an evil look and she laughed. "Seriously, why don't you join us for dinner at the house later on."

"Thanks, but I was really looking forward to this particular can of chunky enchilada soup."

"Smart-ass."

He gave a little salute and ambled off toward his house. She watched him go, picturing herself and Devon alone at the kitchen table, a makeshift dinner, too much wine. God help her.

She pulled out her phone and dialed Daisy. "Can you please come over for dinner tonight?"

"Ever know me to turn down a free meal?"

"Great. Devon showed up, I'm still in my grubbies and I have no idea what I'll cook. So come as soon as you can."

"There's always a catch, isn't there? I just hope the congressman's as cute in person as he looks on TV. Want me to swing by my house and bring a lasagna from the freezer? It's homemade."

"Fantastic. I love your lasagna. I have stuff for a salad and some sourdough bread. A weight watcher's Waterloo."

"You're the only one who worries about your weight. I gave that up for mental-health day. Ten years ago."

By the time Marik showered and dried her hair, Daisy had arrived and introduced herself. While the lasagna bubbled in the oven, Marik set the table in the open dining area at the rear of the living room, forsaking the kitchen table in honor of the social station of her guest. Devon opened a bottle of red wine.

Dinner went so well she actually enjoyed herself. Daisy was adept at conversing with traumatized toddlers and abandoned oldsters in cat-ridden trailer homes. A mere congressman wasn't even a challenge. She was remarkably informed about legislative events and Marik could see that Devon enjoyed her candid opinions, even when they conflicted with his. No one mentioned Burt Gurdman's death or his wife's accusations.

Marik had almost forgotten the pleasure of good conversation. At their working lunches, she and Jace stuck to topics that involved the ranch. Except for environmental issues, she had no idea what his political leanings might be. She wondered, if he had accepted her invitation, whether he'd have joined the discussion or remained as private and closed off as ever.

After dinner, Daisy and Devon cleared the table while Marik loaded the dishwasher. Rinsing plates, she glanced out the kitchen window toward the darkened barnyard and suddenly remembered she'd forgotten to let Bully out. She had shut him in the barn while they worked the stockers.

She dried her hands and stepped out the back door. Hopalong and C.J. swarmed at her feet, nearly tripping her as she came down the steps and out from under the carport.

The night was clear and moonless, the peaked roof of the barn a black silhouette against the stars. She breathed in, feeling a little dizzy from the wine.

Her hand was on the gate when she saw movement by the barn. Bully was already out and Jace was closing the barn door. He was hatless now, barely visible except for the glow of his white T-shirt.

The lighted house behind her disappeared, and for an untethered moment in the muggy night, there was only the disembodied white shirt moving across the yard, phosphorescent with starlight.

She wondered why Jace hadn't brought his son to the ranch yet. Maybe he was waiting for an invitation.

"Thanks," she called, and waved from the gate.

She thought he waved back, but it was too dark to see his face.

Chapter Twenty-One

At sunrise the shadows inside the barn thinned like a watercolor wash and revealed the cavern's earthy innards. It smelled of dust and horse feed and the newly greased tractors. Marik scooped powdered formula into Bully's bucket and set the bucket under the faucet.

Bully saw her coming and trotted to the fence. She hooked the bucket on the wooden railing and held on while he dispatched the milk. The little bull was getting stocky, his coat sleek. He wouldn't be a huge animal, but he had good lines and would make a good heifer bull. The first-time moms needed a bull who wouldn't sire giant calves.

This early the air felt cool, but the afternoon would warm quickly. In a few weeks, farmers in the area would be harvesting wheat. She wondered who would cut the fields for Lena Gurdman.

She rinsed the empty bucket and entered the pasture behind the barn to check on the stockers. Jace was already there, kneeling in the dew-soaked grass beside a calf that was down. Infection was always a concern after cutting and branding. He was probably administering a shot of antibiotics. Sometimes he took Hopalong with him on chores, determined to make Hoppy into a cow dog, but today he was alone. The new steers didn't need any extra trauma. She started across the field toward him.

In his Stetson and denim shirt, it was hard to imagine Jace as the otherworldly apparition she'd seen last night in the barnyard. Must have been the wine.

"Need any help?" she called.

"Nah. This ought to fix him up." He patted the calf on its rump and stood.

She stopped beside him and they watched the calf struggle to its feet and amble away. "This grass is wearing thin," she said. "Think we could move them to the big pasture tomorrow?"

"Sure. We could use a third person when we move. Can the congressman ride a horse?"

"Probably," she said. "But I don't have an English saddle." Jace grinned.

"I'll call Earl or Betty Jane to help out," she said. "It won't take long."

"Good enough."

They walked back across the pasture together. "I updated

the cattle records last night and e-mailed you the new file," he said.

"Great. Thanks."

"And don't worry about my lunch today, since you have company. I'll fix my own."

Jace disappeared into the barn to put the doctoring kit away and Marik walked to the ranch house. There was no sign of her guest, but it was still early and Devon had put in a long day yesterday. A solo cross-country flight was tiring, whether you loved flying or not. From D.C. she estimated ten hours airtime, plus at least one pit stop. She poured a second cup of coffee and carried yesterday's mail to the front porch.

For a few minutes she sat quietly and listened to a bluebird whisper its variegated song. In her father's ragged flower garden a yellow rose defied neglect, and on the ridge the windmills turned lazy circles in the breeze. Up there today visibility would be unlimited. On such a morning she could almost believe the nightmare of Burt Gurdman's death would resolve itself, construction on the wind farm could resume, and she would find a way to know her daughter.

Then she unfolded the Pacheeta newspaper.

The banner headline read, Widow Accuses Neighbor Of Husband's Murder. Beneath the headline a three-column story reported the discovery of Burt's body on Marik's ranch. The story summarized Gurdman's opposition to the wind farm and recounted the incident with the poisoned eagle. It was accompanied by a file photo of the wind towers and a quote from Lena blaming Marik for Burt's death.

Either Deputy Ferguson had talked out of school, or Lena had restated her accusation to the reporter. Marik punched the newspaper with her fist.

The final sentence quoted an official statement from Sheriff Dean, saying no charges would be considered until the medical examiner's report was complete, and that there was no evidence yet to connect a specific suspect to the death. The caveat read like an afterthought.

Marik dialed Keenan McCowan's cell phone. He answered in a shower of interference that sounded like road noise. She had owned a convertible for a brief time and knew that a quiet ride was not one of its selling points, even with the top up.

She spoke above the noise. "Have you seen this headline in the Pacheeta newspaper?"

"An associate faxed me the article yesterday," he said. "I called the editor and requested they print a brief statement from us, that you're sorry for Mrs. Gurdman's loss but deny her allegation. If someone from the paper calls you, I strongly recommend you don't give an interview. The less publicity the better."

"But my neighbors *read* this stuff."

"I know. And when you're cleared, they'll read that, too."

"I doubt it. That's not sensational enough for the front page."

He ignored this. "I'm running a background check on

Gurdman. I'll let you know what turns up. Did Devon get there yet?"

"Yesterday. How did you know that?"

"His office sent me an e-mail saying he wanted to meet with me at your ranch. I'm on my way to Silk right now."

"That's news to me."

McCowan laughed. "Devon's used to taking over. I should be there by ten. I Googled the wind farm and got a map."

"Okay. See you then." She snapped the phone shut. Exactly when had she lost control of her life?

Devon was standing behind the screen door. He had found the coffee. "Good morning. Was that Keenan?"

"Yes. You might have told me we had a meeting this morning."

He came out on the porch, dressed in jogging pants and a gray T-shirt, his hair damp from the shower. "I didn't have confirmation. But I'm glad he's coming. I haven't seen Keenan in years."

Old home week. She forced a smile. "I hope you slept well."

He took a seat in the porch swing. "Like a cat in the sun. And I set up my laptop this morning and answered about twenty-five e-mails. That's all the work I plan to do today." He smiled. "What a gorgeous morning. Look at all this clean air."

"I thought so too until I saw this." She handed him the Pacheeta newspaper.

"Good grief. Has Keenan seen it?"

"Yes, and he's phoned the editor, but the damage is done. By now all my neighbors think I'm a murderer."

"I doubt that, Marik. They've known you and your family all your life."

"Ah, but I left town for several years, and now I have the wind farm. That's enough to make me an outsider. Not that I care."

"Of course you care. You always cared what people thought. Maybe too much."

"Well, I've changed." But she could see he didn't buy it.

She stood abruptly. "I'm going to drive up to the windmills. Want to ride along?"

"I'd love to."

"We can take a bagel for the road," she said. "They're frozen but edible."

He rose and followed her inside. "A bagel will be fine. Tomorrow I'll cook you a real breakfast."

"You cook?"

"Sometimes," he said. "Mostly breakfasts."

She pictured Eden lounging in a vast white bed while Devon served her tiny pancakes with crescents of melon and papaya.

"I make a mean plate of biscuits and gravy," he said, and she laughed aloud.

Devon was quiet as they drove up the white switchbacks toward the ridge. The fine lines around his eyes made him look calmer and more thoughtful than the ambitious young lawyer she'd once known. He scanned the landscape, taking in everything. Through Red Ryder's dusty windshield, all

Marik could see was the angry black headline from the Pacheeta paper. An accusation in print was humiliating and scary, regardless of Devon's influence. Her insides churned with the need to *do something*. Despite the short notice, she was glad her attorney was coming today.

She parked the truck at her usual spot. They got out and stood by the front of the pickup without talking. The river valley stretched below them in hazy repose, patterned by green pastures and distant wheat fields tinged with gold.

Marik's breathing slowed to the rhythm of the windmills. This view inspired her every morning. The land was enduring, human concerns only transient and small.

Devon gazed up at the long white rotors revolving in the wind. Their moving shadows striped the hills. "I've always believed in wind power," he said finally, "but it's incredible to stand beneath these behemoths and listen to them work. They're actually beautiful. So right for this land."

A quick frisson caught in her chest. The last time she'd stood here with Devon, she was a naive college girl who believed in soul mates. There were no windmills then, just the sweeping plains and the wind.

The moment passed in a mist of regret. She pointed to their right along the ridge. "They found Gurdman beneath number 22. Slumped against the base of the tower." She handed him the binoculars. "That's his farm over there. He must have walked across the field, intending to sabotage the dirt movers. Maybe he fell off one of the machines, cracked his own head and crawled to the base of the tower." She shrugged. "Or got hit by lightning."

"There's no ladder on the outside of the turbines, where he might have climbed up and fallen?"

"No. The only access is inside the towers, and the doors stay locked. None of them had been jimmied."

Devon lowered the field glasses and pointed down the slope toward the new construction. "If they found him up here, why is that yellow tape down there by the new roadbed?" She didn't answer right away and he looked at her. "Did they find some kind of evidence there?"

"No. That's something else entirely." She leaned against Red Ryder's headlight. "The construction crew uncovered some old bones up here about two weeks ago."

"From the cemetery?"

"Outside the cemetery. It was an infant, and no infant was supposed to be buried up here. At least not that I knew about."

He frowned. "That's quite a coincidence. Maybe it has something to do with why Burt Gurdman was up here on a stormy night."

"I thought of that, too, but I don't see how. The doctor with the M.E.'s office thinks the bones had been there for years."

"They're testing for DNA?"

"Yes, but it'll take weeks and identification might not even be possible."

"Did you tell Keenan about the bones?"

"Not yet. It didn't seem relevant."

"Tell him this morning," he said pointedly. "It's information the sheriff will already have."

Before they left the ridge, she trained the binoculars on the Gurdmans' farm, scanning the yard for a multicolored dog. But the magnification wasn't sharp at that distance and the house lay shrouded in shadow.

Keenan McCowan arrived before ten. If Devon was surprised by the Shirley Temple hairdo, he didn't let on. Maybe McCowan had always worn it that way.

The men sat in the living room and swapped law-school stories while she made another pot of coffee. Drawing water at the kitchen sink, she noticed the saddle blankets hanging on the corral fence to air. Jace came out of the barn carrying one of the saddles and hefted it across the top railing of the fence, then went back for the other.

The coffeepot gurgled and wheezed. She stood at the open window, suspended between two worlds, and watched him replacing a worn-out cinch, sunshine spilling over the brim of his hat. In front of her was the clean scent of saddle wax and the outdoor life of the ranch, while behind her the conversation had turned to murder.

"I checked with the M.E.'s office yesterday," Keenan was saying. "There's no report yet on the autopsy."

She carried a tray to the dining area. The two men got up and moved to the table. She set out their cups and let them help themselves.

Keenan pulled a folder from his expensive briefcase; down to business. He reviewed the circumstances for Devon, what they knew and what they didn't know.

"Marik has another piece of information," Devon said.

"The construction workers found the bones of a child up on the ridge a couple of weeks ago."

Both men looked at her expectantly. She had no choice but to recount details of the grisly discovery and answer Keenan's questions. She saw his eyes cloud. He knew about Burt's final threat and because of that she'd had to tell him about her baby. But Devon didn't know, and she wanted to keep it that way.

She braced herself for what McCowan might say, but he remembered who his client was. She saw his mind searching for a connection between her baby, the bones and Gurdman's murder. He was clearly irritated that she hadn't told him about the bones before. Maybe he was wondering if his law-school buddy had hooked him up with a psychopath for a client.

"Where are the bones now?" he asked.

"At the OSBI lab, I assume," she said. "I have a card from the agent who was in charge. I can get you his name."

"Good." He made himself a note. "Is there anything *else* the sheriff will find out that I should know?"

"If there is, I don't know it, either."

"Let's request a DNA profile on Gurdman," Devon said. "If there's a connection between him and the bones, that sheds a whole different light on his death."

"It sure does." McCowan gave Marik another hard look.

"I'm sorry I didn't mention it before," she said. He nodded, but didn't absolve her.

McCowan gathered his notes and slid the folder back into his valise. "Devon, good to see you again." He stood and the men shook hands.

"I expect you need a down payment on your fee," Marik said.

Keenan cast a quick glance at Devon. "Don't worry about it."

"I'm not worried. I just want it clear who's paying the bills."

Keenan looked at her a moment, and then he smiled. "Okay. We've got that straight. You can give me three thousand today, until we see if this thing goes to trial."

Three thousand. Shit.

"I'll write you a check," she said evenly, and went to her studio.

When she came out, the men had moved onto the front porch. McCowan accepted the check and the OSBI agent's card.

"We'll stay in touch," he said. "If you have questions or think of anything else, call me anytime."

"Thanks. I will."

Marik stood on the porch with Devon and watched McCowan's convertible drive away. He had put the top up to keep the road dust out of his car.

"He's an excellent attorney, but he needs all the facts," Devon said.

"I got that."

"Good." He turned to her and smiled. "Then let's go flying. This day is too beautiful to waste. You can try out the Skylane."

"You didn't get enough airtime yesterday?"

"This is different. I won't be alone."

She had no good excuse except that she hadn't flown a plane since J.B.'s crash.

"All the more reason to go," he said. "I'll bet that's what your dad would tell you."

It was, indeed.

Devon was right. It was a perfect day for flying. They cruised above the line of the river and over the ranch, where cattle dotted the fields and the windmills looked like Tinkertoys. The Cessna Skylane was a high-tech wonder and truly fun to fly. It had all the latest navigation tools that would make cross-country flying easier and safer, especially in and out of D.C.'s tightly controlled airspace. He spent some time showing her the bells and whistles, then turned over the controls.

They skimmed the Quartz Mountains and Lake Altus-Lugert, giving a wide berth to Altus Air Force Base. From there they cruised west into the Texas Panhandle, joyriding. She couldn't stop smiling, heady with the thrill of being at the controls again. With the yoke in her hands, she felt her father's presence in the backseat, grinning over their shoulders.

"What do you think?" Devon asked, his voice hollow inside the headphones. "Pretty sweet machine, isn't it?"

"It's amazing."

She heard their voices like echoes from an alter-world, the two of them alone above the earth. The land stretched out below them, tranquil and green, breathtakingly beautiful. Up here she was free; she could fly away from the financial problems of the ranch, from the stench of death, from the millstone of regret.

She glanced sideways at Devon. He was smiling, too. "Nothing quite like it, is there?"

He radioed ahead to the small airport in Elk City, and they set down to refuel and have dinner at a legendary barbecue spot. By the time they flew back to the ranch, a magenta sunset marbled the horizon.

"You take the landing," she said. "This strip's a lot shorter than Elk City's."

"Nothing doing. You need to practice for your flight review."

She'd admitted at dinner that her certificate was about to expire. "Okay. But stand by to make corrections."

"Got you covered."

Running into the wind, she lined up with the runway, cut the throttle and raised the nose to decrease airspeed. She wanted badly to grease it in and impress him, but it had been a long time since she'd landed on the grass strip. The uneven surface and fading light made it hard to judge the moment of touchdown.

She put it down with only a slight hop. The pasture streaked by them on the right, the tree line along the river to their left. She braked and raised the flaps, felt the giddy weightlessness of the plane until it rolled to a stop. At the end of the runway she turned it around and taxied back toward the hangar.

Devon gave her a thumbs-up.

"My heart hasn't beat that fast in a long time," she said, laughing. "Damn, that was fun!"

"Yes, it was." His smile was open and young, the way it

used to be when she first knew him. "We'll have to do it more often."

She was thinking how unlikely that was, when his expression changed.

"God, I've missed you," he said, and the look in his eyes broke her heart.

Chapter Twenty-Two

When Keenan McCowan phoned the next day, Marik was in her studio. Devon had gone for a run, the slap of his footsteps fading down the driveway. She had been leafing through her sketchbook, but the drawings seemed naive compared to images in her head: the look on Devon's face after they'd gone flying; Lena Gurdman's tormented eyes; a little girl reading in a schoolyard.

McCowan's news was not good. "The OSBI declined our request for a DNA test on Gurdman, at least for now," he reported. "Their lab had no luck extracting DNA from the bones found on your ranch, so they'd have nothing to compare with Gurdman's profile."

Marik frowned. "So we'll never know who that baby was?"

"The forensic anthropologist confirmed that the child

was female. They've sent the remains to the research center at the University of North Texas. The folks down there are pioneering a method for testing mitochondrial DNA, and they'll try to get something from the immature teeth in the skull. But mitochondrial DNA shows only the maternal link, not the paternal. Even if they're successful, we still wouldn't know if the child was related to Gurdman."

"But it could prove whether or not the child was related to me," she said quietly.

"That's correct. The OSBI has completed your profile and informed the sheriff." He paused. "Which brings me to some hard questions that I didn't want to ask you yesterday with Devon in the room."

Marik glanced out the studio window. No sign of Devon on the quarter-mile driveway. "Look. I don't know who that baby belongs to or who buried it there. I was told by people I trust that my child is alive and well. I have no reason to doubt that." Even though part of her still did.

"Okay. Second question. Did Gurdman try to blackmail you with the knowledge of your adopted baby?"

"Hardly. He announced it plainly enough after the town meeting. He never asked me for money or anything else." She blew out a breath. "It's possible Burt planted the bones up there to stop construction simply out of spite. That's the kind of man he was."

"Which still gives you motive," he said. "If he did that, where in God's name did he come up with an infant's remains? The truth about those bones could be crucial, even if it's just to show they have nothing to do with his murder."

"Or his accident," she said. "Until the autopsy's finished, we still aren't sure he was murdered."

"Sheriff Dean seems sure enough. He's been in law enforcement for twenty-five years and earned a lot of respect from his peers... I checked. He also thinks you're the prime suspect."

"Even good old boys can be wrong."

"And so often are."

McCowan signed off and she heard Devon's running shoes thump onto the front porch. The screen door squeaked open. She came out of the studio and closed the door.

Devon was standing at the kitchen sink drinking a glass of water. In the moment before he realized she was there, she admired the way his T-shirt clung to his lean rib cage. It took a lot of self-discipline to stay in that kind of shape, especially with his schedule. In law school he used to get by on five or six hours' sleep. Probably still did.

When he turned toward her, she caught the familiar, autumn-leaves scent of his skin, and a need flickered. She knew that body; she had molded it in her hands like a sculptor.

She avoided his eyes and moved to refill her coffee. "Good run?"

"Terrific. No smog, no exhaust fumes." He wiped his face with a white towel that hung around his neck. His jaws were shadowed with beard.

"Keenan phoned while you were out," she said, and told him most of what they'd discussed.

Devon frowned. "I realize the DNA labs are overloaded, but I don't see why the autopsy should take this long."

"The understaffed medical examiner would probably be happy to tell you."

"Let's drive to Pacheeta this morning so I can meet Sheriff Dean in person. See if we can get some answers."

She twisted her mouth. "I've already had the pleasure of meeting Sheriff Dean." She didn't want to watch Devon pressure the sheriff on her behalf, even though she hoped it would work. "You're welcome to take the SUV. I need to help Jace move cattle today."

He leaned against the kitchen cabinet. "I get the impression your foreman doesn't like having another man around the ranch," he said. "More particularly, around you."

"Don't be silly. He just doesn't trust politicians. You must get that a lot."

"Not really. Most people are pretty respectful. At least to my face."

She shrugged it off. "The keys are there on the hook whenever you're ready to go."

Within half an hour, Devon had showered and left for Pacheeta. Marik went to the barn where Lady and Gent stood saddled and waiting. Earl Searcy arrived aboard his horse, and his wife in their pickup. Betty Jane climbed out and gave Marik her laid-back smile. "How's the painting coming along?"

"It should be ready by next week."

"Great. I'll pick it up sometime when I can smuggle it into the house without Jackson seeing it. I want it to be a surprise."

Betty Jane drove ahead to the entrance of the target pasture, and the rest of them mounted up. They herded the bawling steers down the main road and around a corner three-quarters of a mile. Betty Jane had parked her pickup crossways on the country road just beyond the open pasture gate. She stood in the bar ditch and calmly blocked the calves' progress until the first ones spied the opening. Soon the herd funneled into the pasture. Jace dismounted to wire the gate shut behind them.

"Good-looking calves," Earl commented.

Marik smiled. "I think so, too. Thanks for helping. Let me know when I can return the favor." The Searcys rumbled and clopped away.

The calves stood blinking in their grassy new home. If the fall market didn't tank and she didn't have to sell off early to pay her legal fees, the ranch would make its first profit from cattle in more than five years.

That afternoon Marik booted up the computer in her studio. It felt good to be alone in the quiet house. "I've turned into a hermit," she told Calamity Jane. Beneath the art table, C.J. gnawed her rawhide bone and didn't comment. Hopalong had gone with Jace to get parts for the pump on the well. Both dogs were growing fast and Marik thought again about their lost sibling. Now that Burt was dead, she might never find out what happened to Zorro.

She downloaded the updates Jace had posted to the cattle records. His spreadsheet made it easy to keep track of every animal. She ought to devise something like it to inventory her paintings. If she did sign on with a gallery, she would need to keep records.

In less than an hour she had set up the file and recorded each painting in the studio by title, size and date completed. On a separate page she posted works she'd previously sold. Listed on two pages, her body of work looked disconcertingly small.

This year she would turn thirty. Van Gogh was dead by thirty-seven and look at the legacy he'd left behind. Was she serious about her work or content to be a hobbyist?

Everything else had always taken precedence over her art. No one could change that except her. She picked up the phone and dialed June May at Wild Things Gallery.

"I'm so glad you called," June said. "We're hosting a reception this weekend for one of our new artists. If you could come, it would be a great chance to see the gallery and meet some of our patrons. We'll have hors d'oeuvres and wine—it'll be fun."

"It does sound like fun. But I have a houseguest this week."

"By all means bring your guest. The more people the better. It's Friday evening, seven to nine."

Browsing through an art show with Devon seemed safer than the long evenings alone with him in the house. "Do I need to let you know ahead of time?"

"Not at all," June said. "I'll just hope to see you then."

Newly motivated, Marik pulled a pencil drawing of a weathered barn from her sketchbook. Old barns were like old houses, with history and character all their own. The smell of turpentine and wet cloth quickened her pulse as she prepared the canvas. She was still working several hours later when Devon arrived. She heard him come in the front door.

"Marik? I'm back."

"In the studio," she called. "Come on in."

He stopped in the doorway. She felt his eyes surveying the room and her at the easel.

"I wondered when I'd get to see your work," he said. "You've been keeping this door closed, so I assumed it was off limits."

She put down her brush and smiled. "For some reason it's harder to let a friend see my work than a stranger."

He went to the gallery wall and stood for a long moment saying nothing. Then he whispered under his breath, "Wow." He looked at her with an odd smile, as if seeing her differently. His gaze went back to the paintings. "Marik, these are wonderful."

"Thanks." Her face felt warm.

"I haven't seen your work since college, and it's really matured. No kidding, these measure up to my parents' art collection."

She laughed. "Now you're exaggerating. I've seen their collection. But thanks anyway."

She wiped her hands and began to clean her brushes. "So what did you think of our esteemed sheriff?"

Devon slouched on a chair by the window, legs stretched out in front of him. "He seems intelligent and straightforward. Has his opinions but is willing to be influenced by the facts."

"Hmm," she said.

"It turns out the medical examiner is an old acquaintance of my father, and Sheriff Dean suggested I phone him while I was there. He's as anxious as we are to get the results. Dr. Boudreau hadn't done the official report yet, but we were able to get some preliminary information."

"Which was?"

He tightened his lips as if she wouldn't like what she heard. "Cause of death was blunt-force trauma with a heavy object. Something jagged. There were traces of shale and gypsum in the wound, but he says the angle and level of violence are not consistent with a fall."

Her stomach tensed. "So he thinks, what, that somebody bashed him in the head with a rock?"

Devon nodded. "Repeatedly. But Gurdman had also ingested something toxic that they haven't identified yet."

Something more toxic than his wife's bitterness? Marik's eyes drifted to *The Ghost Lady of Silk Mountain*. A woman on the edge, driven to jump.

Something skittered in her memory, something about Lena Gurdman's eyes. But the impression was too vague to catch, and then it was gone.

The crowd in Wild Things Gallery bubbled like soda. Marik and Devon piloted through the bodies toward an improvised bar, where a young man with slicked-back hair was setting up flutes of champagne as fast as he could. The evening was warm, and Devon had left his sport coat in the car. He looked flawless, and Marik was conscious of admiring glances from the women who made up more than half the crowd. She wondered if that kind of attention bothered Eden when they went out together. Perhaps Devon's wife was so regal that she outshined even him.

She hadn't mentioned her guest's name to June lest he be hounded by press and hangers-on if he showed up at the gallery. For a congressman, it was an occupational hazard. But after tonight, his privacy would be over. In spite of that, Devon had agreed immediately to attend the event. She wondered if he felt the weight of their aloneness in the house as heavily as she did.

Marik was wearing a dress and high heels for the first time since J.B.'s funeral. She'd have felt more at home in a long skirt and sandals like some of the other women. But one thing about an artsy crowd; any dress code was copacetic. A pair of young women had on jeans with stiletto heels and metallic-embroidered jackets, their short, spiked hair dyed to match. Marik recognized an elderly former governor with his plump wife, both of them rumpled and friendly. It was an impressive turnout; June May knew how to throw an art opening.

Devon snagged two glasses of champagne and they moved away from the bar. Marik had a quick flashback to another party, years ago, when Devon was drinking champagne. She blinked it away and waved to June, who had spotted her from across the room.

"Here comes the gallery owner," she told Devon.

June was so tiny that even in high heels she disappeared behind knots of people as she wove her way toward them. "Marik! I'm so glad you could come." June extended her hand to Devon. "Welcome to Wild Things."

"June, this is Congressman Devon Dulaney," Marik said.

"Of course it is." June smiled with obvious delight. "Every female in western Oklahoma knows that face. Have you met everyone yet?"

June shepherded them around and introduced them both, her face glowing. Marik wondered if the press would show up at Killdeer Ridge now and speculate in print on why Devon was visiting a single woman on her isolated ranch.

Finally June turned them loose to wander on their own. The featured art was an array of stark depictions of stylized crows in leafless trees.

"This fellow may be good at what he does," Devon whispered, "but I'm guessing his stuff is pretty avant-garde for this audience."

Marik studied a crow portrait and sipped her champagne. "You might be surprised." The birds' eyes were sharp as diamonds, the trees set against a flat, bold background like a serigraph. "There's something disquieting about them, sort of ominous yet pleading. I think he's making a statement about the environment."

Devon rolled his eyes. "Okay. I'm in over my head."

The featured art took up one room, and in the other Marik got to see work from other artists represented by the gallery. A few pieces felt amateurish, but she also saw work she admired, particularly a series of conte drawings of working cowboys and ranch women. There were several wildlife bronzes by a well-known sculptor from Colorado.

"Your work would stand up wonderfully here," Devon said.

"I'd be in good company." Marik glanced at him. "She said they would do a show like this for me."

His smile widened. "Make sure I get an invitation. I wouldn't miss it."

She turned to face him, smiling and frowning at once. "Devon. You can't keep flying back to Oklahoma on my account."

His eyes were as dark as the crow's when he laid his palm against her neck. Warmth poured through her like candle wax.

"Marik," he said. "Of course I can."

On the ride home, their headlights spearing down the country highway, they didn't talk. Devon was driving, and once she dozed and awoke to find him watching her.

"Go ahead and sleep," he said. "It's all right."

Near midnight they parked in the ranch yard and walked to the house beneath a sickle of ivory moon. It felt natural, the years and miles between them erased like smoke in the wind. The feeling scared Marik to death.

As soon as they were inside, she said good-night quickly and climbed the stairs. She felt the weight of his gaze as she put one foot in front of the other. She dared not look back.

She couldn't sleep. The room was too warm, the minutes endless in the ticking darkness. She rose from the bed and stood by the open window, trying not to listen for movement in the house.

She never should have phoned Devon. Had she secretly hoped he would come? Second-guessing a decision she'd made years ago?

She felt—or imagined—the vibration of his footsteps on

the stairs. Coming down the hallway. Stopping at her open bedroom door.

"Marik?"

She remained at the window with her back to him, her ribs tight around a flailing heartbeat. This was the part where she sent him away, saved herself from a world of hurt. But her breath was too sad. Too lonesome.

He came into the room and stood behind her, not touching. She felt the warmth of his breath in her hair and in the shiver that laced her skin. Her legs were paralyzed; she couldn't move.

"Marik," he said again.

His arms slipped around her waist. He pulled her against him, the heat of his skin like an electric shock.

A whisper was all the voice she had. "You're married, Devon. I can't do this."

He whispered back, "Of course you can."

Chapter Twenty-Three

She left her bed before dawn, unable to awaken in daylight with someone else's husband. She dressed in darkness and escaped outdoors.

If Bully was surprised to be fed so early, he didn't complain. In the milky half light, she ran fresh water for the horses and fed the stray barn cat, lingering in the forgiving redolence of the barn.

At length she crossed the yard and slipped in the back door to the kitchen. When she came out again with her mug of coffee, the dogs swarmed at her feet. She stopped to rub their ears and praise them, then left them behind. This morning she needed to be alone.

Red Ryder started on the first try and rolled quietly down the gravel driveway. She took the winding road to the windmills, her head buzzing with self-reproach and the memory of Devon's body against hers, the thrill of loving him again. For a few hours last night she hadn't been lonely, the first time in years. But Devon would not give up his marriage, and certainly not his career. She wouldn't want him to. Both of them knew this.

Red Ryder crunched to a stop on the high ridge and Marik got out. The horizon bisected a fat orange sun whose light reflected pinkly from the white towers of the windmills. Wildflowers winked among the sage, and killdeer called from hidden places. The clean beauty of the land filled her up and her vision blurred.

But weeping was just another self-indulgence. She had never aspired to moral perfection, but there were lines she'd meant never to cross.

She inhaled deeply and struck out walking. Past the place where a nameless baby had come to rest beneath the stars. Down the slope to the family cemetery, the wind soft against her face. She entered through the wooden gate and sat in the grass beside her father's headstone. J. B. Youngblood. Husband, father, rancher. She closed her eyes.

Her dad had always forgiven her. Even when she gave away his granddaughter. The memory rose up again, like a thousand times before.

A crucifix on the wall of the hospital administrator's office. On the desk, a photo of two children, a boy and a girl. The pajamas with pink roses her father had brought her. His hand warm on her shoulder.

"It's the right thing. Isn't it?" she asked.

"I believe it is, yes." His yearning for a grandchild outweighed by what he thought was best for Marik.

She picked up the gold pen and scrawled her name. Her father's arm supporting her down the antiseptic-scented hallway…a woman in a seersucker robe peering at them, her face vaguely familiar…

A woman in a seersucker robe.

Marik saw again the skittish eyes, the hopeless downturn of the mouth, and felt the same flicker of recognition as when she was working on the ghost-lady painting.

Lena Gurdman.

That's how Burt Gurdman knew about her baby.

Kneeling at her father's grave, she drew out her cell phone and called Keenan McCowan. It was early and Keenan's phone took a message.

"I think Lena Gurdman was in St. Andrew's Hospital in Redhorse eight years ago last July," she said. "Find out why."

She put the cell phone back in her pocket and stood. The sun was fully up now, the wind rising warm from the south. She kissed her fingertips and pressed them on her father's headstone in the grass.

When she got back to the house, Devon was sitting on the front porch, waiting. She remembered a time when the morning after wasn't fraught with recrimination. But that was then. She parked by the barn and walked toward him with heavy steps.

"Good morning," he said, and smiled. "You sneaked off without me."

She saw no guilt in his eyes. Shouldn't a man who had

been unfaithful to his wife show some vestige of remorse? Even as she thought it, she felt the sting of hypocrisy.

"I needed some fresh air," she said.

He was dressed in casual slacks and a polo shirt, the expensive loafers he'd had on the day he arrived. She sat in a chair facing the sky.

"You look as if you're leaving," she said.

He thumbed the rim of his coffee cup. "I thought it might be a good idea if I went to visit my parents for a day or two."

He was giving her some space. Maybe himself, too.

"I can rent a car in Pacheeta," he said, "if you'd drive me there."

A crow flew toward the trees behind the barn, its caws of protest ringing through the morning. "Just use the SUV," she said. "I won't need it."

"If you're sure." He waited a few beats. "Do you want to talk?"

When she didn't answer, his gaze ranged outward, unfocused. "The last few years, Eden and I have lived in the same house but not the same world," he said. "We rarely talk, and when we do it's about trivial things. We haven't made love since she found out she can't have children."

Marik held up a hand to stop him. "Please don't."

She swallowed hard, bitten by the words *can't have children.* "I'm not cut out to be the congressman's mistress, Devon. You can't fly out here a couple of times a year so we can have sex and tell ourselves things that aren't true, then fly back again. That's a little too sordid for me to live with."

His voice was quiet. "It's not like that. The truth is that I never stopped loving you."

She stood up, her chest hollow. "It's *exactly* like that," she said. "And I can't do it."

She went inside to her studio and closed the door. Some time later, she heard him take the car keys from the peg in the kitchen and drive away.

She was still there that afternoon, trying to work and failing, when Jace came up the driveway and knocked on the door. He stood just inside with his big hat in his hands, a slight frown worrying his forehead.

"I ran off a guy who said he was a reporter for some newspaper," he said. "He was looking for your friend, but I told him the congressman wasn't here."

"Good work," she said. "Thanks."

His head bobbed. "If it's okay, I'd like drive to Amarillo this afternoon and bring Zane back with me for a few days. His school's already out for summer."

Marik smiled. "Of course. It'll be fun to have a kid on the ranch."

The creases tightened around his eyes. "I'm not so sure. He may not be able to cope with the change of routine." His fingers crimped the hat brim.

"Zane is welcome," she said. "Take whatever time you need to be with him."

"I appreciate that." He turned but didn't leave, running the hat brim around and around in his hands.

Marik watched him. "When I was teaching," she said,

"I worked with two autistic students who were mainstreamed into art class. One had to wear a pressure vest under his clothes so he could stand the chaos of a regular classroom for a short time." She smiled. "But he sure could draw."

Some of the tension melted from his face. "Zane likes patterns, and numbers. They tell us he thinks in pictures, and words are like a second language to him. Reza spent hours teaching him to read, but he hardly ever talks."

Maybe that was partly inherited from his father, she thought. This was the longest conversation they'd had about anything except the cattle business.

"I really want to let him see the ranch and be outdoors," he said. His eyes wandered toward the barns and the pen where Bully browsed on grass. "Reza's been talking to him about it, preparing him, but I'm not sure how it'll go. Unfamiliar surroundings will be tough for him."

"Does he like animals?"

"Yeah. He nearly brushed the fur off our old cat. But when the cat got run over, he didn't seem upset. He doesn't process normal emotions. Even his meltdowns are a lot less frequent now, because of a new medication." He grimaced. "I'm still not sure how I feel about that."

"One of my students would freak out if he got paint on his hands," she said. "Which was a little hard to prevent in art class."

Jace smiled. "I'm glad you understand. That really helps." He opened the door and stepped outside, fitting the hat back on his head. "I'll be back tomorrow afternoon." He gave his John Wayne salute and clumped down the porch steps.

After he'd gone, she let Hoppy and C.J. inside and found something to watch on Animal Planet. But she kept thinking about Jace and his son. She shut off the TV and went to the computer in her studio.

The facts about autism were sobering, but it was a video depicting the daily lives of mothers with severely autistic children that impaled her. The women had no lives of their own and the divorce rate was high. They devoted every day and night to their disabled children. "I can never die," one mother said.

Marik stared at the screen and thought about the agony of watching your child struggle and suffer, every day. Compared to the heartache of a child with autism, grieving her own loss seemed egocentric. If her daughter was healthy and thriving in someone else's home, what parent wouldn't choose that for her child rather than a locked-in world where she couldn't communicate or understand?

She was still awake near midnight when the phone beside her bed rang, loud in the darkness. She thought of Jace, then of Devon. But when she answered, no one was there.

Chapter Twenty-Four

Lena had lost track of time. With Burt gone, it didn't matter what time she got up and made breakfast, or when she fixed supper or went to bed. She was dreadfully tired. She'd been sleeping a lot, and when she was awake the days passed in a kind of stupor. She kept waiting for something to happen—the sheriff to come back to question her again, somebody from the church to stop by with a casserole. But nothing happened. Nobody came.

This morning she'd forgotten to feed Borax and the chickens. Thank goodness they didn't keep a milk cow anymore; the poor thing would have burst. It was late afternoon before she went outside to do her chores.

Borax had grass to eat, but the mule still looked at her with accusing eyes until she poured oats in the feed pan. And the witless chickens were nearly frantic scrambling for their feed. By the time she fetched her wire basket to gather the eggs, the sun was setting and the inside of the henhouse was nearly dark.

The electric light in the chicken house had burned out days ago, and she hadn't got around to dragging the ladder and changing the bulb. The dim building smelled rank with ammonia and dust. Several hens had already gone to roost on their nests and refused to move. Lena had to stick her hand underneath them to search for eggs and one of them pecked her wrist. You wouldn't think a chicken's blunt beak could hurt very much or draw blood, but it did. Worse than that, Lena knew that sometimes a snake would curl up beneath the straw, waiting for a fresh-egg dinner.

Maybe she would leave the henhouse door open and let the coyotes have the chickens. What was she going to do with all those eggs, anyway? But she couldn't leave them out there to rot and stink.

She was on her way back to the house with the egg basket when she heard the noise again, like whining. She'd heard it before but thought she was imagining things. Now she could plainly tell the noise was coming from the little four-by-four shed that protected the water pump from freezing in winter. Some animal must be trapped in there.

She set the egg basket on the ground and worked the metal hook loose on the wooden door of the well house. It was hard to do; the door was swollen with humidity and the hook was rusty. The shed was not quite head high, the door even shorter. She squatted beside it and yanked the door open a few inches, leaning back in case something came flying out. Nothing did, so she peeked inside.

She couldn't see anything inside the dark little building. She waited a moment and heard whining again, but nothing moved, so she opened the door wide.

The minute she saw the little animal crouched behind the pump she knew it was Marik Youngblood's puppy. Or it used to be.

The puppy wouldn't come out. Maybe it was scared, or just trying to stay warm. Lena reached toward the animal gingerly. When it didn't offer to bite, she scooted the pup out of its hiding place. Even in the fading light, she could see it was skin and bones, its eyes nearly matted shut. It was filthy and seemed too weak to stand up. The well house smelled of feces.

The poor thing must have been there for days, ever since Burt was gone.

Beneath a faucet that was attached to the wellhead, a shallow pan had a little water in it. Burt never got around to replacing the washer in the faucet and had set the pan there to catch the drip. The puppy had had enough water to keep it alive. But unless it ate bugs or a hapless mouse, it couldn't have had any food for a long time.

Lena turned the tap and ran more water in the pan. She took an egg from her basket and broke it on the concrete floor beside the pan. She didn't know what kind of dog this one was, but she knew some dogs liked eggs. When she was a girl her father had shot their cocker spaniel for raiding the henhouse. And she knew eggs had protein.

The puppy crawled on its belly to the raw egg and began to lap at the edges.

She didn't have any scraps in the house. What else would a dog eat? Then she thought of some canned tuna.

She pushed the swollen door almost shut and went to the house. In the kitchen, she emptied a can of tuna onto a plastic saucer and took an old towel from the rag bag. Outdoors again, she set the tuna inside the shed and laid the folded towel in the back corner, smoothing out a clean place for a bed. The puppy was still lapping at the egg.

What should she do about this dog? She couldn't keep it; eventually someone would come and find out it was the dog Burt had stolen. If she took it back to the Youngblood ranch, Marik was liable to run her off with a shotgun.

She'd done all she could for now. It was a miracle the puppy hadn't died already.

The warped door wouldn't shut snug enough that she could fasten the hook, so she closed it as best she could and took her basket of eggs to the house.

The puppy was all she could think about while she took her shower, toweled her hair and let it hang loose to dry. She wasn't hungry and didn't bother fixing supper. With the TV tuned to the Nature Channel, she wrapped up in a blanket on the couch. Lately she'd been cold all the time. The show was about snakes so she changed the channel and watched a sitcom that wasn't even funny. She dozed off and woke up a long time later with cold feet, still thinking, *What am I going to do with that dog?*

With the TV off, she lay on the sofa in the ringing silence.

Burt wasn't coming home tonight.

Burt would never come home.

Part of her felt a great relief about that, but she also felt sick to her stomach. Maybe nobody would ever come to the farm again. She'd just sit here by herself until cancer ate her up, or she starved to death or went crazy.

Wearing her blanket like a cape, she got up and went to the kitchen. Her hands tremored like an old woman's when she dialed the phone. She listened to the plastic whir of its ringing, once, twice, like an echo chamber in her ear. Her eyes scattered to the teakettle clock on the kitchen wall.

She was shocked to realize it was ten minutes to midnight. She hung up quickly before the third ring.

What did she plan to say anyway? *You were right, Burt took your dog and it's nearly dead.* Or just hang up when she heard Marik's voice, like the other times.

Lena dragged her feet down the hallway, past the closed door to the bedroom where she and Burt used to sleep together. She hadn't opened that door since he was gone. In her own room, shivering beneath her blanket and chenille bedspread, she lay curled up on her side, eyes wide in the darkness. Her body had never felt so tired, but her mind jittered like an old-fashioned movie projector.

What was she going to do about all those eggs in the fridge? She imagined the grocery man's judgmental eyes when she came to town trying to peddle her eggs. She didn't even know his name.

Yesterday she'd looked out in the wheat fields and realized the grain was turning gold. It surprised her that the crop would ripen without Burt to worry over it. What would she do when it was time to harvest? And after that, could she plow the fields by herself? What if the tractor broke down?

What would she do about the cattle, and the hay?

What would she do about the whole godforsaken farm?

Chapter Twenty-Five

On Sunday afternoon Jace's truck came up the driveway and parked by his house. From her studio window, Marik watched a boy with tousled dark hair climb down from the passenger side. He wore tan shorts with a red T-shirt and sneakers. Jace didn't touch him or hold his hand as they went inside. Some children with autism couldn't stand to be hugged or even touched. That must be the case with Zane.

Zane's mother dealt with his special needs on a daily basis. Marik wondered if Reza was relieved to have that burden lifted for a few days while Zane stayed with his dad, or if she was terrified. Probably both. She was brave to let him try.

Marik glanced out her window several times that evening but saw nothing more of Jace and Zane. The little house was quiet, and their lights went off at nine o'clock.

The next morning, not too early, she called Jace's cell phone. "How's it going?"

"We didn't get much sleep. He's not used to being away from home. Or Reza."

She could hear the tension in his voice.

"We drove out and counted the cattle this morning," Jace said. "He liked that. Right now he's playing a computer game. He'd sit there all day if I'd let him."

"Why don't you bring him up to the house for lunch. My houseguest is gone and I'd like to meet Zane."

Jace sighed. "The only things he'll eat are fish sticks or peanut butter and jelly sandwiches."

"Grape jelly okay?"

"Perfect." He hesitated. "Could you cut it in four exact squares?"

"No problem. Does he drink milk?"

"Reza took him off dairy products. She thinks that helped some of his symptoms. He loves Sprite, but if you don't have that, water is fine. No ice."

Shortly before noon, they came up the driveway toward her house. Zane was carrying a spoon in his hand. A security item, no doubt. They stopped at the yard where C.J. and Hopalong stood on their hind legs, wagging and poking their noses through the fence. Jace crouched and let Hoppy lick his palm. Marik couldn't hear what he was saying, just the calm, slow tenor of his voice. Zane stood back from the fence, rocking from side to side.

She came outside and picked up C.J., who was less bois-terous than Hoppy. The pups had doubled in size since she brought them home, and C.J. was an armful. She carried the dog outside the gate.

Zane didn't acknowledge her until she sat down on the grass close to him, holding the puppy on her lap. "Hi, Zane. My name is Marik. I'm glad you came to visit the ranch."

Zane didn't look at her, his face expressionless as he watched C.J.

"This is the lady who owns this ranch," Jace said. "Can you say hello?"

Zane's dark eyes glanced up briefly, then returned to the dog.

Marik rubbed C.J.'s ears and smiled at Zane. "This is C.J. Look, she has brown eyes just like you. Would you like to pet her?" The pup and Zane looked at each other. "It's okay," Marik said. "I'll hold on to her."

Zane took a step forward. When C.J. didn't react, he reached out the hand without the spoon. C.J. licked him, and he drew back quickly.

"She likes you," Marik said, laughing. "Here, pet her head like this."

Zane squatted beside them and tentatively smoothed his hand over the dog's head. He repeated the motion several times and began to hum.

His face was beautiful. He had almond skin and thick, dark hair he must have inherited from his mother, but his square chin and lanky stature clearly came from his dad. Except for the lack of expression, his face gave no hint of his autism.

The petting and humming went on until C.J. got impatient. "Are you hungry, Zane?" Marik asked. "I made peanut butter and jelly sandwiches for lunch."

He nodded.

The three of them went inside and Jace took Zane to wash his hands. She had placed his quartered sandwich on a small plate on the kitchen table, and on another, she arranged six apple slices in a pinwheel pattern.

Zane's eyes fixed on the pinwheel. He laid his spoon beside the plate and began to eat his sandwich. He was left-handed.

"Did you see the cattle this morning?" she asked and he nodded. "Maybe you'd like to ride one of the horses. You could ride with your dad."

No response. He rearranged the apple slices in a straight line, spacing them perfectly.

Jace shrugged, and they fell to discussing the merits of ear-tagging cattle. When they were finished with lunch, Zane gathered his apple slices to take with him. He had not eaten any of them.

Marik handed him a sandwich bag. "For your apples," she said. He slipped the apples inside and she saw a flicker of something behind his eyes.

"Fifty-four," he said.

It was so soft she wasn't sure she'd heard. "What was that?"

His eyes fixed on twisting shut the plastic bag. "Fifty-four," he whispered.

Jace had said he liked numbers. She took a guess. "You saw fifty-four cows in the pasture this morning?"

He glanced up at her, and for the space of an instant she saw a curtain lift. His smile was so sweet it misted his father's eyes.

"That's the first thing he's said since he got here," Jace said.

On Monday morning one of the stockers tore up its ear trying to graze beyond a barbed-wire fence. Jace needed more antibiotics from the co-op in Silk, and Marik talked him into letting Zane stay with her. It wasn't easy; Jace was afraid Zane would panic at being left in an unfamiliar place. But when Marik showed him a box of colored pencils and a drawing tablet on the art table in her studio, he put down his spoon and began to line up the pencils in a row with the points exactly even. She could tell he was counting. He didn't even look up when Jace left for town, nor a few minutes later when the phone in the studio rang.

It was Betty Jane Searcy. "Could I pick up that painting this morning on my way to church? If it's not a good time, just say."

"This morning is fine. And if you're not happy with it, there's no obligation."

Betty Jane laughed. "I'm sure it's wonderful."

While Zane drew a picture with the colored pencils, Marik hunted up enough bubble wrap to protect the painting and carried everything to the living room, thinking not to disturb Zane when Betty Jane arrived.

June May had suggested a price of two thousand dollars for a landscape that size, unframed. That would sure help make up the trauma to her checking account from McCowan's attorney fees, but the Searcys had been so good to her she priced the painting at five hundred. Even then she was afraid Betty Jane would be shocked at spending that much on art.

But her easygoing neighbor handed over the cash without flinching. "Danielle will love it," she said. "And Jackson loves whatever Danielle loves." Betty Jane laughed in her good-natured way and drove off with the picture on the front seat of Earl's crew-cab pickup.

When Marik returned to the studio, Zane was gone from the table. Her heart flipped until she saw him standing at the utility sink, holding his spoon under a gentle stream of water. He was watching the water fill the bowl of the spoon and overflow, again and again. He rocked gently, self-comforting. On his tablet, he'd drawn a black-and-brown-and-white dog, the eyes large and sad.

Marik wanted to wrap him in her arms and hug him, but she knew better.

Her cell phone played its electronic tune and she recognized Keenan McCowan's number. She sat on the painting stool and watched Zane at his water play.

"You were right," Keenan said. "Lena Gurdman gave birth to a baby girl eight years ago last July. Burt is listed as the father."

"The same time and place I gave my baby up. I didn't recognize her at the time, but obviously she recognized me and told Burt."

"There's no record anywhere of their child's death," he said.

Silence filled the line while both of them thought of the implications. "Lena's been a recluse for years," she said. "No one in Silk ever knew they had a child."

"I'll tell the sheriff," Keenan said. "He'll want to question Lena and possibly take a DNA sample, in case the lab at North Texas gets anything from the bones. At the very least, this ought to shift suspicion for Burt's murder off of you."

Marik barely heard him. She was seeing the haunted eyes of a woman in a hospital hallway, a woman who didn't hold with hurting innocent things.

Lena, too, had lost her baby girl. How? What happened to that baby?

"Keenan," she said slowly, "please hold off on calling the sheriff about this for a while."

"Why?"

She wasn't sure how to answer.

"Don't do something crazy, Marik. You're almost home free."

She watched Zane rocking, filling and refilling his spoon. Children were completely dependent on circumstance, and on the adults who cared for them—or didn't.

"Just for a couple of hours," she said. "Please."

Keenan's breath huffed. "You're the client. But at noon I'm calling Sheriff Dean."

"Fair enough." She hung up and pocketed the cell phone.

On the caller ID of the answering machine for her landline, she checked the number for the hang-up call in the night. It was the second time that number had appeared on the machine, and she had no trouble locating it in the Silk phone book. Two times, maybe more, Lena had tried to call her.

She heard Jace's pickup coming up the driveway. He'd made a fast trip, probably worrying the whole time.

"Your daddy is back," she said to Zane. He looked up and turned off the faucet. Marik smiled. "Come on. Let's dry your hands and go see him."

Zane jogged ahead of her down the lane toward Jace, carrying his drawing of C.J. Jace waved his thanks.

"I'll be gone for a while," she called. "See you guys later."

She backed Red Ryder out of the barn and waved at them as she drove away. At the main road she turned north, heading toward Lena Gurdman's farm.

Chapter Twenty-Six

In the midday sun, the Gurdman farm looked like an old photograph, faded and forgotten. Along the cracked sidewalk Lena's pansies had decomposed, and the lawn was grown up in weeds. A window shutter lay askew in the shrubbery, a victim of the wind. Except for the lop-eared mule and four chickens scavenging by the barn, the place looked deserted.

Did Lena have no family to step in and help her after Burt died? Obviously her neighbors hadn't volunteered, and that included Marik. Not that Lena would have accepted help from her.

The mule watched with baleful eyes as she parked her truck on the wind-scoured shale of the driveway. Burt's pickup sat inside the shed; Lena had to be home. Marik walked up the porch steps and pounded on the frame of an aluminum storm door.

She was just about to knock again when the inside door opened. Lena stood behind the glass in a blue flowered housedress. Her tan hair hung in ragged clumps around her shoulders.

"You've got a lot of nerve coming here now," Lena said.

The hoarse whisper was the same as before, but today there was no heat in her voice, no color or expression in her face. Lena Gurdman looked like a dead woman.

Once again Marik was surprised by Lena's height. Behind her meek demeanor, it was easy to miss a physical strength developed by years of farmwork. Her arms below the short sleeves of her dress were sinewy and tanned. Whatever hope or animation might once have inhabited her eyes had burned out long ago.

"I know about your baby," Marik said quietly. "I know why you killed Burt." It was almost true.

Marik saw a glint of moisture in the flat eyes.

"Go away." Lena turned and disappeared into the shadows of the house. She didn't even bother to shut the door.

Wind swept through the farmyard and rattled the fallen shutter. A chicken cackled in alarm, its feathers upturned by the gust. Marik waited a moment, then opened the storm door and stepped inside.

The Gurdman living room was dark and chilly, a house of perpetual dusk. Lined curtains pinched together at the windows, shutting out sunlight and the world beyond.

Neither of the twin lamps was lit. The room looked like a diorama in a history museum, with not a magazine or doily out of place. The scent of cooked food and cleansers hung in the stale air.

Lena was nowhere in sight. Marik stood on the dark carpet and thought of the comfortable, airy ranch house where she'd grown up loved and protected. Lena was here even then.

She heard movement in a back room and waited. When Lena didn't come out, Marik followed the sound to a hallway off the living room. The first door, likely a master bedroom, was shut. Marik walked past it to a second room where she sensed movement, and stopped.

The door had been ripped from its hinges. It hung at an angle from a twisted padlock.

Her chest closed up. Had Lena locked herself in that room, or had Burt?

Lena stood by an open bureau drawer. A gap in the bedroom curtains spilled light across a pink chenille bedspread. A suitcase lay open on the bed. Lena turned, holding a stack of folded clothes on two hands. Her eyes grazed Marik without interest. She leaned over the suitcase to put the clothes inside.

Marik spoke to her bent back. "What was her name?"

Lena's hands smoothed the collar of a folded blouse.

"I called my baby Eva," Marik said. "I don't know what her name is now."

Lena straightened her back slowly and turned around. Their eyes met across the shattered door.

"Sarah Grace," Lena whispered. "My mother's name was Grace."

Marik nodded. "It's a beautiful name." She waited. "That was Sarah Grace buried up by the windmills, wasn't it?"

Lena looked toward the window, but her eyes focused on something much farther away.

"What happened to her, Lena?"

A flutter of confusion passed over Lena's features. Her hands combed at the stringy hair. "I have lemon cookies in the freezer," she said, as if she'd just remembered. "I could make some coffee."

Did the woman think this was a social call? She looked like a bird on a wire, tensed for flight.

"Or tea," Lena said. "You'd probably prefer tea."

Marik met the bewildered eyes. "All right."

Lena edged around the sagging door and walked past her down the hall, leaving a scent like attic dust.

Marik followed her to the kitchen. Speckled Formica covered the countertops, and pilot lights shivered on a freestanding gas stove. An avocado-green refrigerator made a noise like the muffled wheels of a train.

Lena switched on a light. The kitchen was spotless. She ran hot water into an orange teakettle and set it on the stove. Lit the burner under it. "You could sit down," she said.

Marik sat in a lyre-backed wooden chair.

"No, not there. That's Burt's chair."

Marik moved to the next place at the table.

"Thank you," Lena said.

She put tea bags into two coffee mugs and took a plastic

bag from the freezer section of the clacking refrigerator. She put the frozen cookies on a plate and set it in the microwave. Her eyes watched the lighted door of the microwave as the plate revolved inside.

"She got sick," Lena said in that strained whisper. "Her little face was hot as a biscuit. I couldn't get her to nurse. She cried all the time."

The microwave dinged. Lena set the plate and cups on the table with a cracked sugar bowl and powdered creamer. "She cried all night, but I was sick, too, hemorrhaging from the childbirth. You never saw so much blood. When I tried to get out of bed I passed out."

The teakettle sang and Lena moved quickly to silence it. Very carefully she poured scalding water over the tea bags. "I begged Burt to take the baby to the doctor, but he said she'd either get well or she wouldn't. That she was defective anyway."

Marik flinched. "Defective? What did he mean?"

"Sarah Grace was born with a harelip." Lena set the teakettle back on the stove.

Marik watched steam curl from the cups, the water turning copper brown, a sinking feeling inside her ribs.

Lena placed a plastic bear of honey on the table, then she sat down and smoothed her dress on her lap. "The pastor at the hospital said that God loved Sarah Grace just as much as if she was perfect. Burt couldn't, though. He wanted a boy. He could hardly stand to look at her."

"He never took her to the doctor?" Marik said.

"I thought he did. He finally said he'd take her to the

hospital in Pacheeta. She'd stopped crying by then, she was so weak." Lena lifted the tea bag from her cup and placed it on a saucer. "When Burt came back he was alone. He told me she'd died and the hospital had...*disposed of her body.*" Her mouth quivered. "Like a vet would dispose of a dog."

Marik dropped her forehead into her hand. Lena's nose ran and she wiped it with a paper napkin. "I was so sick. There was nothing I could do," she said. "I thought I was going to die."

"Did you call the hospital later?"

She fingered the rim of her cup. "I was afraid to. Burt forbid me to talk about it ever again. I couldn't even say my daughter's name. I buried her in my memory, like it never happened. And after a while it didn't. I couldn't remember parts of it until they found those bones."

The watery eyes looked up. "Sarah Grace was up there on Killdeer Ridge all those years, and I didn't even know. And him treating me like dirt ever since, like everything was my fault."

Wind whistled at the front door and a tree limb scraped the roof. They sat for a full minute in silence. Marik wondered if Keenan McCowan had ever used battered woman syndrome as a defense, and whether it was successful.

"Did he hit you, Lena? Abuse you physically?"

Lena straightened in her chair. "No, he never." Lena sniffed, lifted her chin. "I'd have left him if he did."

Marik watched her and knew she was lying.

"I meant to kill myself instead of him," Lena said. "But there he was all doubled over in the chicken yard, grabbing his gut, and something took hold of me. I remembered Sarah Grace, the way she suffered." She stared into her tea, stirring and stirring. "I had put weed killer in his coffee. If he ever figured it out, I knew he'd kill me, too."

The rock sat right beside the water hydrant. She used it sometimes to prop up the long handle when she watered the chickens. She picked it up without intention, feeling its weight in her two hands, satisfying, substantial. The vision from her bedroom ceiling rose up again, Burt rutting on top of her. She imagined him lifting the rock and bashing the eagle. She saw a puppy with a red collar, a tiny baby with a cleft lip. Her hands became his hands.

She felt his power and his wickedness, and she swung the rock down as hard as she could on the back of his head.

Blood spurted on the ground. Burt slumped forward without a sound.

Her arms lifted the rock again, and again. The third time, he toppled over on his side and she saw his face. It was slack, the eyes closed. His hair was matted with red.

She looked at him, waiting. If he opened his eyes, she'd have to get the gun.

Nothing moved except the wind and a slow trickle of blood from her husband's head. She dropped the rock and sat down hard on the ground.

Her heartbeat felt like a bomb set to explode, but in her head she was calm. She felt removed, like a character in somebody else's dream. She looked down at her half slip and shoes, spattered with blood, and thought that she'd have to treat them with stain remover before they went in the wash.

She sat still until the pounding in her chest slowed down. A drop of liquid landed on her arm. She looked at it expecting to see more blood, but it was water. Drops of rain plopped in the dirt. The wind gusted, picking up force.

She looked at Burt lying on his side, quiet as the bloody rock she'd hit him with. It wasn't a dream. Burt was dead and she had killed him.

She'd have to do something with his body.

The sky rumbled and the peculiar yellow-green light that preceded a storm stretched across the yard. Everything was highlighted in sharp clarity—the dark outline of the barn roof against the sky, the parallel lines of the corral fence. She saw the whole farm in severe detail. Behind the fence, Borax stood with one long ear cocked forward, the other bent over like relaxed fingers.

The smell of ozone on the wind gave her a rush of energy. Her brain felt electrified, and she knew exactly what she had to do. Borax would help her.

She went into the barn and put on her skirt and blouse. Took down the harness from its pegs on the wall. Outside the barn, light slanted between the clouds in golden lines, like an omen. A scrap of rainbow showed in the east and she took a deep breath. She wasn't afraid of rain.

She dragged the harness into the corral and Borax offered no resistance when she fastened it on. She snapped a lead to the mule's halter and led Borax from the pen.

Kneeling beside Burt, she looped a leather strap beneath his arms and secured it to the singletree. His eyes were open now, the pupils fixed. Later she would come back and throw the rock in the stock pond, rake dirt over the bloodstains if the rain didn't wash them away.

She returned to the barn, working quickly now. She took a pair of wire cutters from the workbench and then went into the house and got a sack of sugar from the pantry. She put them both in a plastic grocery bag and hung the handles on her shoulder.

She led Borax into the east pasture toward the big windmills. Wind whipped her skirt and the sky darkened. The rain came like a curtain, drenching Burt where he dragged through the grass.

Halfway across the pasture Borax balked, spooked by thunder. She clucked to the mule and talked to her kindly and they moved forward again. At the pasture fence that bordered the Youngblood ranch, Lena took out the wire cutters and clipped all four strands of barbed wire, her hands slick on the wet handles. She bent the wire back on itself, making a path wide enough not to catch on the mule's harness or Burt's clothes. She led Borax through the gap and started up the incline toward the ridge.

It was hard going uphill in the rain, but the wind was at their backs. The sky was black now and a bolt of lightning crashed so near that Lena jumped. Borax screamed. She held on to the halter and calmed the mule, and eventually they moved on.

On the side of the hill, they passed the Youngblood family cemetery, marked at the corners with red cloth. But Burt didn't belong with the Youngblood clan. She wished she knew exactly where he'd buried Sarah Grace, but even if she did, she wouldn't leave him there. He belonged under those big windmills he hated, where he'd left the dead eagle. Let the buzzards find him tomorrow.

As soon as she unhitched Burt's body, Borax took off for home.

She could hear the singletree rattling behind. Lena was alone in the dark.

Wind plastered her clothes to her body. She dragged Burt to the base of the closest windmill, slipping on the rocky ground, breathing rain through her open mouth. Lightning cleft the sky and stunned her ears. She propped Burt up against the white wall of the tower on the downwind side.

The plastic sack holding the sugar had fallen off her arm. She retrieved it from the mud. Flashes of lightning illuminated the hulking machines that she'd heard grinding at the earth every day. She heaved the sack of sugar toward them into the darkness and let the wind take the plastic bag from her hands. She'd lost the wire cutters somewhere in the pasture.

She trudged toward home in the lashing rain. The wind shrieked over the fields and hail peppered her bowed head like she was being stoned. To the south there was a deep, persistent growling in the black sky. Maybe a twister would sweep her away. A fitting end.

But the tornado didn't come for her. In the farmyard, Borax had pulled the harness into the barn and stood out of the rain. Lena left the mule there and stumbled up the steps to the back door of the house.

She dropped her wet clothes on the kitchen floor and fell into bed while the storm pummeled the house. Before she sank into comalike sleep, she prayed for a tornado, a big one that would take the house, the barn, everything. But her prayers were never answered. She was the woman God forgot.

Marik's hands had gone cold on the tabletop in Lena's hermetic kitchen. Burt Gurdman was a monster. A stronger woman might have left him—and possibly ended up dead. Lena was driven to a different choice.

In the silence that followed Lena's story, Marik remembered an afternoon when her mother had returned from an unexplained absence. Her father, irritated, asked where she'd been. "I gave Mildred Sanderson a ride to the bus station in Pacheeta," she'd said, and looked at J.B. with a defiance Marik had never seen in her mother's eyes. *Why would she do that?* Marik had wondered. *She doesn't even like Mildred Sanderson.* But her mother would not explain.

The black hands of Lena's kitchen clock clicked together. Noon.

"The sheriff knows about your baby," Marik said.

Lena blinked, her eyes vacant.

"He'll figure out you killed Burt, and you'll go to prison."

Lena shrugged. "I've been in prison for years."

"Maybe that's long enough."

Marik stood up and pulled from her jeans pocket the money Betty Jane Searcy had brought her for the painting that morning. She laid the folded bills on the table. "I have reason to believe Sheriff Dean will be here within an hour."

Lena looked at Marik, then at the money. Her mouth quivered.

In the kitchen doorway, Marik paused. "Where will you go?"

Lena didn't answer and Marik wondered if she'd still be sitting there when the sheriff arrived, and whether she'd tell him where the money came from.

Finally Lena said, "I have no idea." She stared at the money, a frown starting at her eyebrows. "My mother's people came from Missouri."

Marik would carry that image always, Lena Gurdman's blue dress patterned with tiny flowers, the untouched tea, the folded money beside a plate of lemon cookies. She walked through the dusky living room and out the front door into bright sunlight.

She breathed through her mouth, thirsting for fresh air. A dry wind ripped through the cab of the pickup as she drove away.

She had often thought there were places in rural Oklahoma where a person could get lost, where nobody would ask questions. Probably in Missouri, too.

Chapter Twenty-Seven

The house seemed too quiet when Marik got home, and too privileged. The rooms echoed like the hollow space in her chest. She was grateful when she saw Jace and Zane come up the path and onto the front porch.

"We've come to invite you for lunch," Jace said. "I bought some fish sticks while I was in town." He winked at Zane and his smile looked hopeful.

Zane's face tilted up at her briefly, flawless and detached. The spoon raked back and forth on his pants leg.

"In case you're not in the mood for seafood," Jace said, "I made vegetable soup, too."

She smiled. "Seafood and soup. My favorites."

Her legs felt tired as she walked with them past the yard where Hoppy and Calamity Jane stood wagging. Zane stopped to put his hand against the fence. He was getting braver. C.J. licked his palm and Zane made a noise that might have been a laugh.

"You've made a friend," she told him. "C.J. thinks you're cool beans." She thought she detected a spark in Zane's eyes, but she might have been projecting.

Jace grinned and tousled his son's hair. Zane shrank away and trotted down the path. His father's smile sagged.

"He's not rejecting you, just the physical contact," she reminded Jace.

"I know." He shrugged. "I appreciate the way you relate to him. It means a lot to me."

"Zane's a sweet kid."

"Yeah, he is." His fists shoved into his jeans pockets. "Sometimes I'd almost prefer the meltdowns, you know? It's like…" His voice trailed off.

"'Do not go gentle into that good night'?"

"Exactly. It's like he accepts his difficulties without a fight."

"I understand what you mean. But I'm guessing that frequent meltdowns would be a lot harder to deal with. And they still wouldn't make him better."

"No." He shrugged again. "Sometimes it's just hard to feel lucky."

The inside of the cottage looked a lot different from when Monte had lived there with his old-man's things. It was still bachelor sparse, but Jace had a stereo system, a computer that was a lot newer than hers and framed pictures on the walls. One of the frames held a poem that had won an award from a National Cowboy Poetry Gathering in Elko, Nevada.

She read it and smiled. "So you like poetry?"

"You sound shocked," he said.

"Kind of, yeah."

"Lots of folks don't consider cowboy poetry as the real thing, but I do. I even write some."

"No kidding. I minored in literature but I never wrote anything. I'd love to read something of yours."

He turned away and headed to the kitchen. "You just did."

She looked at the poem again. "Wow." It was what Devon had said when he first looked at the art in her studio.

Jace dished up the soup and let Zane carry the bowls to the table. It was a scary proposition, but he made it without spilling and Marik bragged on him.

The little house felt homey inside, with Jace's lived-in clutter and Zane's toys on the floor. She thought of Lena's gloomy living room, how it might have been different if their daughter had lived. Or not. It was horrifying to think of Burt Gurdman as someone's father.

She wondered if the sheriff had arrived at the Gurdman farm yet, and what he'd find. Her stomach felt empty, and not only from the aroma of Jace's vegetable soup.

Zane laid his security spoon beside his plate while they ate. He crunched three fish sticks with ketchup and a slice of quartered bread and butter, but he only sniffed the homemade soup.

"Thank goodness for multivitamins that taste like candy," Jace said.

Marik wondered what foods her daughter liked, and whether she ate her vegetables.

After lunch, Zane brought a set of picture cards to the table and they played Concentration. His ability to remember and match the hidden pictures was amazing. After two rounds she stopped humoring him and gave it her best effort, but Zane won every game. Whatever had gone wrong in the complicated scheme of his neural synapses, it hadn't erased an active intelligence. It was sad to realize how much was going on in that eager mind that he couldn't organize or communicate. The frustration must be overwhelming.

"Did you know," she said to Jace, "that a lot of the equipment ranchers and meat packers use to manage cattle was designed by a woman with autism?"

"Dr. Temple Grandin," he said, nodding. "I've read about every book on autism I could get my hands on."

She heard a vehicle on the driveway and saw her red Explorer pass by the window. "Looks like my company has returned," she said. "Time for me to go."

Zane began to stack up his cards one at a time. Jace walked her to the door.

"I hope you don't mind—I've invited Reza to visit us here," he said. "I think it'll be easier for her to let him come and stay with me if she sees where we are."

"That's a good idea. She's welcome to stay at the big house, if she wants. I have extra bedrooms."

"I appreciate that. But I'm hoping she'll stay here with us."

A niggle of disappointment etched through her, indefensible. "Let me know if you need anything," she said. "Extra towels, whatever."

She called goodbye to Zane. He glanced up from counting his cards and offered a limp wave, a big reaction for him. He had not said a single word.

"Thanks for coming," Jace said. "I think Zane had fun."

The afternoon sun hung in the blades of the highest windmill as she walked back toward her house. The day had turned hot and she perspired beneath her cotton shirt. What if Zane had been born to parents like the Gurdmans, she thought, instead of to Reza and Jace, who were giving him every chance to overcome his disability?

Every chance except a mom and dad who stayed together. And maybe it wasn't too late for that.

Devon was waiting in the cool shadows on the front porch. He looked handsome and at ease in jeans and a knit shirt. Was it possible for a man to be too comfortable with himself?

After their last tense words, she wondered where they went from here. His eyes searched her face with the same question.

"I was looking for you," he said.

"Jace's son is here for a visit. I was having lunch with them." She stopped at the foot of the porch steps and hung her thumbs in her pockets. "How are your parents?"

"Doing great," he said. "I swear Mom looks younger than before they put in the stent. They send you their best."

She lifted her eyebrows. "You told them you were staying here?"

"Sure. Why not?"

She said nothing.

His eyes traveled down the driveway behind her. "I didn't know your foreman had a son. He's divorced, then?"

"Separated. Their son has autism, and that's tough on a marriage." She felt a twinge of guilt for discussing Jace's personal life to avoid the elephant in the yard.

"All I know about autism is from watching that *Rain Man* movie," he said.

"Most people with autism don't have a savant quality like the man in the film. Zane's very bright, but he may never be able to live on his own."

"That's too bad." He shook his head. "Have they looked into a group home for him?"

Marik's foot stopped on the porch step. She frowned. "I'm sure they haven't. He's only eight years old."

"My hat's off to them," he said. "I don't think I could deal with it."

She looked up at his calm, advantaged face. "When he's your child," she said, "you don't get a choice."

The point seemed lost on him. She might have said more except for the sound of an approaching vehicle. A white SUV with gold insignia on the door smoked to a stop at the edge of the lawn. Sheriff Dean was at the wheel.

"Shit," Marik said.

The sheriff got out and rounded the vehicle. His face looked even more world-weary than on the day she'd first met him, when they'd found Burt Gurdman's body on the ridge. He didn't bother with greetings.

"I've just come from Lena Gurdman's house," he said. "She's gone."

Marik said nothing.

"What do you mean, gone?" Devon asked.

"Truck's gone, so is Lena. Looks like she's cleared out." His eyes narrowed at Marik. "You don't look surprised."

"Nothing Lena did would surprise me," she said. "Why don't you come in, Sheriff. Have some iced tea."

She crossed the porch and went inside.

They sat at the dining-room table, as if the occasion was too serious for the kitchen. She brought three glasses of sweet tea and slices of lemon on a saucer.

Sheriff Dean stirred his tea with a long spoon. "I came to let you know we won't be filing charges against you in regard to Gurdman's murder."

Marik only nodded and dropped a lemon slice into her tea.

Devon frowned. "Is there something I don't know?"

"Marik's lawyer called me this afternoon," the sheriff said. "He discovered—or Marik did, I'm guessing—that Lena Gurdman gave birth to a baby girl in the Redhorse hospital eight years ago, the same week Marik did."

She felt Devon's breath stop, but she didn't look at him.

"Marik's child is accounted for," the sheriff went on, "but nobody knows what happened to the Gurdman baby. There's no adoption record, no death certificate, nothing."

He waited a moment, watching her, but Marik kept silent.

"When we searched the Gurdmans' house today," he said, "there were two cups on the kitchen table. Still warm."

Now Devon looked at her, too, his face clouded.

"That was Lena's baby they found up by the windmills, wasn't it?" the sheriff said.

Marik nodded. "I believe it was, yes. More importantly, Lena believes it."

"And that baby's death is the reason she killed her husband."

"The strongest reason. But one of many."

"You *had coffee* with Lena Gurdman today?" Devon said.

Marik took a deep breath and met his eyes. "Tea, actually. She served lemon cookies and tea."

"Good God." Devon's face was flushed, but it had nothing to do with Lena Gurdman. She knew he'd counted back the years. Shortly after he was elected to the state legislature, on his climb to Washington. The year they'd stopped spending their weekends together.

"She told you the whole story," Sheriff Dean said to Marik.

"Yes."

"Why?"

"Because we had something in common. Or maybe just because I would listen." Her voice toughened. "She's been abused and intimidated for at least eight years. Maybe for her whole life."

The sheriff took a long drink of his tea and set the glass

carefully on its coaster. "That's a sad thing," he said. "But she's still a murderer." He leaned his elbows on the table, his face intense. *"Where did she go?"*

Marik looked at him, but she saw Lena's faded eyes, her rough hands twisting the cotton dress. "I have no idea."

The sheriff sat in silence for half a minute, his face unreadable. Then he pushed back his chair and put on his hat.

Marik didn't move. Devon saw Sheriff Dean to the door and followed him onto the porch.

An eerie detachment had risen around her like a wall. The sheriff's anger and Devon's suspicion didn't touch her. Even the surreal story Lena had told at her kitchen table was a bloodless dream.

The front door clicked shut and Devon came back inside. His footsteps on the wooden floor were all too real and she braced herself for his questions, the inevitable confrontation.

But he stood quietly beside the table until she realized he was holding something in his hands.

"The sheriff left this for you," he said. "They found it in the Gurdmans' barn." He laid a red dog collar on the table in front of her. It was Zorro's.

Marik laid her head on the table and cried.

Devon had the decency to leave her alone. At least for now.

Chapter Twenty-Eight

She closed herself in her studio, needing solitude. Outside the windows, dusk thickened the trees and filled the hollow eyes of the barn. It looked familiar and comforting. Maybe the loneliness was part of the reason she loved it.

The decisions she'd made in a hospital eight years ago, at a funeral on a windy hill, in Lena Gurdman's kitchen, defined who she was, whether the choices were right or wrong. And the specter of another choice, just as fateful, hovered close at hand. For the moment Devon was being patient. But sooner or later he'd want answers. Maybe he deserved them.

She could hear him in the kitchen rummaging through cabinets, probably cooking dinner. He had changed since they were lovers a decade ago. But had he changed enough? She had thought so, until his comment about Zane.

In the darkened window glass she saw a younger Devon, and a younger version of herself. They were at the victory party celebrating his first election—the state's youngest new congressman.

The party hosts, friends of Devon's parents, had spared no expense for the occasion. There were lavish buffets, influential people. Laughter and live music bubbled through the glittering rooms and into the garden, where candles floated in an aquamarine pool shaped like the state of Oklahoma. Its panhandle was a hot tub churned by jets of water.

On the flagstone terrace, swarms of young constituents gathered around a champagne fountain. Older men, who eschewed the champagne for whiskey neat, slapped Devon on the back when he crossed a room. At his elbow, Marik felt inadequate in her little black dress, though Devon had whispered she looked good enough to eat. A waiter offered them flutes of champagne. Devon took one for each of them, but Marik shook her head.

"You're not celebrating my victory?" he said, frowning.

"Sure I am. With club soda." She held up her glass.

"I guess I'll have to drink both of these, then."

Devon was enjoying himself, and why shouldn't he? With the help of his father's financing, he'd mounted a winning campaign for the special election without dropping his last semester of courses for his law degree. His self-discipline amazed her. For months she'd seen him only on stolen hours sandwiched between speeches and black-tie dinners and hand-shaking tours of the district.

Tonight she had news of her own, news he hadn't needed to hear during the whirlwind campaign. She'd promised herself she'd tell him as soon as they were alone.

Devon was working the rooms, and when she lagged too far behind, he looked for her and caught her hand, drawing her close. She wondered if it was her company he wanted or the impression of a stable relationship. The evening gave a glimpse of what it would be like to be Mrs. Devon Dulaney, second chair to a jealous public. Some women would prosper in that first-lady environment. Marik knew she wasn't one of them, but it was too late not to fall in love. And didn't love conquer all?

The party was still going near midnight. For almost an hour, Devon had been closeted in the host's study with a clutch of monied friends, each with his own pet project and agenda. When Devon came out, his tie loose and his forehead damp, she was standing alone near the open terrace doors, nursing her third club soda.

"I'm sorry," he said. "Let's get out of here before I get cornered again."

"I'll vote for that."

She set her glass on a table and he led her through the crowd. Devon had come to the party with his parents and campaign manager, and she'd driven her own car. They were supposed to drive back to Norman together, finally alone.

He had to express his thanks to the hostess, of course, so they couldn't escape unnoticed. Devon worked his way past outstretched hands and good wishes. At last, they were on the front walk to the parking area and Devon took the car keys from her hand.

"Maybe I should drive," she said. "I haven't been drinking."

"I'm fine, really. Champagne's like drinking air."

He always preferred to drive. And he did seem fine, just too keyed up to be a passenger. She said nothing as he opened the right-side door for her.

Devon talked fast as he drove, adrenaline still high. A senior legislator at the party had invited him to serve on his committee; the chairman of the chamber of commerce wanted him to be keynote speaker at their upcoming event. The car wound through the affluent neighborhood, familiar territory to him. Within a few blocks, she was lost.

He took a shortcut to the interstate, still naming people he'd met tonight, people who wanted something from him or could do something for him. Usually both. They passed into an addition of darker streets where the houses were less well kept, with single garages. Many looked like rentals. At one house the lights were blazing and extra cars lined the curb, narrowing the street to one lane. Rich folks weren't the only ones partying on a Saturday night.

"I think you should slow down through here," she said.

And he did, a little.

"Did you meet Millicent Ramsey?" he said. "She has more money than a Saudi prince. She wants me to—" Something streaked from the darkness behind a parked car and into the headlights.

"Jesus!" Devon slammed the brakes.

A small white face looked toward them for an instant,

blinded. Marik screamed. Beneath the squeal of brakes she heard a nauseating thump and the child disappeared.

Marik leaped out the passenger door and ran around the car. A skateboard lay wedged beneath the left front tire, and on the grass that bordered the street lay a crumpled form, not moving.

She dropped to her knees beside him. A young boy dressed in pajama bottoms and a striped T-shirt lay doubled up on his side, holding his leg. She sucked in a grateful breath when she saw that his eyes were open.

"Are you hurt?" A stupid question.

"My leg," he said, and started to cry.

Footsteps pounded toward them. *"Bobby!"* The voice was shrill with fear. A woman fell to her knees on the grass. "Bobby, my God, what happened? What are you *doing* out here?"

What, indeed? The sick dread in Marik's stomach mixed with anger. Why the hell was a boy his age riding his skateboard at this time of night?

A man appeared from the darkness, but it wasn't Devon.

"Call 911," the woman told him. "Hurry!" He disappeared toward the house.

The woman took the boy's head in her lap, rocking. "I thought you were asleep, baby. Why weren't you in bed?"

"It was too noisy. My leg hurts, Mommy. Is it broken?"

Marik looked for Devon. He was still inside the car— but not behind the wheel. He had scooted over to the passenger seat. She saw his frozen face in the reflection of the dashboard lights, and their eyes met.

She understood immediately. Whether he was impaired or not, he had been drinking. He could not afford to be identified as the driver of a vehicle involved in an accident, especially with injury to a child. His eyes asked her to save his future from imploding before it began.

"I'm so sorry," Marik said to the boy's mother. "He just came out of nowhere between the cars. We…I couldn't stop in time."

"I know," his mother said, stroking his hair. "I came running when I heard the skateboard on the driveway."

Flashing lights filled the narrow street. When she looked at her car again, Devon was gone.

Marik backed away while paramedics stabilized the boy's leg and lifted him onto a stretcher. A policeman took her statement and asked if she'd been drinking. She volunteered to take a Breathalyzer. Her heart was pounding but her head felt clear as ice. When the officer was satisfied and had taken all her information, he said she could go.

She followed the screaming trail of the ambulance to a hospital emergency room. She found Bobby's mother in a waiting room and dropped into a chair across from her. The woman looked surprised to see her.

"How's he doing?" Marik said.

"Looks like a broken leg and some bruises. They're taking X-rays to be sure." She looked tired but relieved. "He'll have a cast to show off at school."

"Thank God it wasn't worse." Marik dug in her purse for paper and a pen. "I gave my information to the cop, but I'll write it down for you. I have insurance."

"Thank goodness for that, because I don't." She pushed long, straight hair back from her face and met Marik's eyes. "Look. I know it wasn't your fault, and I'm not the suing type. If your insurance will pay our medical expenses, I won't cause trouble. If you don't cause trouble for me."

"Trouble?"

Bobby's mother slumped back in the chair. "I'm a single mom. I don't need DHS coming out to my house and saying I neglected my son. Bobby is everything to me. I put him to bed at nine o'clock like always, but a few friends came over, and we must have kept him awake. He got the skateboard for his birthday last week and he's been on it ever since. I guess he sneaked out for an extra ride."

Marik nodded. "I promise you his medical expenses will be taken care of."

Devon had willingly tendered a cashier's check for ten thousand dollars, but he refused to visit Bobby and his mom. In a week it was as if the incident had passed from his consciousness.

Marik never told him why she was drinking club soda that night instead of champagne.

Now she heard his gentle knock on her studio door. She took a deep breath and huffed it out. "Come on in," she called, without moving.

Devon carried a tray with two dinner plates and a bottle of wine, already opened. He set the tray on her worktable. The food smelled delicious—something Italian—but her stomach recoiled.

"I appreciate your trouble," she said, "but I don't think I can eat."

"Just drink, then."

"That I can do."

He poured two glasses and handed her one. She accepted the wine and turned back toward the window.

Devon sat down. "I'm sorry about your dog. I shouldn't have given you the collar."

"No, I'm glad you did. I wanted to know." The wine melted through her, softening the tension in her shoulders.

"And I'm sorry about everything you've been going through." He paused. "But I have to know about the baby. You had a baby less than a year after my first election."

"Yes. A little girl."

"And you gave her up for adoption without even telling me."

Still she didn't face him, but watched his reflection in the darkened window. "Yes."

He shook his head. "Do you know how many years Eden and I tried to have a child? She was willing to adopt, but I couldn't do it. I wanted a child that was—" he looked at his feet "—really mine."

Her hand fisted on the stem of the glass. She turned toward him. "Adopted children *are* really yours."

It was a lesson that had taken her a long time to learn.

Now that she faced him, she saw the hurt and anger in his eyes. "How could you not tell me I had a child?" he said.

In the eight years she had dreaded this moment, she'd

thought of a thousand things she might say. When he'd first stepped off the plane in her hangar by the river, she had almost forgotten the reasons she had chosen not to be the congressman's wife. Tonight her memory had improved.

"I didn't tell you," she said, pronouncing the words deliberately, "because you're not her father."

He sat back, astonished. For a long moment he said nothing, scanning her face. "You're telling me you were seeing someone else? At the same time when I wanted us to get married?"

"If you recall, we hadn't really been together for months."

"Except when we *were* together." He stared at her a long moment. "You're not telling me the truth. If there was someone else, I would have known."

She met his eyes and said nothing.

"Who is listed as the father on her birth certificate?"

"Not you."

"You put 'unknown'? I can find out. I can file for paternity rights."

"No, you can't. Someone else is listed as the father."

His hand slammed the table. The sound echoed in the quiet house. "Dammit, Marik! This is wrong. How could you do this?"

Heat flashed up her neck. "Do what? Have a child that isn't yours? Not want you to be her father? What if I told you she had a disability, that she wasn't perfect? Would you still want to claim her?"

His face drained. "She's handicapped?"

It was like seeing the core of him naked.

"No, thank God. She's healthy and whole, as far as I know. She has a good family that loves her, and you are not going to do one thing—*not one thing*—that might upset that little girl or damage her happiness." She stood straighter, her voice hard. "If you try to find her, I swear I'll ruin you. Your career, your marriage, your reputation. I'll dedicate my life to it."

He shook his head, his expression incredulous. "My God, Marik. Who are you?"

She thought about it only a second. "Apparently I'm a hard-assed Oklahoma rancher." She set her glass on the table before she left the room. "I'll drive you to the airstrip tomorrow morning."

She didn't stay to watch his Cessna Skylane launch into the blue bowl of the sky. Even as her tires rattled across the cattle guard, she was calling Daisy Gardner's number on her cell phone.

"Hey, stranger," she said when Daisy answered. "Let's have dinner tonight and lots of wine. I'll even cook."

"There's a threat. How about I'll cook, you bring the wine."

"Even better. See you about six?"

"Six is good. Will the congressman be joining us?"

"Nope. It's women only."

She glanced out the side window at the silver silhouette disappearing toward the sun.

Daisy made an enchilada casserole heavy with jalapeños. They washed it down with a peppery shiraz while Marik narrated her encounter with Lena Gurdman, the tale of Burt's overdue reckoning and Sheriff Dean's final visit to her house. She stopped short of telling Daisy about the five hundred dollars she'd left on Lena's kitchen table. There were some things better kept to oneself.

"Even if they catch her," Daisy said, "no jury in this county would convict."

Melted cheese strung from their forks. Marik's lips were on fire.

Daisy dipped out a second helping. "I'll pay for this tomorrow, but it's worth it tonight. You ready?"

Marik held out her plate.

"What about Devon?" Daisy said. "Did you sleep with him?"

Subtlety was not high on Daisy's list of virtues. Maybe that was a good thing between friends. "None of your business," Marik said.

"Ah, you did." Daisy looked pleased. "Will he be making a return visit soon?"

"I seriously doubt that."

"Uh-oh. Did he find out about your daughter?"

"Yes," Marik said. "And immediately assumed paternity."

Daisy's fork stopped working, the hazel eyes on alert. "What did you tell him?"

Marik finished a spicy mouthful and compounded the fire with a swig of wine. "I told him to take a hike. That he's not listed on her birth certificate as the father."

Daisy sat back in her chair, eyeing Marik with open admiration. "Really. Do you think he bought it?"

"I made sure he did."

A slow smile pleated Daisy's cheeks. "A wise man once told me that sometimes there's a difference between telling the truth and doing the right thing."

Marik knew she was quoting J.B. She frowned. "What makes you think I wasn't telling the truth?"

"Are you kidding? I knew Devon was the father the minute I saw those dark-chocolate eyes of his."

Marik stared at her.

"Close your mouth, for heaven's sake," Daisy said. "You have food in it."

"The little girl in those pictures didn't have brown eyes."

"Well, your daughter does."

Marik put down her fork. "That wasn't my daughter?" A different kind of heat rose in her throat. "You conned me!"

"I had to do something to make you back off. I'd already threatened to have you arrested." Daisy cleared her throat. "Sometimes there's a difference between telling the truth and—"

"I ought to kick the shit out of you."

Daisy met her eyes. "You don't have enough time. Tougher broads than you have already tried."

Marik's neck felt like it might explode. "You betrayed me."

"Technically, I never said that girl was your daughter. I just let you assume what you would."

"That's bullshit and you know it. A lie by implication is still a lie."

"Yeah, you're right. I lied."

Hadn't she always known that Daisy would do anything to protect what she believed were the best interests of a child?

Marik shook her head. "I'll never trust you again."

"Sure you will," Daisy said gently. "Your long-term memory will start to go when you hit forty. Besides, one of these days you'll understand I was doing what's right for your daughter."

"I can't believe you trust me so little that you resorted to lying," Marik said.

"Like you lied to Devon, when you thought he might disrupt your daughter's life?"

The point wasn't lost on Marik. "I threatened him with everything but cutting and branding."

Daisy lifted her glass like a toast. "Girl, there's hope for you yet."

"So. Where *is* my daughter?"

Daisy snorted. "Nice try."

Marik set her glass down hard. "If I trust you again when I'm forty, how old do *you* have to be before you finally trust *me?*"

Daisy looked at her thoughtfully. "I would trust you with my life. But I'm not sure yet that I can trust you with your daughter's. I'll let you know when it happens."

Chapter Twenty-Nine

On Saturday afternoon, Jace brought Lady out of the corral and saddled her while Reza and Zane stood by—a bit nervously, Marik thought. Zane rocked from one foot to the other, raking his spoon against his pants leg.

Reza Rainwater was a full head shorter than her husband, with dark, worried eyes and a slight roundness that made her look maternal. She looked cute in her loose cotton pants and tank top, her dark hair pulled back in a ponytail. Her devotion to Zane was plain on her face.

The afternoon was warm and breezy, summer closing in. Marik watched the Rainwater family from her studio, where she'd been working on a sunset painting. That morning June May had e-mailed her the artist agreement from Wild Things Gallery for her approval and signature.

Marik had read it carefully and signed. She phoned June to tell her, and they had set a date for her one-woman show.

June told her they'd sold four of the crow pictures the night she and Devon had visited the gallery. The possibility of selling four paintings in one night left Marik speechless. If that happened, maybe she could call herself an artist as well as a hard-assed rancher.

Marik watched Jace mount up and walk Lady around the circle driveway, demonstrating the mare's gentleness. Zane began to flap his hands, his signal of excitement. Jace dismounted and lifted Zane onto the saddle, then mounted up behind him. He walked the horse around the barnyard, holding Zane around the middle. She heard a childish shriek and Zane's hands flapped wildly. Reza's laughter floated through the window.

Marik smiled, but it was a bittersweet moment. If Jace and Reza reconciled, it would be a great thing for Zane. It also meant Marik was likely to lose the foreman she'd come to depend on and trust.

She went back to her work. Half an hour later she heard Jace calling for Zane. Reza's voice was high-pitched and frantic. Marik jogged through the house, down the porch steps and toward the small pasture where they had gone to ride the horse.

"He just disappeared," Jace said. "He was right behind me when I helped Reza up so she could ride—and then he was gone!" Lady, trained to stay put when her reins hung to the ground, pricked her ears forward and whickered. Zane was nowhere in sight.

Reza's face looked frozen and pale. She kept calling Zane's name, and Marik could tell she was trying hard not to panic.

"I'll check the barns," Marik said. "Would he have gone in the house maybe, to the bathroom?"

"I'll look," Reza said, and ran for the cottage.

"I'll head for the pond," Jace said, his face grim. But he hadn't gone three paces when a movement caught their eyes. Zane had emerged from a small grove of trees along the fence line just behind the barn.

"Zane!" Jace yelled and Reza came running back.

Zane was coming through the deep grass of the pasture, his progress slowed by something he was carrying. He held a mottled dog, brown and white with a black mask across its eyes.

"Oh my God!" Marik said. "It's Zorro."

She hurried toward them, afraid to run for fear she would scare Zane. Jace and Reza were close behind.

Zane looked at them, his eyes lit with rare emotion. Quite clearly, he said, "Look what I found." He set the dog down in the pasture.

Marik fell to her knees beside Zorro. The puppy looked thin, her hair matted and dirty. She licked Marik's hand with a dry tongue.

"Zorro! My poor baby." She pressed her cheek to the spotted head, laughing, tears spilling from her eyes. "This is the dog Gurdman stole," she told Reza. "I was sure she was dead."

Zane stroked down Zorro's back to the tip of her limp

tail. Cockleburs clung to her paws. Had Zorro been at the Gurdman farm while Marik sat in Lena's kitchen? How did she find her way home? Had Lena set Zorro free before she drove away? Marik would never know.

Jace peeled a burr from Zorro's paw. "She looks dehydrated. Let's get her some water. Want me to carry her, Zane?"

No chance. They helped him get a secure hold under her body, and all of them trudged across the pasture. At the barn hydrant, Marik ran water in a shallow pan and Zorro lapped until her knees gave out, then she lay down beside the bowl and lapped some more.

"Thirsty," Zane said, and they all laughed.

"She sure was," Marik said. She wiped her eyes on her sleeve. "Tomorrow I'll take her to the vet and get her checked out."

Zane sat beside Zorro, stroking the dog's side.

"You saved her, Zane. She might not have made it another night on her own," Marik said. "She's your dog now. We'll keep her here at the ranch with C.J. and Hoppy, where she has lots of room, but whenever you come to visit you can play with her and take care of her."

Zane nodded. He looked up at his parents and smiled.

At the ranch house, they fixed a box in Marik's studio, with the old blanket that still carried the smell of Zorro's littermates. She was in no shape for reintroduction to C.J. and Hoppy just yet. Zane stayed beside the box until his parents tore him away with a promise that he could check on Zorro the next morning after breakfast.

"If she's strong enough tomorrow, you can help give her a bath," Marik told him.

When the Rainwaters left, Marik took Zorro on her lap and spent an hour working the mats and burrs from her fur, talking to her in a low voice. That night she went to sleep with one arm dangling over the bed into Zorro's box. By morning, the box was empty and Zorro was curled up beside Marik's pillow, trail dust and all.

Chapter Thirty

From the top of Killdeer Ridge, Marik watched a yellow school bus wheeze up the winding road toward the wind-mills. The first cool front of September had blown through in the night, a lucky break for the twenty-three fourth graders aboard the bus. A week before, temperatures were still hovering at the hundred-degree mark. Leading the bus, a pickup emblazoned with the GPP&L logo created a white plume of dust that dispersed in the wind.

Construction on the last wind turbines had kicked into high gear during the summer months. Ten of the new windmills were already in service, and the other fifteen would come online within weeks. One day in July, an un-assuming envelope had arrived in the mail containing the power company's lease payment for all seventy units. She'd never seen so many zeros on a check.

The first thing she'd done was pay off her bank loan for the stocker calves, then most of the mortgage on the ranch. For the first time in a decade, Killdeer Ridge Ranch was almost debt free. Soon she'd have the honor of paying income tax on ranch profits.

She had raised Jace's salary to a respectable level. Reza and Zane had moved to the ranch in July. Reza lost no time in transforming the foreman's cottage with Victorian ruffles and doodads that were probably charming, if you liked that sort of thing. At Silk Elementary School, Zane and two other students had a special teacher all to themselves, and that was a contributing factor in Reza's decision to move from the city. According to Daisy, who kept track of such things, the teacher was a marvel with the kids.

It hadn't taken the teacher long to win Zane over. Already he was mainstreamed into music class, where he surprised everyone with his love of dancing. He still rarely talked, but every evening he played with Zorro. Zorro was still smaller than the other two dogs, her growth stunted by the trauma of her kidnapping. Otherwise she was back to her inquisitive self and devoted to Zane. The two of them spent hours together, and it was fun to have a child on the place. J.B. and Monte would have got a kick out of watching Zane and Zorro together.

Reza had seemed a bit lost when she first arrived. With Zane at school and Jace busy on the ranch, Reza had idle time that didn't suit her. Jace said she missed the job she'd had to give up when they moved. Since Marik was devoting more time to her painting and the business side of the ranch, she asked Jace privately whether Reza would consider part-time housework. Some women might be insulted by the offer, and the last thing Marik wanted was to hurt Reza's feelings. But the next day she came knocking on Marik's door, her dark hair tied up in a perky ponytail and a smile on her heart-shaped face.

"Part-time work is perfect for me," she said. "I can do it while Zane is at school and be finished in time to pick him up."

Marik had heard rumors of women who actually loved to clean house, and apparently it was true. Reza was thrilled with the idea. Her thoroughness put Marik to shame.

On weekdays, Reza prepared lunch in Marik's kitchen. The meals were geared to Jace's prodigious appetite, and Marik had to switch from driving up the ridge every morning to walking. Even so, her jeans fit tighter. The daily hikes gifted her with unexpected benefits. She worked out problems of composition and design while she was walking, and the extra endorphins increased her appreciation of the view from the top.

Last week, she had allowed Jace to haul away the remains of her father's wrecked airplane from the hay barn. She planned to fill it with old-fashioned square bales where Zane and Zorro could climb.

Today the north wind was cool and dry, and it carried with it the scent of autumn. The change of season stirred her blood, and so did the chatter of children's voices from the open windows of the school bus.

The bus rocked to a stop. The power-company truck parked close to Red Ryder and Brent Lawson got out.

Inside the bus, the clamor increased and young faces appeared at the windows, exclaiming. The windmills looked small from the road, and the children were always surprised by their gargantuan size up close. This was the third group to visit the wind farm since school had started.

Marik heard the teacher's voice from inside the bus, admonishing students to stay seated until she came back to get them. The bus door sliced open and a plump young woman in slacks and a flowered shirt got out and walked toward her, smiling.

"Hi, I'm Lynn Petree."

"Marik Youngblood. Welcome to Killdeer Ridge Ranch. Here comes the man with the hard hats."

Brent joined them and introduced himself. He was in charge of community relations for GPP&L, and he was good with the kids, personable and handsome. "If you'll have the kids make a double line at the back of my truck, Marik and I will get them each outfitted with a hat. It's a requirement for safety reasons."

Marik watched the young teacher respond to his smile. "They'll love it," Miss Petree said, and hustled off to organize the group.

Marik stood at the truck bed, wearing her own hard hat for this occasion, and helped Brent fit a hat onto each child's head. The power company had invested in several dozen hats especially made to fit small noggins, each with the GPP&L logo—great PR for tiny taxpayers. Invariably some of the kids asked to take their hats home. To alleviate that disappointment, the company had commissioned four-inch plastic models of the wind towers, complete with moving rotors, which Brent gave out as souvenirs at the end of each field trip.

Brent and Marik had established a routine. He did the spiel about how the windmills produced electricity, and she answered questions about the ranch—mostly whether the windmills scared the cattle. Each visit had gone smoothly so far, and she enjoyed the kids. But today, because of yesterday's phone call from Daisy Gardner, her stomach flittered like bird wings as she fastened the straps on one helmet after another.

"I hope you realize the magnitude of what I'm about to tell you," Daisy had said. "This is a leap of faith for me."

"Will you stop babbling and come to the point?" Marik said good-naturedly. "My oil paints are drying out here."

She heard Daisy take a deep breath. "This group that's coming Tuesday from Sand River Elementary."

"Yeah?"

"There's a special child in that class."

"You mean a special-needs child?"

Daisy hesitated. "No. A little girl you've been wanting to see."

Marik's breath froze in her chest. "Eva?" she whispered. "Eva's coming here?"

"She isn't Eva anymore," Daisy said. "Don't forget that. And I'm trusting you to keep this knowledge to yourself."

The painting on Marik's easel blurred before her eyes. She had to swallow twice before she could ask, "How will I know her?"

Daisy made a noise that was not quite a laugh. "Believe me. You will."

"Okay." She took a breath. "Daisy…thanks."

"Just don't do anything stupid. I'll call you tomorrow evening."

Marik had hardly slept that night. Now, watching the face of each child who came to the front of the double line, her heart jackhammered in her ears. So many boys in this class—she had thought girls usually outnumbered boys. There were dark-skinned girls, red-haired girls, blond girls—how would she know?

Then a little girl stepped in front of her and smiled, waiting for her hat. Marik looked into a pair of dark eyes that were familiar. Except for the eyes and a deep dimple in one chcek, the girl looked just like Marik's fourth-grade school picture.

Marik smiled, and her hands shook only a little when she fitted a hard hat on the girl's head. "Is that strap too tight?"

"No, it's fine." Another smile. "Thank you." And she turned away so the next child could step up.

Marik breathed. There was no lightning, no parting of the clouds. After waiting nine years, meeting her daughter was just that easy. Except for the weakness that suddenly assailed her knees. She sat on the lowered tailgate of Brent's pickup.

Brent fitted Miss Petree with a hat, to the giggling delight of her students, and they trooped behind him like hungry calves toward the nearest wind turbine. Marik brought up the rear, riding drag on the herd.

When they'd assembled beneath the towering windmill, Brent called for a moment of silence. The children's necks craned upward, listening to the slow shush of the blades, the humming song of the wind. A little thrill ran through Marik's center.

Brent began the lesson. "These towers are three hundred twenty-eight feet tall. Each one produces enough energy to power more than twenty thousand homes. The blades are called rotors. They're a hundred ten feet long and each one weighs about seven tons. How many pounds is that?"

Furtive calculations on little fingers. "Fourteen hundred pounds?" someone guessed.

Brent grinned. "Close, except you left off a zero. Fourteen *thousand* pounds. The rotors might look like they're moving slowly, but at the tips, they reach speeds of a hundred fifty-six miles per hour." He waited for the gasps of appreciation.

"Who turns them on and off?" someone asked.

"The windmills are monitored and controlled by computers inside the trunk of the tower. Would you like to take a peek inside there?"

"Yeah! Cool!"

Brent climbed the short metal stairway to unlock an oval door in the tower, and Miss Petree organized the children in single file. One by one they climbed up and stuck their heads inside the door, peering upward at the cables and computers and a ladder that let servicemen climb to the top. The girl with the dark eyes, near the end of the line, carried a yellow pencil and a hard-backed tablet. She was glancing back and forth from her tablet to a distant windmill.

Miss Petree saw Marik watching her. "Sierra is our little artist," the teacher said. "She's always drawing."

Sierra. Like the mountains. Marik approved.

"I saw an article about you and your paintings in the Pacheeta paper," Miss Petree said. "It said you were going to teach some basic art classes on Saturdays at the community center in Pacheeta."

"Yes. We're still working out the dates."

"I'll bet Sierra would love to know about the class, if children can attend. She really has a gift, I think, and her parents are very supportive."

A gust of wind tugged at Marik's jacket. She hugged it around her.

Before they reboarded the bus, Miss Petree handed out juice boxes. A boy with glasses and an infectious smile collected the remains in a big trash bag. Sierra had wandered to the crest of the ridge and was gazing across the pasture below, her pencil working. Her profile held a dreamy expression.

She walked toward the girl, thinking of the gift of Daisy's trust, her throat tight. Sierra looked up when Marik stopped beside her.

"Hi," Marik said. "I'm an artist, too. Could I see your drawings?"

Sierra's smile was shy. "I'm not really an artist. I just like to draw."

She handed her tablet to Marik. On the first page she'd

drawn the wind towers, and Marik could see a rudimentary grasp of the concept of perspective. She was also using shadows to give depth and dimension. The second drawing was of the gravestones half hidden in pasture grass.

"Who's buried down there?" Sierra asked.

"My family. Parents, grandparents, a few others." Marik handed back the tablet. "I like your drawings very much. You have a natural talent."

"Thanks." She shrugged, self-deprecating. Holding on to the clumsy hat, she tipped her face upward. "I love these big windmills. That sound they make. It's kind of—" she seemed to search for a good word "—mysterious."

Marik smiled. They stood side by side, looking up at the turning blades. "I like to think the windmills are listening to the ancient secrets of the wind. Trying to catch its magic spirit in their arms."

The dreamy look filled Sierra's eyes again. "I'd like to stand on top of one. You could see all the way to tomorrow." She laughed. "My dad says that."

A melting filled Marik's chest. "I'm going to teach some art classes in Pacheeta soon. If you'd like, I could let you know when they'll be. You'd be welcome to come free of charge."

"Really? That would be so cool. I'll ask my mom."

"Good. I'll send word about the classes to Miss Petree."

The teacher whistled and the children flocked toward the bus. At the door, Brent handed out the model windmills. Sierra disappeared up the steps and in a few minutes the bus lumbered away.

Marik and Brent stood on the hill, waving. "That was fun," he said.

"Yes, it was," she said, with more feeling than he knew. "And they learned something. You do a really good job with them."

"Thanks," he said.

He had an open smile and straight white teeth that must have benefited from preteen orthodontia.

"You know," he said, "there's a new Italian restaurant in Pacheeta that's supposed to be good." His eyes moved from the retreating school bus to her. "Would you be interested in trying it out with me? Maybe this weekend?"

She looked at the crinkled blue eyes beneath his hard hat. A tiny crescent-shaped scar beside his mouth gave his face an asymmetrical illusion she found appealing. "You're not married, are you?"

He grinned. "Definitely not."

"Then yes," she said. "That would be fun."

"Great. I'll phone you."

He strode off toward his truck and Marik was once again alone on Killdeer Ridge.

She looked out across the valley, the yellow-green pastures and the river beyond. Was that the arc of a migrant eagle in the sky? Maybe that was wishful thinking; it was too early for them. But they would soon return, certain as the seasons.

She walked to her truck and opened the passenger-side door. A wreath of autumn-colored flowers lay on the seat, and she carried it down the hillside toward the cemetery.

A killdeer called from the ridge behind her, and the hum of a lightplane echoed in the distance. Her boots crunched through the grass.

The red flags on the corners of the fence were gone now. She entered the gate and knelt beside a fresh grave, no more than three feet long. The lab in Texas had been unable to extract DNA from the infant bones found on her land. Since there was no known family to claim the remains, the OSBI had returned them to her. Marik had ordered a headstone like the others in the plot, inscribed with the name Sarah Grace. A hundred years from now, someone would find that stone and wonder about her story.

She placed the wreath on the small grave. Next to it lay the one marked Leasie Youngblood, 1876–1895. The ghost lady of Silk Mountain.

Marik sat in the grass beside J.B.'s stone. Perhaps they had done the right thing after all, in giving up her baby to a loving adoptive mother and father. She imagined an art room with long tables and half a dozen students at work, some of them senior citizens, some younger, one a dark-eyed child. *Your granddaughter,* she told J.B.

Someday Killdeer Ridge would belong to Sierra. But Marik was learning, slowly, the patience of the wind. She would wait for the day her daughter chose to find her.

Author Note

Across the central plains and prairies of the United States, wind power turbines are blossoming like wild flowers in spring. Experts say that one unit can produce enough energy to power more than 20,000 homes. The turbines don't require water or any other natural resource except the wind, and they don't put out solid waste or emissions into the air. Using wind for producing energy instead of coal or petroleum from even one wind turbine has as much environmental benefit as planting a square mile of forest each year.

The engineering is a marvel. The windmills are about 328 feet tall, including blade length. As a base for each turbine, a construction crew digs a hole 21 feet in diameter and 17 feet deep and fills it with 30 truckloads of concrete. The cylindrical trunk of each tower arrives in three sections borne on semitrailer trucks, each section weighing more than 40 tons. The housing at the top that holds the generator and gearbox is called the nacelle, and it's bigger than a bus. Each fiberglass blade, or rotor, is hollow and about 115 feet in length. On Oklahoma highways, it's not uncommon to see a single rotor traveling to its destination on the flat bed of a semitrailer rig.

From the generator inside the nacelle, electric current passes down cables inside the trunk of the tower to a transformer on the ground. From there it runs through electrical lines to a substation, where it can be distributed to homes and businesses. Building those lines to service the growing number of wind farms has become a major undertaking in the central states.

You can't truly grasp the scale and wonder of these giant windmills until you stand beneath them and watch their graceful blades plying the sky. I'm an Oklahoma girl, born to the wind. So I guess it's natural that the first time I saw these windmills I fell in love, not only with the concept of clean, renewable energy, but with their stark beauty and haunting sound—the whispered heartbeat of a windswept land.

Discussion Questions

We invite you to use the following discussion questions to enhance your reading of *The Wind Comes Sweeping*.

1. The American frontier in the 1800s was a challenging and often lonely place, especially for pioneer women. Discuss other circumstances, in history or in modern life, where women live with extreme isolation and solitude. Could you?

2. Near the end of the story, Marik recognizes that the loneliness of ranch life may be part of what she loves about it. Do you think women are more susceptible to feelings of loneliness than men? Why?

3. Lena is a sympathetic character but not very likable. How did you react to the way Lena dealt with her unhappy situation?

4. Do you think Marik's decision not to tell Devon the truth about the father of her baby was justified?

5. Some states allow for "open adoptions" and others do not. Marik had consented to a closed adoption. Do you agree with Daisy's firm stance on protecting the privacy of the adoptive parents and child? Did that belief justify her showing Marik the photos of a different child?

6. Daisy says that sometimes there's a difference between telling the truth and doing the right thing. Do you agree? Under what circumstances?

7. Wind energy development is blossoming across the U.S., especially in the Great Plains states. What do you see as the advantages and disadvantages of wind power? Would you object to having wind turbines in a field near your home?

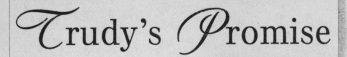